⁕{ A }⁕
Saloonkeeper's
Daughter

The Longfellow Series of

American Languages and Literatures

❧

Marc Shell & Werner Sollors, SERIES EDITORS

A Saloonkeeper's Daughter

DRUDE KROG JANSON

Translated by
GERALD THORSON

Edited, with an Introduction, by
ORM ØVERLAND

THE JOHNS HOPKINS UNIVERSITY PRESS
Baltimore & London

The Johns Hopkins University Press
2715 North Charles Street
Baltimore, Maryland 21218-4363
www.press.jhu.edu

Library of Congress Cataloging-in-Publication Data
Janson, Drude Krog, 1846–
[Saloonkeepers datter. English]
A saloonkeeper's daughter / Drude Krog Janson ; translated by Gerald Thorson ;
edited, with an Introduction, by Orm Øverland.
p.   cm. — (Longfellow series of American languages and literatures)
ISBN 0-8018-6881-5 (pbk. : alk. paper)
I. Thorson, Gerald.   II. Øverland, Orm, 1935–   .   III. Title.   IV. Series.
PT9150.J36 S25 2002
839.8'236—dc21
2001003756

A catalog record for this book is available from the British Library.

In memory of

Gerald Thorson and Anneliese Staub Thorson

⟫{ }⟪

Contents

⁂ ⁂

Translator's Preface

Drude Krog Janson, a member of a prominent Norwegian family, arrived in Minneapolis with her six children in 1882. Her husband, Kristofer, a recognized author, had come there a year earlier. Because he had been enthusiastically received by Norwegian immigrants on his lecture tour of the Midwest in 1879, and because his views were liberal, the Unitarian church had offered him support to establish a church for Scandinavian immigrants in Minneapolis.

Minneapolis was a burgeoning American city in the 1880s, and it attracted, among others, Norwegian immigrants. As one of the fastest-growing cities in America, Minneapolis grew from a population of 46,867 in 1880 to 164,738 in 1890, but the number of Minneapolis residents born in Norway increased at an even greater rate—going from 2,667 in 1880 to 12,624 during the same period. Kristofer did start a church in Minneapolis and, eventually, others in neighboring communities. When he lectured in Minneapolis, he often attracted several hundred Scandinavians.

That Minneapolis society of Scandinavian immigrants was where Drude Janson placed Astrid Holm, the main character of her novel, and what we find in the novel are Astrid's observations, concerns, and reactions to her new environment. In describing Astrid's situation, Janson also expressed her own views.

Astrid arrives in the city in 1879 with her two brothers and the family's maid to join her father. Although Astrid's status and experiences are far different from Janson's, Janson expresses her reactions to her own situation through the mind of Astrid. The novel is in that sense autobiographical. This helps the reader to see the narrative as an authentic story of life in Minneapolis in the late nineteenth century. That ring of authenticity comes clearly from the mind and craft of an artist at work. For the contemporary reader, the novel provides a glimpse of an immigrant society, a culture in exile, and the immigrants' responses to the social scene. A bustling but raw city, Minneapolis had contrasting social classes, neighborhoods, and leisure activities. These the novel depicts, giving a realistic description of its characters and their problems.

A Saloonkeeper's Daughter is interesting also in the ways in which it reflects literary movements in Europe and in America. Drawing on the realistic and naturalistic trends in Europe and in America, Janson has written an American novel that anticipates the works of such writers as Theodore Dreiser, Stephen Crane, and Sarah Orne Jewett. Astrid and Sister Carrie are similar in their aspirations and many of their experiences: each aspires to become an actress, and each is confronted by men who try to dominate them. When Dreiser drew on Helen Campbell's *Prisoners of Poverty* (1887), an exposé of the working conditions of women in Chicago, in describing Sister Carrie's search for work, he was using the same primary source that Kristofer Janson used when he wrote his novel *Sara* (1891). Drude Janson had already reviewed *Prisoners of Poverty* in the Norwegian feminist publication *Nylænde*.

Perhaps more interesting for the contemporary reader is the author's perspective on women's issues. Even though it comes out of the heart and fervor of the women's movement in the late nineteenth century, it is applicable to those same concerns expressed by feminists today. In Drude Janson's novel we get an unusually up-to-date study of the problems of gender and class. Most of Astrid's difficulties grow out of the fact that she is a woman in a society dominated by males. Her professional opportunities are limited, and she becomes one of the sexually pursued. Here we find Janson's involvement in the late-nineteenth-century concern for women's liberation. Her novel clearly reflects her active participation in the feminist movement.

A Saloonkeeper's Daughter is, then, a novel for the contemporary reader. In its style and content, it is a novel ahead of the trends and concerns found in most American writers of the 1880s. Furthermore, it is the work of an artist.

I want to dedicate this translation to the memory of my wife, Anneliese Staub Thorson, who encouraged me to translate the novel and who typed the various versions of this text. I also want to thank my daughter Helga, who insisted that I send the manuscript to the Longfellow Institute.

—*Gerald Thorson*

Introduction

D rude Krog Janson (1846–1934) is hardly a forgotten name in American literature: she fell into oblivion so rapidly that she seems never to have been noticed much in the first place.[1] Yet her first novel, *A Saloonkeeper's Daughter* (1887), written and published in Minneapolis, is a remarkable contribution to American literature. It deserves recognition.

One reason she has been neglected is the multilingual nature of American culture. Literary histories are silent on the fiction, drama, and poetry that came out of the late-nineteenth-century Midwest, partly because so much of it was in languages other than English.[2] In the decades around the turn of the nineteenth century, Norwegian, along with German, Yiddish, Spanish, French, Swedish, and other languages, were American literary languages and should be considered no more foreign to America and the many American experiences than the language of England. Much literature in these languages was written by native or naturalized Americans and intended for American readers who read books and newspapers in English but also enjoyed reading in the language with which they had grown up in an American immigrant home or in another country. A great variety of languages have been used by and for Americans and have expressed American concerns.

The identification of American literature with the English language is in the process of reevaluation. Languages such as Spanish, French, Dutch, and Swedish were languages of government in the early colonial period of various parts of what is now the United States; German was an important language for literature and communication in eighteenth-century Pennsylvania. Preceding them all, of course, were the Native American languages, some of which are still the preferred languages in certain American homes and communities. One of the writers who used Norwegian in the United States was Drude Krog Janson. For an important period of her life, she was an American writer. She can now be reconsidered, in translation, for the distinctive qualities of her contribution to American literature.

EUROPE

Drude Krog Janson was 36 years old when she immigrated in 1882. She was of a family prominent in both government and business. Higher education was not available to women, but her father, a member of parliament and a minister in the Lutheran Church, saw to it that his daughters received a private education. The young man who came courting from neighboring Bergen in 1867, Kristofer Janson, was also of a prominent family and about to conclude his theological studies at the university in Kristiania, now Oslo, the capital.[3] He was exceptionally gifted, had a colorful, charismatic personality, and was a promising author. His first book, *Fraa bygdom* (From the countryside) had been published in 1865 and received considerable attention, not the least because it was written in the recently constructed version of Norwegian, Landsmaal, promoted by liberals as an alternative to the written language that Norway shared with Denmark.[4] Drude accepted her suitor, and they were married in 1868. She demonstrated her independence, however, by retaining her maiden name, Krog, an unusual practice at the time.[5]

Their marriage was unconventional also. Nina Draxten, who communicated with members of the Janson family for her *Kristofer Janson in America* (1976), writes that both Drude and Kristofer were "determined it was to be a partnership. . . . Both were earnest advocates of the emancipation of women. They had agreed to be completely honest with one another, scorning all hypocrisy and intrigue."[6] They remained true to their agreement, even though their honesty and openness did not always make life easy.

In 1869 Christopher Bruun invited Kristofer Janson to teach in his new folk high school (*folkehøyskole*), Vonheim, in the Gudbrandsdal Valley. This was the first school of its kind in Norway, inspired by schools in Denmark founded by the bishop and poet N. F. S. Grundtvig (1783–1872). These coeducational boarding schools were intended as an alternative to traditional academic education for rural youth. Ideologically, they were nationalistic and romantic. Theologically, they were liberal. Pedagogically, they stressed the importance of the living—that is the spoken—word. On all counts the folk high school was a natural home for Kristofer, whose increasing liberalism made him uncomfortable with Lutheran orthodoxy as well as with traditional education.[7]

Paradoxically, their move to a remote valley was important for Drude's intellectual development: she attended classes and took part in the life of the school, where all lived together as in an extended family. In his memoirs Kristofer claims that Drude was more suited for the institution than he: "I was fortunate in having a wonderful folk high school mother in my wife. She not only won the trust of the students but had them confide in her and became their friend. She had far greater talents than I had in this respect since I sat all day in my study and was more taciturn by nature."[8] Drude acknowledges her debt to Christopher Bruun in her autobiographical novel, *Mira:*

> Every day she sat among the other students and listened to him as he in powerful words described the progress of world history. He gave her portrait after portrait of the world's men of intellect who had suffered and fought and with joy given their lives for the cause of truth. As she listened enraptured to the strong but calm warmth of his voice and saw the fire of enthusiasm that burned in his eyes, new and unknown vistas were opened in her own mind.[9]

Another man soon became an even stronger influence in her life. A short time after the school had moved to the neighboring valley of East Gausdal, Bjørnstjerne Bjørnson (1832–1910) acquired and moved to a nearby farm, Aulestad.[10] It was natural that the Bjørnsons and the Jansons should become close friends. Bjørnson was a towering figure in Norwegian society, and Kristofer Janson had also achieved considerable renown. In 1876 the Storting (parliament) selected him, along with Bjørnson and Henrik Ibsen, as recipient of a new annual lifetime pension for writers.

The Jansons built their home on a hillside overlooking Aulestad. Bjørnson was a frequent visitor, and as Janson wrote in his memoirs, "he sat many an evening alone with my wife and myself and spoke of his innermost concerns." So close were their relations that Kristofer asked Bjørnson to intervene for him with Drude because he felt she was unduly influenced by Bruun, with whom he increasingly differed. "When Bjørnson realized the situation, he became angered. He tried to make my wife, who was spell-bound by Bruun, understand who I was and my importance for the school, for Bruun, and for the people of the valley." In the fall of 1879, when Kristofer was in the United States, Drude accompanied Bjørnson and his wife Karoline to Gothenburg on their journey to Vienna.[11]

Drude Krog Janson was intellectually and emotionally drawn to exceptionally gifted men: first Kristofer; then, in Gausdal, the older Christopher Bruun and Bjørnson; and in Minneapolis, the far younger Knut Hamsun (1859–1952), who was to become one of the great novelists of his time, and Claude Madden, a young musician, the model for Mr. Gerard in *Mira*. The arena available to a gifted and intellectually ambitious middle-class woman for self-realization beyond the purely private and personal, except in the sphere of social activity, was extremely limited—especially in Europe but also in the United States. Given the state of education for women, the few who had acquired the learning and the inclination for an intellectual life, which was then the domain of a male elite, could not always find the intellectual challenges they sought in the company of other women. Although a few women in the United States were seeking professional careers by the 1880s, they were exceptions even in this country. A woman of the upper middle class who pursued a professional career, moreover, often did so at the cost of her standing in society. It may be that Drude Janson's tendency to attach herself to gifted men should be understood as a way for her to realize her intellectual and creative potential.

The attraction was mutual. Testimonials in praise of Drude Janson are remarkable both for their quality and for the quality of those who have praised her. Bjørnson found her company stimulating and used her as a model for the main woman character in his comedy *Geografi og Kærlighed*. In August 1883 he wrote from Paris to Georg Brandes (1842–1927) about his play in progress, stating that this character was based on "my staunch friend, Drude Janson, who, God knows! has never thought of divorce. What swine we writers are who in such ways place our best friends in salacious relationships even though they may themselves live in the most secure ones in the world. It is because I always used to say to Drude: 'Oh Drude! I have such mortal anguish that a Spanish captain should come and take you!'—Now I am inclined to believe he never will." Brandes, too, one of the first-rank European intellectuals, was an admirer of Drude. He had met her in Kristiania in May of 1880, when Kristofer was lecturing in the United States. "Among the ladies," Brandes writes in his memoirs, "I became very interested in Kristofer Janson's wife, Drude Janson. She had grace and an original mind. I met her three or four evenings in a row and have never seen her since." According to Bjørnson, who wrote to Brandes on May 27, Drude had been no less impressed: "Drude Janson, who came home in a wild Brandesintoxication, has now been under my treatment and been sufficiently restored to be able to send you a sane greeting."[12]

The years 1878–79 wrought great changes in the lives of the Jansons. Kristofer's growing commitment to the Unitarian faith became so problematic for Bruun that he convinced a teachers' meeting to dismiss Janson, who got the news from his wife while they were visiting Aulestad. In their break with orthodoxy, the Jansons were influenced by Bjørnson. Drude, however, seems to have been more ready than her husband to embrace a rationalistic faith. Certainly the religious views Drude gave to the protagonist in her first novel are more liberal than the "conservative" Unitarianism of her husband.[13]

Kristofer Janson, whose popular public lectures and readings now were the main source of income for his family, was glad to accept an invitation from Rasmus B. Anderson (1846–1936) to tour the American Midwest in 1879. Like so many other European liberal intellectuals, Janson had long been interested in America and had his own ideas of its potential, especially for the development of the individual. He had expressed his views in a play fittingly titled *Amerikanske Fantasier* (American fantasies).[14] Now he had the opportunity to make his own observations, and on returning home in June 1880, he wrote a new book about the United States, *Amerikanske Forholde* (American conditions).[15]

Meanwhile Drude had taken care of the family, living for the most part in Gausdal but visiting Bergen and Kristiania, where she had an active social life. She had embarked on a literary career as the translator of her husband's books from Landsmaal to Dano-Norwegian for his Copenhagen publisher.[16] Both her own work and the prominence of her husband gave her access to the circles that would have interested her. The couple's decision to spend the winter in Italy also helped to make her exclusion from the American tour more palatable. They made arrangements for their children on a farm near her father's vicarage and traveled through Europe, visiting

Hamburg, Dresden, Prague, Innsbruck, Venice, and Florence on their way to Rome in the fall of 1880. It was her first visit, his second. In Rome they had the company of a group of Norwegian intellectuals, writers, and artists; Ibsen was prominent among them. Their circle also included the painters Eilif Petersen and Kristian Ross, who did Drude's portrait, and Camilla Collett, a pioneering feminist and novelist, who wrote a long letter to Kristofer praising his work for women's rights but criticizing him for giving priority to the republican cause: "We must dethrone the 'sovereign' half of our nation's individuals . . . and install the other half in their rights." Drude herself went to Capri with Camilla Collett. After months in such company and life on the Via Purificatione, Drude may well have been concerned about the effect of immigration on her social and intellectual life. Moreover, her outlook was also darkened by a severe illness and then by the death of one of her children before she was able to follow her husband home to Norway.[17]

MINNEAPOLIS

In Rome the Jansons had had their first intimations, in a letter from Bjørnson, of plans initiated by Rasmus B. Anderson to bring Kristofer to Minneapolis as a Unitarian missionary. Drude encouraged the skeptical Kristofer to consider Anderson's proposal, which had arrived just before she joined him in Norway in May 1881. Janson had become convinced that the ministry was his true calling and that in Lutheran Norway there could be no place for one with his Unitarian faith. In the fall he went to the United States, leaving his wife and their children in her father's home in Fana. Bjørnson had returned from his American lecture tour in May, and his accounts of the cultural and religious life among the immigrants may have given her doubts about how she would fit in among them. But she had made up her mind. In *Mira* the narrator explains that "there are moments in life, in particular when great decisions have to be made, that you have to go where the hand of fate points, whether you want to or not" (24).

Both Jansons were committed to a new life in America. After having organized two congregations, one in Minneapolis and the other in Brown County, Kristofer returned home in the spring of 1882 to assist Drude in arranging their affairs. They made a visit to Bjørnson at Aulestad for the celebration of the twenty-fifth anniversary of his still popular novel *Synnøve*

Solbakken. Then the whole family and their maid Anne set off for Minneapolis, where they arrived September 14 and "moved into a flat on Franklin and Thirteenth, an area heavily populated with Scandinavian immigrants."[18]

Drude took part in her husband's work, but it was a duty for her, not a calling as for Kristofer. He was very active in his ministry, traveled frequently, was constantly involved in newspaper polemics, and continued his writing. This level of activity was made possible, as so often is the case, by a wife who not only shouldered the responsibilities for their household but also acted as his secretary and assisted him in the church. Draxten observes that whereas Kristofer performed on a public stage, Drude's efforts, no less necessary to the success of the enterprise, were less visible. "To an extent, Janson saw this situation, for he often wrote Bjørnson that Drude's life was by no means easy, but he seemed to fail to realize that while his efforts got recognition, she had no such rewards."[19]

Drude Janson did not feel at home in Minneapolis. To a friend in Gothenburg she wrote in April 1883 that everything was unfamiliar and she longed for home.[20] It may be necessary both to avoid exaggerating her negative reactions to Minneapolis and to appreciate them. In the early 1880s, Minneapolis was a new city, not far removed from frontier conditions. "The city they had come to," she wrote in *Mira,* "was at that time still in the unorganized and chaotic stage of a frontier town" (25–26). The first settler family had come to the west side of the river in 1850. Minneapolis was incorporated in 1867, but the present Minneapolis may be said to date from 1872, when St. Anthony and Minneapolis were made one city. In 1880 Minneapolis already had a population of 46,867, and by the end of the decade it had grown to 164,738, exhibiting one of the highest growth rates of American cities in the decade. In this period the Norwegian-born population grew from 2,667 to 12,624.[21] There were few among them with a background similar to Drude Janson's and still fewer with her intellectual interests. Minneapolis could not boast a Brandes or a Bjørnson in any nationality or language. Although Drude had advanced liberal ideas, it must be appreciated that she also had the social prejudices of her class and that she found it difficult to adjust to a situation in which she was expected to mingle with people who would have kept their distance in the Old World. As she writes in *Mira:* "The people in Winter's congregation . . . belonged to the lower immigrant class of whom some had been lucky in good times. Among them were saloonkeepers and their fat, silk-dressed wives, the proper families of craftsmen, unsuccessful journalists, deprived individuals, and women who had come over as servant girls but who had been lucky in marriage and now were among the leaders of the congregation" (26).

One aspect of immigrant society in particular caused Drude distress: the widespread abuse of alcohol. Kristofer had noted the vice of drunkenness on his first lecture tour and wrote in *Amerikanske Forholde* that occasionally a member of the audience might vomit. Bjørnson had used this as a counter-argument when Anderson suggested that he make a similar tour. "When I heard about Janson's audiences in such places, the idea makes me shudder," he wrote from Cambridge, Massachusetts. His experience confirmed his foreboding. Bjørnson may have been a spokesman for the common man, but he certainly did not like him when he came too close and did not show respect. From Albert Lea, Minnesota, he wrote to his wife February 2, 1881, that it was "one of the Synod's worst holes, where half the audience was drunk, where everything is black ignorance"; and from Fergus Falls, Minnesota, he wrote to Anderson that it was "a crude, swinish hole, nothing but ill-bred people," who were "so stupid, so ignorant of anything but money and sprees."[22] In the sixth ward of Minneapolis, where much of the Norwegian immigrant population was concentrated in the 1880s, there was also a concentration of saloons.[23] That Drude Janson reacted in much the same manner as her husband and Bjørnson is evident from her first novel.

All was not squalor, however. There were, in particular, two mitigating factors. Because of Kristofer's stature as an author and an intellectual and because of his close cooperation with the Unitarian Church, the Jansons had more dealings and relations with educated Anglo-American residents and visitors than immigrants usually did. Moreover, there were a few other well-educated and enlightened Norwegian immigrants in Minneapolis in the 1880s. Some, such as the physician Karl Bendeke, had a university education from Europe; others, such as the prominent judge and attorney Andreas Ueland, were American-style self-made professionals. With these and others the Jansons had frequent social relations. In 1885 Ueland married Clara Hampson, who soon embarked on a long career of public service, which eventually earned her a plaque in the state capitol. She, in particular, would be inspiring company for the older Drude.

Their situation improved considerably the second year, when they moved to a house of their own on suburban Nicollet Avenue, where they kept a horse as well as a cow. "Out here some of the wild prairie woodland still remained," she wrote in *Mira.* "In these pure, clear fall days it shone in purple and gold. . . . She could sit for hours and look at the last sunlit cloud pale out there in the west and see how the stars lit up, one by one."[24] Drude preferred the Minnesota countryside to the city, and she looked forward to summer, when Kristofer concentrated on his rural congregation in Brown County and they lived in the vicarage the congregation had built for them.

Shortly after Drude immigrated, her sister, Wilhelmine Behr, left Norway to avoid the social scandal of her husband's business failure. Settling first in Chicago, in 1885 she too moved to Minneapolis. Late in life her daughter Dina wrote her memoirs, including recollections of life with the Jansons, with whom she stayed for long periods. Although on the one hand she remembers the care with which her aunt distributed thin slices of meat on Sundays, an eloquent reminder of the mundane endeavors of the housewife to make ends meet, she also remembers their active social life: "Every Saturday evening there was a reception with music and tea at the Jansons. Many of the great musicians and lecturers, violinists and pianists who gave recitals in the city would come here. . . . these evenings were great and unforgettable occasions for us and important for our development." Drude may have had to be careful with how she sliced the meat, but the Jansons paid a private instructor to teach their and her sister's daughters German, history, and mathematics—a priority not uncommon in upper-middle-class families at the time.[25]

Drude Janson's first years in Minneapolis were, in spite of her bouts of loneliness and her heavy and not always inspiring workload, a period of intellectual and emotional growth. She had been interested in feminism in Europe but had not developed anything like the principled and radical stance of a Camilla Collett. In the United States she met a society in which women, although certainly in an underprivileged position compared to men, enjoyed more freedom and more career possibilities than their European sisters. Minneapolis was a repressive society for women, as were other cities. A married woman was, for instance, not allowed to teach in the city schools.[26] But Drude nevertheless saw and heard of women doing things unheard of in Bergen and Kristiania. Even the *History of the City of Minneapolis Minnesota* (1893), where women are for the most part limited to the roles of wife or dispenser of charity, or both, recognizes the presence of woman physicians, one of them, Adele Stuart Hutchison, honored by a biography. Although not listed in the *History*, there was at least one immigrant woman who practiced medicine in Minneapolis, Milla C. Svanøe, who advertised her practice in the Minneapolis newspaper *Budstikken*.[27]

Women clergy were still rare in America in the 1880s, but there were some among the Unitarians; one was Marie Jenney, who married the novelist Frederick Howe. The Unitarian Theological School in Meadville, Pennsylvania, had begun to accept women students as early as 1864. In his memoirs Kristofer writes admiringly of women clergy:

> I got to know them as not only eloquent and well-educated, but also as very competent administrators. One of them, Mary Safford, one of the most modest and feminine people I have met, was so appreciated as an administrator that she was called on to help new congregations get their machinery in good working order.
>
> The solemn and even contemptuous dismissal that the notion of a woman clergy had been met with at home has therefore struck me as strangely comical. There were always women speakers at Unitarian conferences. At a great meeting of feminists in the large Universalist Church in Minneapolis, there were only women speakers for the four days of the conference, and several of them were ministers. I had to admire the competence, wit, and eloquence demonstrated by these women, but then they were of course the leaders of the movement.[28]

The great meeting was the convention of the Women's Suffrage Association in Minneapolis in October 1885, attended by both Jansons.

That spring and summer Drude had experienced a state of depression. She wrote to Bjørnson on November 17, telling him that the suffrage convention, one of the greatest experiences in her life, had helped her out of it. Her letter is such a moving document of the impact these courageous pioneers had on an immigrant in, we may say, a state of readiness, that it deserves to be quoted in some length (here partly in Nina Draxten's translation, partly in her paraphrase):

> "You can't believe what it meant to me to see those women, most of whom have become gray in the service of ideas to which they had dedicated their

lives—and yet remained so youthfully fresh and warm, so keen and intelligent that anyone not a beast or mean-spirited person (and there are plenty of those among both the Americans and Scandinavians) had to love them."

The pearl among them, Drude continued, had been Lucy Stone, the president of the Association. An elderly woman with a round, childish face, pink cheeks, a charming smile, she had a voice the like of which Drude had never known. "One dared not move while she talked for fear of missing a single sound; her fine humor, the depth of her commitment, the deep seriousness with which she presented the cause she loved were all so captivating that she reached even the stupidest person." The last night, when she had delivered her farewell address, she had held her audience enthralled even though it was so vast it filled the huge Universalist church to the entrance. None of the others, Drude continued, was the equal of Lucy Stone, but every one was a true, serious woman.

This experience may not have been the sole cause of the lifting of Drude's depression; nonetheless, she felt not only elated but dedicated afterward: she had "resolved to become as fine a person as possible," she wrote to Bjørnson.[29] Her involvement in the women's movement may be seen in her polemics with the editor of *Budstikken,* who had joined other newspapers in writing critically of the International Women's Congress in Washington, D.C., in 1888; in her contribution to Kristofer's journal, *Saamanden;* and in her articles in the Norwegian feminist journal *Nylænde.* One of these articles is a long review of Helen Campbell's *Prisoners of Poverty* (1887), a book about the plight of women workers in sweatshops that was an important source for Kristofer's novel *Sara* (1891).[30]

A chance meeting between Kristofer Janson and a young immigrant in Madelia in Brown County during the summer of 1883 marked the beginning of another important event in the life of Drude Janson. In his memoirs Kristofer tells of becoming aware of "the tall, straight man with gold spectacles and an aristocratic, intelligent face who worked in a sawmill and spoke Norwegian." He engaged him in conversation and offered him work as his secretary. The young man was Knut Hamsun, who lived with the Jansons as Kristofer's assistant for about a year, returning to Norway in August or early September 1884. There has been much speculation on the relationship between Drude Janson and Knut Hamsun, most of it based on two letters, one from a friend of the Jansons, Peder Ydstie, to Torkel Oftelie, the other from Hamsun himself to the Danish writer and critic Erik Skram, in 1888. Drude became fascinated by the ambitious writer-to-be. He, on his part, sought her advice, showed her things he had written, and appreciated her encouragement. In a letter to the Norwegian writer Arne Garborg (1851–1924) in 1886, he mentions three in particular who had given him "so much hope. Bjørnson, Janson, Mrs. Janson." To a friend in Wisconsin he wrote that the lady of the house "is a very gifted woman. She has read my last work of fiction and says that she has never before come across such a wealth of colors and so powerful an esthetic sensibility. But she thinks I should wait a while. I had determined to have it published in Chicago but now it is best that I wait and look it over when I have developed a more critical eye for its faults." Drude's feelings may have gone beyond intellectual interest. Anderson, who corresponded with both Jansons and who also knew Hamsun, claimed that "Mrs. Drude Janson was delighted if not to say infatuated with him. She said to me that it was bracing and invigorating both mentally and physically to be in the same room with Knut Hamsun."[31]

According to Ydstie, Drude confessed her love for Hamsun to Kristofer and asked him for a divorce. Then, still according to Ydstie, Hamsun backed off when he realized what was involved. Drude was after all twelve years his senior and the mother of six children. So she again talked with Kristofer, who in all accounts is said to have been the kindest and most gentle of men, and they were reconciled. Hamsun's version in his letter to Skram is an unpleasant not-kiss-and-tell story. He was ill and expecting to die, he explains:

> Well, I had an absolutely desperate desire to go down to a bordello in the city and sin. Have you ever heard anything so crazy? When I was going to die! I wanted to sin on a grand scale, kill myself doing it. I wanted to die in sin, whisper hurrah, and expire in the act. I am ashamed to tell it. . . .
>
> I told Mrs. Janson in so many words about my desires and Mrs. Janson must have been a human being at one time and she answered that she could well understand me. Imagine, that's what she answered. But it may have been because she was so indulgent with me then, more than I deserved, embarrassingly indulgent.
>
> I sold my watch to be able to pay for this step, secretly sent for a carriage since I was too ill to walk, and was ready to set out. Then it so happened that

the Mrs. could not understand me after all. She caught wind of the affair and sent the carriage away. . . . I was extremely upset. An afternoon passed, a night, and a morning. And then I had an opportunity actually to sin in the very house where I lived; the opportunity was offered to me in so many words.

And then I wouldn't.

Can you understand it? This is something that has been with me ever since. I was once offered a key—a red ribbon in the curtain, a certain hour, one knock on the door—and then I wouldn't. If I had been allowed to beg for the key, then I can't say what may have happened. So little may mean so much for me. Are there more such people or am I the only idiot in the entire world?

Drude Janson was clearly not the average Minneapolis housewife, and there were probably more radical cultural differences between the language of the Janson household and that of most Anglo-American Minneapolis households than the more obvious linguistic ones. But it is nevertheless difficult to get Hamsun's story to tally with a consistent understanding of Drude's character. Næss believes that Hamsun misunderstood her and that her affection was intellectual rather than erotic: "And when she would sit at Hamsun's bedside and openly discuss his most intimate problems with him, then she was probably driven by the curiosity of a polite woman."[32] When Drude wrote to Bjørnson in 1896, "It is true the Spanish skipper came," it was not to Hamsun she referred but to a young violinist, Claude Madden, whom she met several years later, in 1891. No Hamsun-like character appears in the autobiographical *Mira*, but it is difficult to believe that the passionate woman portrayed here should have had only an intellectual interest in the attractive and gifted Hamsun. Regardless of how their relationship may be interpreted, however, it is Hamsun who comes out the lesser of the two. "Why does Hamsun want to hurt you? Have you ever done him anything but good, I must ask," the novelist Amalie Skram (1846–1905), wife of Erik Skram, wrote to Drude in 1898 after Hamsun had attacked her in a Kristiania newspaper for publishing *Mira*.[33]

Drude had not been in good health, and the sudden departure of Hamsun may have contributed to her depression. More important, however, is the effect this aspiring writer had on her ambition to write. Seeing how self-confidently Hamsun comported himself with the established Kristofer may also have encouraged Drude to greater independence. Her relationship with Hamsun certainly contributed to increased emotional independence in her relations with Kristofer. Drude Krog Janson herself eventually returned to Europe with her youngest children after her divorce (two older sons remained in the United States), but that is not part of the story of *A Saloon-keeper's Daughter.* Her first novel, which takes the protagonist from Europe, through an American ethnic experience, and into a life then possible only in America, remains an American document.

THE NOVEL

On January 29, 1886, Drude Janson wrote to Bjørnson thanking him for sending them his two plays, *Geografi og Kærlighed* (Geography and love) (1885) and *Kongen* (The king) (1877). She had found the former "highly amusing" and insisted that the protagonist could be no other than Bjørnson himself. Draxten observes, "If she recognized the heroine, modesty may have kept her from acknowledging it."[34] She may, however, have heard from Bjørnson or others that he had used her as model for the protagonist's wife. Her implication would then be that Bjørnson had made them a married couple in his play. Be that as it may, she was now ready to begin writing on her own, and in her novel she made Bjørnson himself an important character. A review of *Geografi og Kærlighed* in *Budstikken* (August 10, 1886), which claimed that Bjørnson's plays were beyond the artistic resources of the Norwegian-American theater, may also have given her an idea for her novel.

Drude began writing that summer. Life was better in rural Brown County. More of it could be spent on herself. Much of her own experience and the life around her went into her novel. The result is a remarkable bildungsroman, a story of the Unitarian minister as a young woman, a woman who against great odds establishes herself as an intellectually and emotionally independent person.

A brief look at some characteristics of Kristofer's fiction may demonstrate how her novel departs from his work. Kristofer began writing in a romantic tradition; but by the time he composed his American fiction, he had embraced the newer literary ideal of realism. His work, however, not unlike that of the later Frank Norris, is given to melodramatic excesses, especially in his

endings, that spoil it for today's readers. He was dedicated to the cause of
women's rights, and feminist themes are prominent in his fiction. Feminism
was also a frequent theme in the journal he published with Drude's assistance in Minneapolis. It was called *Saamanden* (The sower) and included a
regular column titled "The Woman Question." But he tended to portray
women characters as victims of an oppressive male society who often saw
suicide as the only way out of their trapped lives.

Both *A Saloonkeeper's Daughter* and the novel Kristofer wrote that same
summer, *Bag gardinet* (Behind the curtain) (1889), were embedded in the
local community. To a certain extent they are romans à clef. Indeed, Drude
placed characters with the names of well-known, living people in her novel,
thus giving it one characteristic trait of the historical novel. Readers in Minneapolis immediately began to discuss who was who. "It would be difficult
for us to form an opinion of its artistic merits, if we were good judges (which
we are not) knowing the originals of her characters so well," Ueland wrote
to Anderson, then U.S. minister to Denmark, on December 4, 1887, shortly
after its first publication in Copenhagen with the bowdlerized title *En ung
pige* (A young girl).[35] Later readers, too, have engaged in the exercise of
identifying the fictional characters with real-life Minneapolis citizens. Draxten claims that the protagonist is based on "Mathilde Ilstrup, a beautiful and
popular young lady who took part in amateur theatricals and was the daughter of a saloonkeeper." But neither she nor her father seems to have had
much in common with the corresponding characters in the novel. According to Hansen, Ilstrup, "always prim and silkhat-bedecked," was a respected
citizen and had a fine saloon in the Skandia Bank block on the corner of
Cedar Avenue and Fourth Street. His daughter favored roles that the fictional Astrid Holm despised, such as that of Inger in the popular vaudeville
Petter og Inger, and was the darling of the immigrant community, easily winning a popularity contest organized to raise money for Janson's congregation with more than eight hundred votes above her closest competitor.[36]

Such searches for the key to the roman à clef may offer more entertainment than enlightenment. An understanding of how closely Drude based
her novel on ethnic Minneapolis, however, may help us appreciate her de-
votion to realism. Although her account of an amateur theatrical is colored
by her own evident disgust, it gives a good idea of the quality of the local
theater. Some theatricals were relatively sophisticated affairs for a small so-

cial elite, but most were more like the shows to which Pete took the wondering Maggie in Stephen Crane's 1895 novel *Maggie: A Girl of the Streets.*
In either case they were as much social as cultural events. Advertisements
were for "Theater and Ball." Refreshments, beer and sandwiches, were
served during the performance; and after the actors had taken their bows,
there was dancing, often far into the night. The short-lived Scandinavian
Theater Society in Minneapolis (1882–85), a dedicated group that produced
fifty plays in the course of three years, followed this practice. A reviewer in
Budstikken, most likely the editor, Luth Jæger, a close friend of the Jansons,
complained about the custom and concluded: "The society should have too
much respect for itself and for its audience to run such a catering business
on the floor as well as in the galleries and thus create a disturbance that
drowns out all sound from the stage."[37]

Artistic failure could not always be blamed on the audience. Luth Jæger
may have entertained Drude with accounts of the ludicrous results of the
combination of ambition with lack of talent when a dramatic society decided to produce a tragedy by the Danish Adam Oehlenschläger (1779–1850)
in 1878, an event that evoked laughter rather than tears from the audience
in the Pence Opera House.[38] Her experience, as well as the stories of her
friends, gave Drude material for her use of the immigrant theater in her
novel; we may enter into the spirit of the author's realism and her blending
of fiction and reality and say that Astrid Holm should have known better
than to set out on her theater venture. The episode, then, is also about
Astrid's failure to understand her society and her failure to understand that
the subtleties of Bjørnson's comedy would be more than her group of ama-
teurs could convey and the audience could appreciate. (Later in the novel,
Bjørnson is surprised that she tried to do such a thing.) Thus, an appreciation of the realistic aspects of the novel helps us to see that the protagonist's
theatrical adventure also shows her naïveté and that her failure is an important step in her intellectual and emotional development.

However, a reading that merely recognizes the historical accuracy of the
novel will not do justice to the novelist's intentions and achievements. Consider the way in which images of nature become motifs in the novel and
achieve symbolic significance. In the opening chapters, Astrid's capacity for
both joyous ecstasy and depression are brought out in her response to two
contrasting natural settings: the garden in Balestrand drenched in moon-

light and the dismal darkness of the lake, Svartediket. Both scenes are dominated by steep mountains; but in Balestrand the mountain is a benevolent, protective sentinel, a "loyal giant," whereas the mountains that cast their shadow over the lake are "dark, forbidding," and threatening. These two settings symbolize the protagonist's struggle with her own depressive states. The Svartediket motif is not merely threatening, however. It offers a way out, indeed a release from the overwhelming troubles of the world: it invites suicide. At the very end of the novel, a flowering garden with its promise of fruition dominates the mind of the protagonist. Clearly, the author did not wish to move us to tears by the sad story of her protagonist but rather to have her emerge victorious from her struggle and be a model of achievement for her readers. Writing in a way that demonstrated her artistic independence from her husband, she created a novel with a protagonist who develops the strength to live an independent life.

American women had few novels that encouraged them to venture bravely out into life on their own, practicing a self-reliance and embarking on careers that were the prerogative of males. Not that American fiction does not have its share of remarkable and strong women characters, but for most of the nineteenth century there was little space for them in the male professional world; and the defiant ones, those who transgressed the law, usually suffered defeat. Hester Prynne is a harbinger of a new kind of woman, Hawthorne explains, one whose time had not yet come. It may be instructive to read Drude Janson's first novel in the light of *The Lamplighter* (1854), by Maria Cummins, also a Unitarian, albeit of an earlier generation and of a more conservative kind than the later immigrant. Drude Janson was surely acquainted with this immensely popular novel, which was also available in a Danish translation.

In her instructive reading of *The Lamplighter* in the context of earlier novels by Catherine Maria Sedgwick and Susan Warner, Nina Baym describes a female bildungsroman tradition and suggests intertextual readings that may also do good service to Drude Janson's novel. If, as Baym demonstrates, Cummins's novel may profitably be read as a rewriting of Warner's *Wide, Wide World* (1850), then *A Saloonkeeper's Daughter* may be read as a rewriting of both the story of *The Lamplighter* and the typical Kristofer Janson story of a victimized woman. Both Drude Janson's Astrid and Maria Cummins's Gertrude grow to independent human beings and seek employment in which they can be guides for others; both achieve this in defiance of "unjust patriarchal authority."[39] In the case of Astrid Holm, this patriarchal authority is embodied both in her father and in Smith, the man who almost overpowers her. In Drude Janson's novel, however, employment is not a temporary adventure before the haven of marriage. Rather, Astrid's career as a minister begins as the novel comes to an end, her ordination taking the structural place of the wedding in so many novels, including *The Lamplighter.* Moreover, the relationship she looks forward to with the physician Helene Nielsen is one that will be supportive of her career, not an end to it.

Yet another intertextual reading may be suggested. A couple of years before Drude Janson began writing her first novel, Sarah Orne Jewett published *A Country Doctor* (1884), her novel about a woman who chooses to follow her calling to be a physician rather than enter into a marriage with an understanding, loving, and gentle young man. This, too, is an exceptional novel in American literature of the 1880s in presenting a heroine who successfully enters a profession still thought to be the exclusive domain of men. From her situation in an immigrant community in Minneapolis, Drude Janson had a similar sense of new openings for women.[40]

In the novel it is Bjørnson who explains to Astrid that American society was more advanced than the Old World in both the encouragement it gave for self-reliance and the possibilities it offered for self-realization—primarily, of course, for men, but increasingly also for women. In a fine article on Drude and Kristofer Janson, Gerald Thorson, the translator of this edition, sees Astrid Holm as a Cinderella and Bjørnson as her fairy godmother.[41] The novel, however, offers a moralizing twist to the fairy-tale motif: Bjørnson lectures Astrid on the challenges and potential rewards of a life of hard work and dedication and gives her a program of study rather than access to a prince.

Three other men are obstacles and cause pain and sorrow and bouts of despair and depression. Her father, the saloonkeeper, and Adolf Meyer, the worthless character who tries to seduce her, are conventional, one-dimensional characters. The third, Smith, the attorney who is given no other name, is less easily dismissed. When he first enters the novel, at the gathering of society women where Adolf Meyer has begun to realize his plan to spread slanderous suggestions about Astrid Holm, Smith not only stands up in her defense but also does so by questioning the double standard in sexual ethics for men and women, thus allying himself with Bjørnson. He is clearly in-fatuated with Astrid and sees her fine qualities regardless of her social situa-tion. As his ardor increases, however, Astrid enters into a depression caused by her suppressed awareness of allowing herself to be drawn into a rela-tionship that may offer a superficial advance in life but that does not involve her own emotions. As she remains aloof, Smith increasingly becomes the male brute, and the turning point comes when he speaks of her as his pos-session. By not giving him a name beyond the nearly anonymous Mr. Smith, the author has made him into a negative male force rather than an individ-ualized character.[42]

In the end Helene Nielsen and Astrid Holm form the nucleus of a new family that will include faithful old Annie and Astrid's brother. Together, they will forge a meaningful life for two independent women realizing their own special gifts in the service of mankind. Not in the immigrant commu-nity, however—for it is declared too backward and unready for the kind of life represented by Helene and Astrid—but in the larger American society. Thus, *A Saloonkeeper's Daughter* is also a novel about immigrants entering America. Fittingly, it was better received here than it was in Europe. After serialization, beginning in October 1888, in *Illustreret Ugeblad* (Illustrated weekly), published by the Chicago and Minneapolis publisher Christian Rasmussen, a book edition by the same publisher had six printings by 1894.[43]

⌒

HAVING LOOKED INTO A PROMISING AMERICAN FUTURE through the eyes of her protagonist, Drude Krog Janson herself found that Astrid's country was not for her. In this she is not alone among American writers, whose books have remained American even though their authors settled or reset-tled in the Old World. In 1893, after her own frustrated love affair with a young musician was followed by the harrowing experience of having the new woman in Kristofer's life come to live with them as a member of the family, Drude left the United States with her four youngest children and settled in Dresden, Germany. Her and Kristofer's marriage ended in divorce in 1897. She published three other novels and several articles, mostly for the Nor-wegian feminist journal *Nylænde*. *A Saloonkeeper's Daughter* is her most vi-brant and engaging work.[44]

In Nina Draxten's *Kristofer Janson in America*, there is an outdoor family photograph of an elderly Drude, probably taken not long before Kristofer died in 1917. She sits in the center with a daughter and children on either side and flanked by the second Mrs. Janson and Kristofer and a son-in-law. The parties are to all appearances reconciled after all they have gone through, including the acrimonious attack by Drude on her rival and Kristofer in her autobiographical novel *Mira.*

Drude Krog Janson died at age eighty-eight in Copenhagen in 1934.

—*Orm Øverland*

Notes to the Introduction

In various ways, Dag Blanck, Kimberly Clarke, Ruth Crane, Susan K. Ebbers, Øyvind Gulliksen, Lene Johannessen, Sherry Linkon, Nils Axel Nissen, Harald S. Næss, Petter Næss, Sverre Øverland, Gerald Thorson, Dina Tolfsby, and Bjørn Tysdahl have been helpful in the preparation of this work for publication. In particular, thanks are due to Jay Martin and Gayle Graham Yates.

1. Important sources of information on Drude Krog Janson are Sigrun Røssbø, "Drude Krog Janson: Norwegian-American and Norwegian Author," in Dorothy Burton Skårdal and Ingeborg Kongslien, eds., *Essays on Norwegian-American Literature and History* (Oslo, 1986), 49–60; and Nina Draxten, *Kristofer Janson in America* (Boston, 1976). Another valuable source is Kristofer Janson's memoirs, *Hvad jeg har oplevet: Livserindringer* (Kristiania, Norway, 1913). For the literary and cultural context, see my *Western Home: A Literary History of Norwegian America* (Northfield, Minn., 1996). Translations from texts in Norwegian are mine.

2. Isaac Atwater, ed., *History of the City of Minneapolis Minnesota* (New York, 1893), lists seventeen newspapers in languages other than English in Minneapolis in the 1870s and 1880s. Of these, one was in French, two in German, and the others in the Scandinavian languages.

3. The Janson family's stately eighteenth-century rococo home, Damsgård, remains a sight worth visiting in Bergen. Kristofer Janson's maternal grandfather, Jacob Neumann, had been bishop of Bergen and was the author of a pamphlet (1837) warning the peasantry against emigrating to the United States.

4. That the official written language, Riksmaal (now Bokmål), was as closely related to Danish as are American and British English was a consequence of the long union of Denmark and Norway (1380–1814). Landsmaal (now Nynorsk) was the creation of Ivar Aasen (1813–1896) and was based on rural dialects, mainly those of western Norway. His first grammar was published in 1848, and his definitive grammar and dictionary were published in 1864 and 1873. When the young Kristofer Janson wrote in Landsmaal as early as 1865, he was recognized as champion of a national culture, then a liberal cause. In 1885 the Storting (parliament) gave Landsmaal an official status.

5. To begin with, she used her maiden name only intermittently, but writing her first novel made her more conscious of having an identity independent of her marriage. In January 1886 she wrote to Karina Anderson: "You can see I have resumed my maiden name, something I have long thought of doing, feeling I should not drop it simply because I married." Quoted in Draxten, *Kristofer Janson in America*, 147. Letters of the Jansons to the Andersons are in the Wisconsin Historical Society, Madison, Wisconsin.

6. Draxten, *Kristofer Janson in America*, 79.

7. See Kristofer Janson, "Bishop Grundtvig and the Peasant High School," *Scandinavia* 1 (1884): 161–165, 197–201.

8. Janson, *Hvad jeg har oplevet*, 176–177.

9. Drude Krog Janson (as Judith Keller, a pseudonym), *Mira* (Copenhagen, 1897), 12.

10. On Bjørnson, see note to page 46 of the novel.

11. Janson, *Hvad jeg har oplevet*, 168, 169; Bjørnstjerne Bjørnson, *Kamp-liv: Brev fra årene 1879–1884*, ed. Halvdan Koht (Oslo, 1932), 1:81, 86.

12. Bjørnson, *Kamp-liv*, 1:162, 2:97–98. Georg Brandes, *Levned: Et Tiaar* (Copenhagen, 1907), 360. Georg (Morris Cohen) Brandes had a strong impact on the intellectual and literary life of Sweden, Norway, and Denmark. He was influenced by and personally knew Hippolyte Taine, Ernest Renan, and John Stuart Mill; he also corresponded with a large number of contemporary writers, among them Henrik Ibsen and August Strindberg, and had an important part in their development. He wrote a great many books and was for several years a professor in Berlin. Prejudice against both his ideas and his ethnic background, however, kept him from a professorship at the University of Copenhagen until 1902.

13. Janson, *Hvad jeg har oplevet*, 176. Draxten, who emphasizes the independence of Drude (*Kristofer Janson in America*, 80), disagrees with Røssbø about who, of the two, led the way. According to the latter, Drude "gradually . . . gave up her Grundtvigian Christian faith to follow her husband as he moved toward liberal Unitarianism" (50). A comparison of the religious views of Astrid Holm in *A Saloonkeeper's Daughter* with those expressed by Kristofer in *Jesus-Sangene* (The Jesus songs) (Minneapolis, 1893) makes Draxton the more convincing of the two. Janson, moreover, allied himself with the theologically conservative wing of the Unitarian Church, not the liberal one as suggested by Røssbø.

14. Scholars have been unaware of *Amerikanske Fantasier*, which was not published in Norway but in Chicago in 1876. Anderson, who played a central role in having Janson come to Minneapolis, was an important figure in the development of a Norwegian-American literary culture. See Lloyd Hustvedt, *Rasmus Bjørn Anderson: Pioneer Scholar* (Northfield, Minn., 1966).

15. Before he returned home, he went to Cambridge to visit Longfellow. Their meeting was not long, and Janson was somewhat surprised when he became convinced that the prominent but aging American poet had little understanding of Whitman. He did not get an enthusiastic response from Longfellow when he brought up the name of Victoria Woodhull, either. He also visited other cities in the East, and among those he met in Washington, D.C., was Frances Eliza Burnett, later to achieve fame for her best-sell-

ing *Little Lord Fauntleroy.* Janson, *Amerikanske Forholde* (Copenhagen, 1881), 58, 62; Janson, *Hvad jeg har oplevet,* 188–189.

16. It may be necessary to explain that although Norway was in a political union with Sweden after 1814, the close cultural ties with Denmark remained throughout the nineteenth century. Thus, Ibsen, Bjørnson, Janson, and most other Norwegian writers of prominence published in Copenhagen. Drude Janson's first translation was *Fraa bygdom,* as *Fra Norge* (From Norway), in 1868.

17. For Kristofer's account of their Roman winter, see *Hvad jeg har oplevet,* 190–198. The entire letter from Collett is reprinted.

18. Draxten, *Kristofer Janson in America,* 80. In the year of their arrival, 29,101 Norwegians came to the United States.

19. Ibid., 189.

20. Røssbø, "Drude Krog Janson," 51. Drude Janson to Stina Hedlund, wife of Sven Adolf Hedlund, editor of the *Göteborgs handels-och sjöfartstidning.* She had visited the Hedlunds in Gothenburg in the fall of 1879. Bjørnson, *Kamp-liv,* 1:86.

21. Atwater, *History of the City of Minneapolis,* 90–96; Carl G. O. Hansen, *My Minneapolis* (Minneapolis, 1956), 52.

22. Eva Haugen and Einar Haugen, eds., *Land of the Free: Bjørnstjerne Bjørnson's America Letters, 1880–1881* (Northfield, Minn., 1978), 181–182, 209, 217–218. The synod refers to the dominant, conservative church body among the Norwegian Americans at the time.

23. Hansen, *My Minneapolis,* 134.

24. Draxten, *Kristofer Janson in America,* 96; Janson, *Mira,* 27–28.

25. Dina Kolderup published her memoirs (in Norwegian) as installments in the *Seattle Western Viking* in every other or every third issue in 1963. The quotations are from October 4 and 25. The information in the text about keeping a horse and a cow is also from Kolderup.

26. When asked what he thought about this, Kristofer Janson's response was that "he considered them more fit than the unmarried, especially if they had children of their own." Draxten, *Kristofer Janson in America,* 279.

27. See Atwater, *History of the City of Minneapolis Minnesota,* "List of Physicians and Surgeons," 910–911; and the biography, 929–930; *Budstikken,* July 6, 1875. The name of the immigrant physician suggests that she was from Bergen, and she would thus have been known to the Jansons.

28. Janson, *Hvad jeg har oplevet,* 229. Mary A. Safford, who worked in partnership with Eleanor E. Gordon and was ordained in Humboldt, Iowa, in 1880, may well have been a source of inspiration when Drude decided to have her protagonist become a Unitarian minister. On these and other woman ministers in the Midwest, see Cynthia Grant Tucker, *Prophetic Sisterhood: Liberal Women Ministers of the Frontier, 1880–1930* (Boston, 1990). A useful reference book is Catherine F. Hitchings, *Unitarian and Universalist Women Ministers,* 2d ed. (Boston, 1985).

29. Draxten, *Kristofer Janson in America,* 146–147. She missed another feminist meeting in Minneapolis in the 1880s. In April 1882, just a few months before Drude arrived,

Aasta Hansteen, a pioneer in the Norwegian feminist movement, had lectured in Minneapolis, speaking of the "crying injustice" of Norwegian legislation and heaping blame on the clergy. See *Budstikken,* March 14, 28; April 4, 11, 1882. In her autobiographical novel, Drude gives an account of a period of depression and the following awakening (*Mira,* 91–97).

30. Draxten, *Kristofer Janson in America,* 194–197; Røssbø, "Drude Krog Janson," 53; Øverland, *The Western Home,* 167. The review, "Amerikanske kvindeslaver" (American women slaves), runs in three issues of *Nylænde* 2 (1888): 209–212, 241–250, 273–282.

31. Janson, *Hvad jeg har oplevet,* 220. Rasmus B. Anderson gives a very different version in *Life Story* (Madison, Wis., 1915), 307–308. One reason why Kristofer was looking for an assistant was that Drude was in poor health (Draxten, *Kristofer Janson in America,* 106). Peder Ydstie's letter (undated) is in the Torkel Oftelie Papers, Norwegian-American Historical Association, St. Olaf College. Hamsun to Svein Tveraas (April 11, 1884), Hamsun to Skram (December 26, 1888), and Hamsun to Garborg (June 13, 1886) are in Harald S. Næss, ed., *Knut Hamsuns brev 1879–1895* (Oslo, 1994), 97–101. Draxten has Hamsun in Minneapolis in October, presumably leaving in November (124). As the Næss edition of Hamsun's letters makes clear, however, Hamsun was sick in bed in Minneapolis in June–July and was writing letters from Norway by September 23. See Næss, *Knut Hamsun's brev,* 50–51.

32. Harald S. Næss, *Knut Hamsun og Amerika* (Oslo, 1969), 46.

33. Næss, *Knut Hamsun's brev,* 46 n.

34. Draxten, *Kristofer Janson in America,* 147.

35. Ibid., 177. For this edition Kristofer Janson wrote a patronizing preface, recommending the book and assuring readers that it was in all respects a realistic story.

36. Ibid., 169. Hansen, *My Minneapolis,* 149, 82.

37. Much of this paragraph is based on Øverland, *The Western Home,* 94–95. The review was March 28, 1883. Of course, some theatrical events were different and aimed at a more refined audience, and the Jansons and their friends were involved in some of them. Kristofer Janson, for instance, directed a production of a Danish play at Harmonia Hall in 1888. The next year, at the People's Theater, he was on the program when a play by Bjørnson was produced. See Hansen, *My Minneapolis,* 83. For a valuable study of the theater among Swedish Americans, see Lars Furulund, "From Vermländingarne to Slavarna på Molokstorp. Swedish-American Theater in Chicago," in Philip J. Anderson and Dag Blanck, eds., *Swedish-American Life in Chicago: Cultural and Urban Aspects of an Immigrant People 1850–1930* (Uppsala, 1991).

38. Hansen, *My Minneapolis,* 40–41.

39. Maria Susanna Cummins, *The Lamplighter,* edited and with an introduction by Nina Baym (New Brunswick, N.J., 1988), xxiii. Drude's reading can, of course, only be assumed. Both her strong interest in feminist organizations and the wide reading necessary for the notices she wrote under the heading "The Woman Question" in Kristofer's journal, *Saamanden,* must have made her aware of Lillie Devereux Blake and her novel *Fettered for Life or Lord and Master: A Story of To-Day* (New York, 1874). The relationship

between Astrid and Mr. Smith may then be read as a rewriting of the story of the tragic marriage of Flora Livingston and Ferdinand Le Roy.

40. The best-known portrait of a woman successful in a profession may be that of the journalist Henrietta Stackpole in Henry James's *Portrait of a Lady* (1881). Whereas this one verges on the comical, Lillie Devereux Blake's portrait of the successful journalist Frank Heywood, a woman disguised as a man, verges on the improbable. Both portraits, then, serve as reminders of the limited range of activity available to women. Nan, the daughter of Mrs. Meg in Louisa May Alcott's *Jo's Boys and How They Turned Out* (1886), is another instance of a fictional physician, and Annie Nathan Meyer's *Helen Brent, M.D.: A Social Study* (1892) is yet another.

41. Gerald Thorson, "Tinsel and Dust: Disenchantment in Two Minneapolis Novels from the 1880s," *Minneapolis History* 45, no. 6 (summer 1977): 216.

42. Smith's visit to a prostitute after he has been rejected also serves as a counterpoint to Astrid Holm's reflections on her prospective marriage to Smith as prostitution.

43. The Copenhagen edition, *En ung pige,* was reviewed in *Budstikken,* December 6, 1887. For the number of Minneapolis printings, see the "Thor M. Anderson Bibliography: Norway in America," in the University of Oslo Library, also available at <http://www.nb.no/baser/tma>.

44. Several sources refer to a novel, "Ensomhed," published in Minneapolis in 1888. I have not found any evidence of such a book. The "reviews" in *Budstikken* (November 11, 1888) and *Normanna* (November 24, 1888) are of a public reading of a manuscript by Kristofer Janson.

⊰ A ⊱

Saloonkeeper's

Daughter

〜

A Novel by

DRUDE KROG JANSON

The old attic was such a splendid place for a young girl. All the old broken furniture up there fascinated her—a sofa with three legs, a huge cracked mirror in a gilded frame tossed in a corner, a broken rocking chair. But what was best of all was an old chest filled with the most marvelous treasures. Her greatest pleasure was to sneak up there in the afternoon after school, open the chest, and take out what was in it. Old theater costumes, faded and tattered, looked quite good in the partial darkness, and the sequined finery glittered almost like real gold. She thought she was lovely when she put on the blue silk coat with gold sequins, pulled on the once-white theater gloves that reached up to her elbows, and threw a white embroidered veil over her tousled black hair.

Apparently the rats thought so, too. They ran in packs up there, and they had become so accustomed to her that they no longer ran into a corner when she came. Instead, they sat quietly, looking at her. She had no fear of them either, for they were the audience for her little impromptu plays in which she was always the queen and heroine.

Astrid was often alone. Her two sisters had both died, leaving her with two little brothers who were so much younger that they provided little companionship for her. She loved her mother passionately, but lately her mother's poor health kept her in bed most of the time. Her mother had been an actress with a road company, and all the treasures that were her daughter's joy were from that time. Astrid, however, knew nothing about that because her father did not want his children to know about their mother's "common" origin. So he had all his wife's visible memories from those days packed away in the old chest and stored in the dark attic, where the spiders were allowed to spin their webs undisturbed. When he came home from the office in the afternoon, Astrid's father never suspected that his daughter's greatest enjoyment had been among those things which he thought were hidden and forgotten. He was a respected merchant who thought that he had bestowed a great honor upon his wife by raising her up to his level.

Astrid never had much to do with her father. All the love her heart could hold went to her quiet, melancholy mother, who was always very affectionate and loving. She had very few friends because she could never take anyone home with her for fear of disturbing her sick mother. Therefore, all the time that she was not with her mother in her mother's bedroom she was thrown on her own resources. It was then she acted out her plays and lost herself in fantasy. Her only entertainment outside the home was when her father took her along to the theater, which he did a few times. There she received new nourishment for her play times. She especially liked *The Feast at Solhoug.* That light blue silk dress belonged to the mild Signe, but the black velvet dress belonged to the proud Dame Margit, the role she liked best to play.

Two years passed by. Astrid was almost seventeen years old. Her play in the attic had become more and more neglected. Now she read everything she could lay her hands on. To her mother she would read aloud the new literature as it appeared. She noticed that her mother was especially fond of listening to tragedies and comedies. At those times her mother's eyes would sparkle, and a pale flush would appear on her cheeks as she lay and listened intensely. Astrid liked to read aloud. Even if she did not understand everything, the words stirred her imagination and she did not read them poorly. Those hours of reading aloud bound mother and daughter even more closely.

Astrid was late in maturing. She still looked like a child, and on her mouth flickered a bright childish smile. Deer-like, she would lift her chin attentively; her large gray-blue eyes looking ahead of her expectantly as if she were dreaming of all the delight that life promised her.

Then her father decided that it was time for her to attend confirmation class. When the pastor spoke to her of sin and judgment and hell, his words passed her by; for those were impossible subjects for her. Life lay in a radiant light, and she had no use for such words. They did not belong to her dream world. But when he spoke in quiet, warm words about goodness, what joy there was in devoting one's life to what one loved, and when he de-

picted Israel's strong characters for her as persons who had followed the call
of their inner being, then her eyes opened wide. A strange new feeling went
through her, and tears ran down her cheeks. She herself did not know why.

Not long after Astrid was confirmed her father had to make a business
trip to Bergen, and he asked her to accompany him. She became ecstatically
happy. She had never been beyond the outskirts of Kristiania, and this would
be like a trip around the world. They traveled through Lærdal and on to the
Sognefjord. Her father had a brother in Balestrand, where they stopped over
for a few days.

Those days became for Astrid a single beautiful dream. In the evening
she sat on the shore and looked at the broad waves gently lapping the shore.
The moon cast its trembling golden path out over the sea and the mighty
snow-topped giants stood their eternal night vigil. Then she felt so strange
that she wanted to throw herself down in adoration and jubilation. How
puny and paltry all her fantasies now appeared in comparison to this contact with pure divinity.

Later, after the others had gone to bed, she sneaked out into the large
apple orchard among the powerful old trees that cast their mysterious shadows over the greensward in the moonlight. Ripples from the fjord sounded
to her like soft sighs. Then she was the princess running around in the enchanted forest. The fragrance of the flower garden reached her, virtually in-
toxicating her. In the middle of the garden stood an old walnut tree, spread-
ing its mighty branches. How wet, shiny, and fragrant its leaves were! She
filled her lap with them, sat on the grass, and leaned against the moss-
covered trunk. She put together a wreath of fragrant leaves while the sea
rocked and rocked her into her fairy-tale dreams with its quiet whisper. It
was the elf king, singing for her about his yearning and his love. What joy
to be alive! She threw herself down on the dewy grass, half closed her eyes,
listened to the quiet rippling of the water, and in deep draughts drank in the
cool breeze of the mild September night.

The next day they left for Bergen. The sea lay like a sunlit mirror. Astrid
sat on the deck of the ship looking back at the place where she had just experienced so much. There it lay in all its luxuriance in that dreamy bay of
the fjord, guarded and shielded by the loyal giant beside whose foot it
stretched itself out as confidently as a child in its mother's arms. It knew the
giant could be trusted, and under its mighty shadows flowers and fruit could

take root. Astrid felt as if she shared a secret with that place, as if it had un-
veiled all its splendor for her alone. She threw it a kiss just as the steamer
passed the point and hid the bay from her view.

Then her father approached her. She was struck by how old and wrinkled he looked. She wished she could speak to him about her dreams and
inner feelings, but she could not. She thought that was mean of her, but
she could not help it.

"How did you like it at Hoel?" her father asked. Hoel was the name of
his brother's home.

"Very well," Astrid answered briefly. She could say no more.

"Quite a nice place," her father said curtly. He seemed nervous. "But God
only knows how those people can continue to live there year in and year out.
I have already had enough of it. Come, let's go down to eat dinner."

He went down below, but Astrid remained sitting and staring back at the
blue mountains.

{ 2 }

They were one week in Bergen. Since they had no friends there, they
stayed at a hotel. Her father was out on business most of the time,
so Astrid was left on her own. One day one of her father's business
acquaintances drove them on a long trip in the area surrounding Bergen. It
was a beautiful day, and nature stood clothed in its first autumn splendor.
Astrid reveled in this proud nature where poverty and wealth were thrown
together in a strange mood, making this city's environment one of the most
picturesque to be found anywhere. Every moment she would burst out in a
happy or admiring cry. But when they drove around the dark lake, Svartediket, she became quiet. It was so impressive, almost frightening. She sat
with open mouth listening to the man from Bergen explain how people had

often drowned themselves there—that from that cliff this one or that one had jumped off. Oh, God, how unfortunate they must have been to do such a thing. And she had always thought that life was so beautiful! Oh, the poor, poor people! She imagined a woman standing up there on the cliff on a wild, stormy night, her hair disheveled, her face raised toward heaven, every hope destroyed.

"Oh, oh, oh," she said without realizing it and shuddered.

"What's wrong, Astrid?" her father asked. "How pale you are."

"I'm just a little cold," she answered.

"It has become quite late," said the man from Bergen. "It is best we hurry home."

Soon they were out in the sunshine again. Before them lay the city, bathed in the rays of the setting sun—light, overflowing, and vigorous. Behind them lay Svartediket with its coal-black water, its dark, forbidding mountains, and its horrible reminders.

The next evening they went to the theater. A famous Swedish actress had the leading role. That evening she played Hjørdis in *The Vikings at Helgeland.* Astrid had never seen the play before, but she had read it several times, and she looked forward to the performance immensely. From the moment the curtain went up, with the storm roaring and the waves crashing on the shore and those strange, wild, strong characters exchanging words with each other, Astrid was spellbound. She heard and saw nothing else. It was as if she had received a new pair of eyes. Never before had it been like this. How great Hjørdis was, and yet how frightful. Astrid sat breathless when the curtain came down. She pressed her hands to her breast. This was living! If only she could act like that! If only that day would come!

When Astrid went home that evening, she had resolved to become an actress. She trembled with the thought, unspeakably happy. She felt as though her call had been consecrated that evening. Now she understood what the minister meant when he talked about the joy that came from feeling the call from within. She had become strangely moved that day in confirmation class without understanding why, but now she knew. She would follow her call and be true to it. But she could not say anything to her father. No, she had to wait until she came home to her mother. Oh, how she missed her. Her mother would understand her. She smiled. Her thoughts turned to the old attic and the theater costumes. Now her whole being revolved around this alone. But now she would no longer act for the rats. No, she would go out in full daylight, and she would be triumphant.

When they arrived at the hotel there was a telegram for her father. Astrid turned pale. It was as if a cold hand seized her. She thought immediately of her mother. Not now, not now! What if she died! What would she do without her? Her father opened the telegram calmly. He thought it was a business telegram. But it read: "Karen is worse. Come home as soon as you can. Stina."

Her worst fears were realized. Her mother was very sick. She lay alone waiting for her daughter. Perhaps she was already dead.

"Oh, can't we leave right away, father? Isn't there a steamship leaving tonight?" asked Astrid, her lips white.

"Hmm," her father muttered nervously, walking up and down the floor with the telegram in his hand. "What shall I do? This has come at a very inopportune time. I have to stay here through tomorrow. But I'll try to get everything done by noon. The *Olaf Kyrre* leaves at twelve o'clock. How . . . very . . . awkward! Poor Karen!"

Astrid could not think of going to bed. She took off her dress, pushed her hair back from her warm face, and let it hang loosely down her back. She packed her things together with feverish haste—as if it were important to be ready in a hurry. As soon as everything was ready for departure, she threw a shawl around her and sat by the open window. The cold air blew on her, but she was so burning hot that she found it refreshing. She looked out into the dark night. She saw her mother's face in front of her, pale and distorted with pain. Oh, God! That she should be so far away, unable to be with her and take care of her! She remained staring out into the night. Unwillingly, all sorts of shapes became confused with the face of her mother. She wanted to chase them away, but they kept returning. It was as if they flickered right in front of her eyes, those dramatic characters she had just seen. There came the old, proud Ørnulf, like a branchless tree in the forest that would not snap off in the storm, singing his magnificent ode. There was the noble Sigurd, with his silent, burning love. And first and last there was the dangerous but fascinating Hjørdis. Astrid looked unwillingly at the dark sky. If only she could get up there and join the wild procession, riding her black, snorting steed! Then her mother's apparition appeared again—so quietly. She was pale and suffering.

"Oh, mother," Astrid sighed. Her head fell on her folded hands. "You must not die. What shall I do without you?" She lay there a long time without moving. Finally, an indescribable tiredness came over her, and a cold shiver ran through her. She stood up, closed the window, and went quickly to bed.

The next day at noon they left Bergen. The first sunny autumn days were gone, and the real fall announced itself with a rain storm. They had a rough journey. Astrid was very seasick, but that was almost good for her, for then she was not able to think of her mother. She lay as if dead most of the time until they came into the Kristiania fjord.

Aunt Stina, her father's sister, stood on the pier in Kristiania. She lived near them and had promised to look after her mother and Astrid's two little brothers while they were gone. Astrid did not dare ask her aunt how everything was. She just stared at her, full of anxiety.

"She is a tiny bit better, but terribly weak," her aunt replied to her father's hurried question.

God be praised! Then she was not dead. Astrid would get to see her again. She took her brothers in her arms and kissed them, again and again. And when she came to her mother, oh how well she would take care of her. Her mother would not die!

{ 3 }

What her aunt had said—that her mother was terribly weak—was true. Astrid shrank back when she saw her lying there so white, so white, with large bright eyes. Astrid fell down beside the bed, put her arms around her mother, and began to sob. It was as though all the joy and dread she had experienced since she last saw her mother now found an outlet in her tears. "Mother, mother," was all she could say.

"Astrid, my dear girl," whispered her mother, stroking Astrid's black hair again and again.

"How wonderful it is to be with you again. Now I shall never leave you. I shall take care of you until you are well again. Then the two of us will have many lovely times together," said Astrid as she began gradually to gain control of herself.

Her mother smiled wistfully. She almost looked as if she didn't believe that she ever would be well again. And yet, for her children's sake, she wanted so much to live.

She actually did become better. Her happiness at having Astrid with her again and feeling her love gave her new life. Astrid was happy.

"See, mother. It was just because I was gone that you were so ill," Astrid smiled the day after her return.

"Yes, and now you must tell me everything that happened on your journey," said her mother.

"Not yet, mother. Aunt Stina says I must not talk too much to you today. Anyway, it can wait. It's enough just to be able to see you again," she said, kissing her mother gently.

Mrs. Holm lay looking at Astrid. She felt that some change had come over her daughter, a new awareness. She had suddenly become an adult.

A few days later Astrid was sitting by her mother's bed. Her eyes beamed, and her cheeks were flushed. "Now, dear mother, I must tell you all that has happened, and then you shall hear what your little girl has made up her mind to do."

Then she told her about the beautiful Sognefjord, the overwhelming blue mountain, the wonderful garden, Bergen, and Svartediket. But when she came to Svartediket a shudder went through her and she said, "Oh, mother, so many have drowned themselves there. Can you imagine how unhappy you would have to be to do that? Of course, I have read about people doing it, but I never thought they actually did. Oh, and it was so dark, and the water was as black as coal." She stopped a moment, overcome by the memory. Her mother said nothing, just lay there strangely staring.

Astrid continued in a more cheerful tone. "But I have kept the best until now, dear Mother. We went to the theater and saw Mrs. Hvasser play Hjørdis in *The Vikings at Helgeland*. Oh, God, how wonderful that was! You can't imagine how she acted! And do you know what, mother?" She got on her knees beside her mother's bed. "I have decided to become an actress. I think I have the talent for it. After all, that's all I ever thought of. You should just see," she continued, half laughing, half embarrassed, "how I have acted out comedies up there in the old attic. When I wasn't with you or in school, I was almost always acting out comedies. In the old chest I found so many marvelous outfits that I dressed up in, and I played Dame Margit and Signe and Ragnhild and . . ."

"Why have you never told me this before, Astrid?" Her mother's voice was so full of anxiety that Astrid jumped up alarmed.

"Why? I don't know, mother. I suppose that I was afraid I would no longer have permission to be up there if anyone found out. At that time I didn't tell you everything as I do now that I have grown up."

Her mother turned pale. Then a light flush appeared on her cheeks, and she raised herself up on one elbow with more strength than she had shown in a long time and said: "This is not new to me. I have suspected it would come. You were too much like me. Yet, I have hoped and prayed that it wouldn't be so. Astrid, my little girl!" She fell back on her pillow again. "You don't know what awaits you there, Astrid, but I know it all too well. You see . . ." Her voice became hoarse and she half whispered, "I, too, have been an actress."

"You, mother?" Astrid jumped up in the air. "Then it was your . . ."

"Hush, Astrid. Yes, those were my old costumes. Your father was afraid someone would find out I had been an actress, so they were packed up and put up there. I have never mentioned it to anyone."

"But to be ashamed! Was father ashamed of it? Isn't it rather a great honor?"

"Father didn't think so, and he could be right. He was afraid it would ruin his reputation. I wasn't a great actress. I was never regularly employed at an established theater. I defied my own father when I made my debut. But it was a fiasco. I had too much feeling and imagination and too little talent, they said. I'm afraid it will be the same for you, Astrid. Yet I dreamed constantly of the theater. Then one day I ran away with a road company. I was only seventeen years old. What a life I led there! All the finest and the best in me was offended every day. I loved acting passionately, but the others thought only of pushing themselves forward and making life as miserable as possible for the others. Then the director pursued me with his repulsive advances.

"In the meantime, my father died, and our home was broken up. Then, quite by accident, I became acquainted with your father. He proposed marriage and a good home. I was tired—and so disillusioned. But Astrid, and that is the curse of it, I have never had a happy day since I left the road company either. Your father and I were so different. We could not understand each other. In the first year after we were married I often felt the temptation to do what those unhappy people you told me about did—to cast myself down into the black water. I was so lonely and unappreciated. Then you children came along. Time dulled me little by little. But that is what has broken my health. And now—are you going to repeat the same thing? Your father will never give his consent to it."

"Then I shall do it without his permission. You shall be victorious, mother, through me. I shall hold out longer than you did."

"No, no," said her mother anxiously, grabbing Astrid's hand. "It will never go well! Promise me, Astrid, never to go on the stage without your father's permission. Promise me."

"But mother . . ."

"You must promise me."

Astrid noticed her mother's fear. She heard the hoarse whisper, and she was afraid this might kill her.

"Mother, sweet mother. I'll do anything you wish if only you stay with me."

Her mother closed her eyes. The tension in her face relaxed. She squeezed Astrid's hand. She was unable to say anything more. Astrid thought she looked like a corpse. She sat quietly and held her mother's hand for several hours without moving.

Those were the first serious hours in Astrid's life. A shadow had come over the sun. For the first time she had looked into another life full of disappointment, loneliness, longing, and that was the life of the one nearest and dearest to her in the whole world. "Poor, poor mother," she thought. Tears ran down her cheeks as she sat looking at the white face. "How beautiful you have been; how beautiful you still are! But, oh, how much you have suffered!"

She started thinking of her father, and realized at once that he had moved a thousand miles further away from her in this last hour. He would never understand her, just as he had never understood her mother. She had only pure hatred for him. In this hour she had come to realize that her mother's life spirit had been broken. She would never be able to keep her. With an instinctive fear she thought of life together with her father. Just a moment ago she had been so jubilantly happy. And her call . . . She smiled painfully. God knows how this would turn out if it should depend on her father. And then there were her little brothers to think about.

For the first time Astrid faced sorrow, and with it came worry and responsibility.

Later in the evening Mrs. Holm awoke in a burning fever. She kept calling for Astrid, who comforted her by placing her hand in her mother's. Astrid did not move from the bed.

Three days later Astrid's mother died.

{ 4 }

August Holm had never experienced adversity. His parents had been well-to-do. True enough, they had both died when he was young, but he was too much of a boy to really feel any sorrow over losing them. Moreover, he was one of those individuals incapable of genuine emotions toward anyone or anything except himself. After an indolent performance at school, where he did not really learn much of anything, he was set up in his father's wholesale business. He was the oldest of four children, and when he came of age he received his inheritance and traveled abroad to Germany and France for a couple of years. There he played the role of the dashing young gentleman. Shortly after the death of his guardian, who had also been his father's business partner, August returned home and took over the business. His sly business sense, together with the respectable name of the firm, made it possible for him to keep the company going for some years even though he lacked any real competence.

Shortly after he had taken over the firm, he went on a trip visiting customers along the coast. In one of the small towns where he stopped, a road company was playing at the theater. In order to while away a boring evening he went there and fell madly in love with the prima donna, the eighteen-year-old Karen Linde. She was not such a good actress, but she was spectacularly beautiful, and he found her enchanting in her pure, simple spontaneity. This was something completely different from what he was accustomed to seeing. He tried to make advances, but he soon realized that this would not get him anywhere. Like all spoiled, egotistical people, he was spurred on by her rebuff and became so completely absorbed that he did not give up until she agreed to marry him.

As soon as he had his own way, however, he, like all egotists, found that the joy was gone. He thought that he had done her a stupendous honor, and he often let her hear about it. He was, of course, the fine gentleman, the son of an old patrician family. He had shaken the hand of Charles XV and waltzed with Queen Louise. He was the one who had entertained the king and given the welcoming speech when the king came to the city. All this he told her each time he became irritated over having let his passion run away with him that one time. It had been an expensive pleasure, he often thought when he saw her walking quietly around, sick and melancholy, like a strange plant that had accidentally come into his garden full of all the deep-red tulips and poppies of his self-love. Gradually he became accustomed to her and forgot his irritation. He came and went when he desired, and she became for him, like any other piece of furniture, a household possession that he could not easily dispense with. She seldom contradicted him, and this was a great comfort since he liked best to hear himself talk.

He began to pay a little more attention to his daughter. "She is becoming damned beautiful, but cursed like her mother," he thought. "I had best keep my eyes on her." He always tried to put a damper on her bursts of enthusiasm by coming out with some moral platitude about self-control. "It isn't proper to carry on that way," he would say—or words to that effect.

Lately he had become extremely nervous and unsociable. His face had become more sallow, and the smug smile no longer played around his thin lips. He had become insecure and hesitant. For the first time in his life he felt the earth shake under him. Business went poorly. That it had done for a long time, but in the last year it had gone down severely, and his credit had given out. Partly to strengthen his credit and in part to ask his brother in Balestrand for a loan, Holm had made his trip. He had taken Astrid with him both to get her away from her mother for a while and to give himself company so he wouldn't have to brood alone all the time.

The trip was unsuccessful. His brother assured him that he had tied up all his money in his property and that it barely gave profit. His brother, a hard-working, enterprising man, apparently didn't have much confidence in Holm's business, especially since times were bad everywhere in the business world and bankruptcy was the order of the day. He definitely was not moved by Holm's long, pious speeches or his promises about what high interest he could pay and how brilliantly the firm would prosper if he only received this loan in this momentary setback. Whatever it was—whether it was because he could not or because he would not—was not clear to Holm. In Bergen it hadn't gone any better. They had smiled and been polite, yes. They had even treated him and his pretty daughter to a drive. But there were no firm assurances, and he had come home a little more depressed than when he left because now he was convinced of his impending ruin.

Holm stood with mixed emotions beside his wife's body the day following her death. He felt himself stripped of much of his imagined greatness, and never in all the years they had shared had his feelings for her been so close to genuine as when he now stared with actual tears in his eyes at her fine, pale face, where melancholy had engraved its mark all the way to death. "Poor Karen," he said softly. "It was, though, at the right time you went away."

Astrid fell apart entirely in her sorrow at her mother's death. After their last conversation she had forgotten herself and her worries and had thought only about her mother and all her hardships. But now that her mother was dead she could not control herself. She went up to her room. Now Aunt Stina and the others could take over. She would have nothing to do with that lifeless mask. That was no longer her mother, with her beautiful eyes and loving smile. She was gone from her forever . . . forever. She broke out in a most fervent cry. "Mother! Mother!" She gasped intermittently and sobbed so her whole body shook and she thought her heart would break. Finally, she quieted down a little. There came a tense sob at times as if from a child who has received punishment. At last she closed her swollen, tired eyes and fell asleep. She slept around the clock, her young body exhausted from sleepless nights and sorrow. Her aunt, who, after she had heard of her sister-in-law's death, had moved in with them to help them through the funeral, looked in on her several times but went away again when she saw that Astrid slept. The last time she came up, Astrid lay with her head buried in her pillow, sobbing.

"So, child," she said reassuringly, stroking her head. "Pull yourself together now. Remember that it was the best thing for your mother, sick as she always was. She is well off now, that's for sure."

"Oh, mother! Mother!" Astrid sobbed.

"Yes, it is hard now, but you'll see it will soon be better. Now you must pull yourself together and come and help me. There is so much that has to be arranged for the funeral. Your father has set it for Wednesday," said her aunt in a friendly but firm tone. Aunt Stina, who was a very practical person, thought it was healthiest to handle the situation in a sensible way and not let Astrid succumb too much to her emotions.

This had its hoped-for results. At hearing the words funeral and help, Astrid began to calm down. Life waited for her. She was not—like her mother—finished with it. She lay with vacant eyes and stared ahead of her. It was strange what a grave-cold aura had come over life, and still she would have to get up and go down to meet it.

⌇

THE FUNERAL WAS OVER. ASTRID HAD TRIED TO BE as composed as she could. She went around automatically and did everything her aunt told her to do. Only when she saw her youngest brother's light, curly little head did everything fall apart again. But she tried to be brave. The pastor's words were like a dream. She followed along to the cemetery and saw them lower the casket. All the flowers were removed, and she saw only the dirt and heard the gruesome thud on the coffin when the dirt fell on it. Then they went home. She held her youngest brother by the hand.

That same day Aunt Stina put on her hat and shawl, kissed Astrid on the cheek as she lay quietly on the sofa with her eyes closed, and said: "Yes, now I must go home, Astrid. God only knows what it looks like at home when the servant girls have been able to fritter away the time for so long. Now you must get busy and take care of the house and boys. I shall look in on you to-morrow."

Then Astrid was alone. How infinitely lonesome and helpless she felt. Her brothers were out on the street playing, their sorrow already forgotten. Her father had gone to his office, but if he had been home she would not have felt any less lonesome. Now, at least, she had peace to lie and think about her mother. How good it was to lie so quietly and close her eyes and dream. She was a child again, and her mother was with her.

"Is the young Miss lying alone in the dark?" asked a voice. A strong ray of light shone on her tear-stained eyes.

It was Annie, the faithful old servant who had been with them as many years as Astrid could remember. She held the kitchen lamp in her hand and stared with a worried face into the living room.

"Shouldn't I light the lamp? It isn't good for the young Miss to lie here alone in the dark."

"Thanks, Annie. Oh, it doesn't really matter one way or the other," Astrid said with a deep sigh.

"Don't say that, young Miss. Things will get better. And now the blessed angel has found rest. She really never had it so good."

"But what shall I do without her?" sobbed Astrid.

"Oh, young Miss, it has to be that way. We'll have to live—even if it won't be easy. Then, too, the young Miss has both of her little brothers."

Annie lit the lamp and puttered around in the room a little. When she heard footsteps out in the hall, she hurried out. She knew that Holm would not like to see her in the living room. Astrid got up and pretended she was busy at something.

Holm came in. He looked so pale and tired that Astrid felt pity for him. So he, too, had been fond of her mother! She thought she had more affection for him now than she had had for a long time.

"Are you here, Astrid?" he asked. "Where are Harald and August?"

"They are playing out on the street."

"It is best you get them in. Don't let them stay out any longer."

Astrid went out after them, and Holm walked restlessly up and down the floor. "Hmm. I must talk with her in the morning. I'll have to leave in eight days. It's the only way out. Over there I can still have a rosy future. Here all paths are closed."

Astrid came in. "They are coming now," she said.

"Hmm," he said without listening. "I would like to have a long talk with you tomorrow morning after breakfast, Astrid. There are some things I must discuss with you. This evening we are both too worn out after this emotion-filled day. Ask Annie to have breakfast on the table at eight o'clock. Good-night, my girl." He kissed her absentmindedly on the cheek and went to his room.

Astrid brooded a little over what it might be he wanted to talk to her about, but she soon forgot about it. She felt so tired and despondent that she cried herself to sleep.

THE NEXT MORNING AFTER BREAKFAST, instead of going to his office as usual, Holm said, "Come with me to the living room, Astrid. I want to talk with you."

She followed him and remained standing by the window, looking inquiringly at him. For a long time he just paced the floor. Suddenly he turned to her and, stroking his long mustache rather ostentatiously, said: "What would you say about going to America, Astrid?"

"America?" shouted Astrid with open eyes.

"Yes. America. I have decided to go there."

Astrid could not answer. Her white face became blushing red. Then she threw her head back suddenly. "It's just as well I tell you at once, father, that I shall become an actress."

Her father, who was again walking up and down the floor, turned suddenly and stared hard at her with his small blue eyes. "Aha," he said slowly. "Have we already come so far? But there will be nothing of that, Astrid. Do you hear?" he added, walking right up to her and looking at her almost threateningly.

"Why not?" asked Astrid, her lips quivering. "It's the only thing I want to do—and the only thing I feel called to do," she added defiantly.

"That's all nonsense! I won't hear another word about it, Astrid. I have had enough of that already in the family," he mumbled to himself.

Astrid shuddered. That he could talk about her mother that way the day after she had been laid in the earth! She wanted to reply, but instead she broke out crying.

"Listen now, Astrid. It's no use, even if you beg me on your knees. I hope you will be a sensible girl. It cannot be otherwise. So now we shall not discuss this matter any further. In eight days I'm leaving for America. You and the boys will stay here for the present. I shall ask Aunt Stina and Uncle Meyer if you can live with them this winter. You can help around the house, and I'll pay for the boys. In the spring you can join me in America. Business is going downhill here, and the times are so bad that there is no future for a man who wants to make a go of it. America is the right place for me. There a man with knowledge and experience can get ahead. It's a republic and a land of free institutions. I belong there where one is free of all this aristocratic nonsense."

In spite of her sorrow Astrid could not help looking at her father with big eyes. Was it her father who talked in this way? He who always talked with the deepest respect about the royal family? How often when she was a child he had come home in a flurry when the king was in the city. Then he had appointments here and there and had to have his best finery on. She remembered so clearly one afternoon when she was a little girl and had been allowed to go out with him. They had waited so long and it was so cold that she froze, but her father had said that the king would come soon, and she thought to herself that the king must be someone terribly important. She meditated on whether he was like God and if God could come riding in a carriage pulled by four horses. Her father caught her astonished look and realized that he had not always spoken in this manner.

"Hmm, yes, that is to say," he stammered, a little embarrassed. "Of course, I once had different notions. But lately I have come to believe that a republic is the best form of government, absolutely the best form of government. So, my girl," and he hurried to get away from this dangerous subject, "you have now heard what I have decided to do. As soon as I'm gone you can move over to Aunt Stina's. Annie will be let go. I shall pay her a quarter of a year's wages. The house and all furniture will be sold. So now I think there is nothing more to talk about for the moment and, anyway," he looked at his watch, "it is late. Where's my hat? Oh, here it is. Be sensible about this, girl. There is nothing else to be done, Astrid." He was already by the door. Then he turned. "And about that other nonsense: we won't talk about it anymore. You will never get my permission. Believe me, I understand this matter better than you do."

How good that he went now. She thought she would suffocate while he stood there and talked. She was totally confused. America? Move away? She sank down in a chair, placed her head in her arms, and tried to pull herself together. She thought of her promise to her mother. She couldn't break it. Again she saw his ice-cold look and heard the hard, almost mocking, tone in which he told her that nothing could come of it. She realized that there was no use to beg him. She must wait—God knew how long—maybe until she became old and gray. And then it would be too late.

Would she ever amount to anything in the world? She had had such wonderful dreams! Oh, to be free! And now she was going to America. To America! Perhaps, when it came down to it, that was the best. She lifted her head. There is so much freedom there. Maybe there could be freedom for her, too. At any rate, she might just as well venture out and see a little of the world. It was impossible to stay here now. Her mother was gone. She would be destroyed here. Oh, how helpless she was now that she didn't have her mother to help her.

She went out into the kitchen to find Annie. She needed a trustworthy soul to talk things over with.

"Annie," she said, "do you know what? We are going to America."

"My goodness, young lady, what is it you're saying?" said Annie. She had to sit down in a chair, still holding the bowl she was drying.

"Yes, father will leave in eight days. The house and everything will be sold, and you'll have to go away, and we shall live with Aunt Stina this winter and travel to America in the spring."

"Oh, God! Wasn't that what I always thought. Something terrible would happen when the blessed angel was gone. Oh, you poor things will be going out into the wide world alone!"

"You can come with us, Annie. Oh, can't you do it? If only father would . . ."

"Oh, whatever happens, he won't have anything to say about it if I pay for the trip myself," said Annie with a self-important toss of her head. "And that I shall do before I let you motherless waifs travel alone in the wide world."

{ 5 }

One quiet, sunny evening at the beginning of the month of June, the English steamship *John Bull* left Kristiansand's harbor and put out to sea. The dock was full of people. Some smiled and waved to those on board. Others looked up with tear-filled eyes and pale cheeks to catch their last glimpse of the dear ones they had just said good-bye to— perhaps forever. On the ship there was much commotion and restlessness. Sailors ran back and forth. Chests and suitcases were piled up on the deck and lowered into the hold. The anchor was hoisted and sails were raised. The passengers stood and stared toward land, waving their handkerchiefs as long as they could still glimpse that black spot where they knew their dear ones stood. Then they began to look around, gather their things together, and get settled as well as they could. Some remained sitting, motionless, staring at the blue mountains they would not see again for such a long time, possibly never. Many, many memories moved through their minds.

Two young boys with light curly hair were already playing among the immigrants. They had found a playmate their age and their fresh shrill laughter disclosed that they did not take the departure very seriously. On the contrary, they were full of excitement over all the strange new things they found. Nearby an elderly woman sat on a large chest. She followed the small boys anxiously with her eyes and warned them from time to time not to climb too high. She had a large black straw hat on her head and a gray shawl over her shoulders. She looked a little worn out and exhausted and her red eyes showed that she had been crying. There was something determined and decisive about her, as if she had made an important decision and knew exactly what she had done. Sitting there on her trunk she looked as if no power in the world could budge her from it before she wanted to leave it. It was

Annie, the old maidservant in the Holm household, and the little boys were Astrid's brothers. Annie had kept her resolution to follow the motherless waifs, as she was accustomed to calling them, over to the United States.

Astrid sat in the ship's stern, leaning her arms on the railing and staring intently toward land. She had no loved ones on the dock, no one who had waved to her. She was happy that she finally had come this far, yet she still could not take her eyes from those blue shadows bathed in the reddish hue of the evening sun. She loved them. She stared and stared, and, without her realizing it, tears ran slowly down her cheeks and fell one by one on her lap. Now she was on her way, too.

Oh, what a hard year it had been! She thought again of all that had happened since her mother's death. Life had seemed so empty. She thought about the morning her father had forbidden her to follow her calling and had told her that they were going to America. God, how awful the days had been after father had left. Aunt Stina told her that he had gone bankrupt and that the creditors would come and take the house and everything they found and that now they owned nothing. She never forgot how she felt when she sneaked up to the old beloved attic, got on her knees in front of the chest of drawers, laid her head on it, and cried as she did that morning her mother died. Then she took the shawl edged in white lace that she had so often cast over her shoulders in her plays without realizing it was her mother's, kissed it again and again, and put it on. That shawl no one would take away from her! Not long after that her uncle came in a carriage to take her and the boys to his house, and Aunt Stina welcomed them lovingly.

Astrid never felt at home with them. Her uncle was always busy at the store, so she never saw much of him, and her aunt was so different from her mother. She was clever and capable, but it was as if she could never speak with Astrid about anything but practical and domestic things. Since Astrid had no interest in these, there was no point of contact between them. In addition, Astrid was very slow-witted about anything that had to do with kitchen work. She always looked as if her thoughts were every other place but there. So it was not strange that her aunt lost her patience once in a while. She gave long lectures to Astrid, making clear to her that she would never get out in the world or amount to anything if she didn't pull herself together and try to learn something. There was never any real disagreement between them, however, because her aunt was always friendly and kind to her. But Astrid was fed up with all the speeches and felt so disgusted over her own incompetence that she felt she was living the life of a slave.

Astrid read English diligently on her own, for she had no money to pay for lessons. That was much more fun than to work in the house. Her few friends had stayed away after her father's bankruptcy, and she had been too proud to seek them out. So she was almost always alone or together only with her aunt. Sometimes other ladies, her aunt's friends, came to visit. These tea parties did not interest Astrid at all. They usually talked about the best way to put up pickles or to preserve plums, or about their maids, or about some gossip they had heard. Only once, when the conversation turned to the theater and what they had last seen there, did life come into Astrid's face. Aunt Stina had taken her along to the theater a couple of times, and those were her only happy moments. But how she sobbed afterwards when she lay in bed and images of what she had just seen went through her mind. She felt like a bird trapped in a cage. Still, the crying did not hurt her. It was as if weeping relieved her of all those vague, oppressive yearnings that usually haunted her and filled her nights with delightful dreams.

When she was alone, Astrid's thoughts turned more and more to America. It was good that she would soon get away. She could no longer stand it in Norway. Gradually, all her dreams were focused on America, for she was so young and vibrant with hope and zest for life that she had to dream. In America she would begin to live again, and she dreamed of endless sun-lit plains where people were happy, where all could follow a call, and where no one treated others harshly because of prejudice.

Then came a letter from her father. He wrote that he was in the wine business and was earning good money. He said that he was lonesome for them. He wrote affectionately, and Astrid became excited. She forgot the bitter feelings she had had toward him before he had left and how cowardly she thought it was of him to run away from everything at home. Now she thought only about how lonesome he was over there, and she became hopeful that when they would be reunited they would both understand each other better. He sent tickets for the children and even for Annie, as Astrid had asked him to do. And now—now she was out at sea.

In the distance she could still see something like a faint dark blue shadow. That was her last glimpse of Norway. How refreshing it was out at sea, and how wonderful it was to breathe here! The sun sank. It was the first time she had seen it go down into the sea. The large glowing ball seemed to drop into the water and pour its purple hue in trembling streams over the rippling surface, and the horizon changed from red to a faint violet blue. Then dusk fell slowly as she sat there in the quiet, light summer night, took deep breaths of fresh sea breezes, and dreamed of the unknown land toward which she was sailing.

The next morning the sea was more turbulent. It rolled in deep broad swells. Astrid ventured up on deck, but she soon had to go down again. The boys, however, ran and frolicked as if nothing were wrong. They thought it was fun to see the large billows come and to feel the ship rock in powerful rhythm. Old Annie crept bravely up on her trunk.

After two days they landed in Hull. They had second-class tickets, but since they could not manage alone in the strange city, they went ashore with the emigrants in steerage and were taken with them to a large hotel. There were not many modern conveniences, but for Astrid it was a delight to be able to sleep on solid ground again. She saw nothing of the city but dirty, narrow streets darkened by fog and smoke. It rained constantly with a fine drizzling rain. The next morning they were transported like cattle by train to Liverpool. They were packed in so tightly that Astrid did not get much chance to look out on the quiet, green meadows that they traveled through with lightning speed.

The harbor in Liverpool looked like one big forest of masts, but Astrid had eyes only for the mighty Atlantic ship that lay there with flags and pennants fluttering gently in the fresh ocean breeze. She was overcome by a strange feeling when she boarded the ship that was to transport them to the New World. It was as if all energy swelled up and rose in her. She unconsciously stretched out her arms and could have broken out in a loud cry of joy. All her youthful strength streamed through her again with an uncontrollable courage that had lain dormant so long.

The weather was heavenly, and Astrid soon became accustomed to the sea. She could walk up and down the deck for hours without getting tired as she bathed her face in the fresh ocean breeze or stood by the railing and stared down into the ship's foaming wake, letting the pearls of foam blow up in her face. How strange it was, day after day, to see only heaven and sea, to feel so small and still be carried so surely forward. The ship plied its sure course without rest or pause, huffing and grunting as it cut the waves proudly and surely. For Astrid there was something strangely impressive in this steady course—a feeling of being carried forward eternally with a divine power that was totally incomprehensible to her.

Eventually, they passed the banks of Newfoundland. The evenings began to get darker. Right after the sun had gone down and the gilded skies faded, darkness descended. Then the activity began on deck. Most often Astrid crept up on some piled coils of rope that lay at the foot of one of the masts. From there she could look out over almost the entire length of the ship. There was not so much to see on first class. One or another English "Milord" or other fine gentleman walked pensively up and down the deck, well wrapped in his gray overcoat. Most of them, though, had retired to the splendid illuminated lounge, where, through the windows, she could see groups of well-dressed ladies and gentlemen.

There was much more activity among the emigrants in steerage. In one place a group gathered around a blond fellow who danced the Norwegian *halling* and a couple who danced the Irish reel. In another place the dancers were in full swing to the music of an accordion that sent out some husky hurdy-gurdy tones. Not far away from there Moody's and Sankey's hymns ("Pull for the Shore" or "There Is a Fountain Filled with Blood") were sung with fanatical fervor. In between one heard, "Come to Jesus! Who will come to Jesus? Hallelujah! God be praised." In yet another place a pastor from first or second class gathered a flock of solemn listeners. In second class an elderly man with a powerful physique and brown locks sang Wennerberg's "Psalms of David" with a vibrating theatrical voice, accompanied by a young and innocent woman's voice. The dashing tightrope walker, who had traveled around the world, stole a kiss from the young girl with the shabby silk dress and waving feathers. How unfortunate that just then a waiter came rushing along with a lamp, for the light fell right on the couple, causing all around them to break out in noisy laughter.

Over there sat the young girl with the beautiful face and the happy, dreamy smile. She had laid down her crochet work—that eternal crochet work—and stared, like Astrid, out over this strange, motley activity. Astrid was aware that this young girl was going over to marry and that she was expecting to meet her fiancé in New York. How strange it must be! "I wonder if I would be happy if a fiancé met me. No, I would rather be an actress."

When she tired of watching all this and darkness fell all around her,

Astrid lifted her head upward. There the deep blue vault was set with millions of shining stars. She had never seen them sparkle like this at home. The ship sped at full sail like a swan on the mirror-clear surface of the water. A fresh breeze filled the sails so that they bulged in their shining whiteness against the dark star-filled backdrop. How strangely wonderful it was just to lie there and gaze and drift between heaven and earth.

The next day they saw land. Shouts of "Land!" "Land!" were heard over the entire ship. Far away they spied a thin blue strip of land. It was Long Island, stretching its long arms out into the ocean to bid them welcome to the New World. Astrid stared with mixed emotions at that blue line, watching it get closer and closer. She was happy as she gazed full of hope and youthful courage at the promised land. Yet she was also sad because the voyage was over. When would she again see the sun set on the ocean and feel the fresh air fill her breast and let the salty spray splash on her face? She sighed, remembering all those marvelous evenings she had had on board. She would most likely never experience their equal again.

There were many signs of the approach to land. One pilot boat after another came scurrying out. They looked so proud of themselves with their fine towering structures and bulging white sails. Late in the afternoon the steamship sailed into New York's harbor. What a commotion and what beauty! How open it lay there with its fully outstretched arms so arrogantly confident in its rich splendor. It could easily welcome a large share of the world's rejects, the poor, and the homeless! It was confident of being the entrance to a better life, to human value, and to human rights. Hope and courage for the future would fill even the most forsaken when such an individual was welcomed by all this beauty after her lonely voyage and anxious brooding on what the future might bring. The shores on both sides of the harbor were decked in the luxuriant splendor of early summer. Attractive villas and terraced gardens created a marvelous setting. Ships came sailing toward them. Star-spangled banners waved from the ships' masts. They were full of people who, when they saw the Atlantic voyagers, shouted and swung their hats and waved their handkerchiefs. One after another they came, always filled with multitudes of shouting and welcoming people.

Astrid stood quietly, as if taken up in a splendid dream. Without knowing it she had folded her hands. Her large, dark eyes beamed. The boys shouted with delight and threw their caps up in the air, and some strange twitches appeared around old Annie's mouth. They dropped anchor in the middle of the harbor since they had to wait till next morning for a place at the pier. The sun went down and bathed the homes and gardens in its golden beams. It shone on the city that lay there in the inner bay, casting its light on those mighty buildings and church steeples. The harbor, too, was lit up with the thousand masts and fluttering banners and flags catching the last rays of the sun.

After dark a little steamer sailed around the ship. It sent up red, green, and blue rockets that shot whistling up into the dark sky and were reflected in the dark water under them like sparkling, falling stars. White two-storied cruisers, splendidly illuminated, glided out over the sea like fairy castles.

Finally, everything quieted down little by little. A few ships came sailing by, but there were no longer happy crowds of people aboard. On their ship, too, all became quiet, almost as if it were deserted. Tired from shouting and happiness, the small boys had been asleep for some time, and old Annie now slept more securely than she had since she left Norway. Only Astrid lay there supporting her head in her hands and staring over the railing into the black night at the thousand lights that shone out from the buzzing, swarming strange city.

Such was Astrid's entrance to the New World.

❊{ 6 }❊

Late one dusty afternoon they arrived in Minneapolis. It was burning hot on the train, and people sat, sleepy and tired, staring blankly at each other. Because they had stopped over in New York only one day, Astrid had not been able to see much of the noisy city where the commotion almost overwhelmed her. She was so much the stranger and so alone that she could not stroll far from the hotel where they had been given a room.

Then they were put on a train together with a horde of immigrants and sent off to Minneapolis. How tired she was after sitting upright for three days and nights, able to steal only a few moments of sleep. Little August had lain on her lap at night. He slept contentedly, not realizing the aching knees he caused his sister. But now it would soon be over. They had already begun to pass through the outskirts of Minneapolis. How ugly it was—flat and dusty, with a few poorly constructed little houses scattered on the naked prairies. God forbid! People could not live here. How they could stand to live like that, she could not understand. As the train moved on, however, it began to look a little better. The houses were more attractive and arranged along streets. But it was not beautiful—even if it was a sin to say so. Most likely it would be prettier in other areas. She hoped they would be living in an attractive district.

They arrived at the station. Father was no doubt there. Her heart pounded as she looked for him. God grant that she would now become really fond of him. Yes, there he was. He saw them and came over to them. She could hardly breathe. Was that the way he looked? He came to them, took the boys lovingly in his arms, and kissed them. Then he kissed her, too. But there was something strange about him, as if he were in a hurry. She thought he looked a little embarrassed when he turned to her. He placed them all in a carriage, and they drove down a street swarming with people. How lively it was! People were pushing and shoving as if they wanted to get away from each other. How droll some of their clothes were! There were several attractive, elegant buildings, but scattered among them were several old shacks that seemed to have been overtaken by surprise by their more splendid neighbors. Painted signs and flags hung out from the roofs, and strange painted wooden figures stood along the street, multicolored and life-like. How different from Kristiania! The attractive buildings became fewer and fewer and the shacks more numerous as they drove down the street.

Finally they stopped outside a small building and her father helped them out. "This is where we live," he said to the boys without looking at Astrid. She stepped out of the carriage with the others and followed them to the house as if in a dream. She saw a barely distinguishable sign over the door on which the word *Saloon* appeared in large letters. She smelled a strange, unpleasant odor.

They went up a narrow, steep stairway. Holm opened the door to a room.

She looked around. It was nicely furnished, but it was so dark. And the same odor followed her. She sat on a chair with her coat still on. Holm looked at her furtively while he took care of the boys.

"Aren't you going to take your wraps off, Astrid?"

"Oh, of course," she said as if in a daze and took off her hat.

"See here," Holm said with forced joviality. "The boys will sleep in here with me, and here, Astrid, is your room. It isn't large, but it won't be so bad when you get it fixed up. Here is the kitchen and dining room. And look! I have bought this sofa, which can be opened up at night. It is for Annie. We must get along as well as we can to begin with. But now you must wash off the dust and eat a little and then get to bed. You are most likely tired out after the long journey. Tomorrow you can unpack and get settled."

Astrid looked around in her little room. It was small and square, with white walls and a single window from which the sun was shut out by the wall of the neighboring building. A bed, a little table, two wooden chairs, and a second-hand rocking chair made up the furniture. She began to arrange things a little. She might as well take it as it was. It was not exactly as she thought it would be, but when she had a chance to pretty it up a little with some of her knickknacks and hang curtains on the window, then maybe it would not be so bad. If only the odor had not been there. She did not know what it came from, but it seemed as if she had not been able to breathe since she had entered.

She washed herself and the boys as well as she could while Annie set out a little food according to Holm's instructions. While they ate, the boys jabbered and told their father all the remarkable things that had happened on their journey. Astrid attempted to eat, but the food stuck in her throat. Every once in a while her father stole a glance in her direction as he chatted with the boys.

"Well, now I'll have to go downstairs," said Holm as they got up from the table. "Try to get some sleep now, little boys," he added, patting Harald on the head. "How sleepy and tired you look!" Then he kissed August, who was his pet. "You get to bed soon, too, Astrid, and don't worry about me. I'll come up when I'm finished." He nodded and went out.

As in a stupor, Astrid followed the boys into their room and got them in bed. Tears ran down her cheeks when she kissed them goodnight. She did not know why, but this evening she kept thinking so often of her mother.

She had been in such good spirits and so happy on the voyage, but now the terrible feeling of loneliness returned to her. She went into the living room. It had become dark. She leaned out the open window and stared down at the street. The gaslights were lit, but they stood so far from each other that people walked in the dark. A couple came walking along. They were most likely engaged, for she held him by the arm. They talked Norwegian together. She could hear them clearly when they passed underneath her window. Three, no four, young fellows came out of their house. What in the world were they doing there? And there came yet another. How loudly they shouted, all at the same time. They, too, were Norwegians. Were they all Norwegians around here? Two men appeared over on the other side of the street. They seemed to be staggering. Then the oppressive, suffocating feeling came over her again. All at once she heard a racket, and the door below crashed open. A strong light fell through the door out on the street. Someone came tumbling out head first.

"You won't get a glass more. You're as drunk as a swine." She recognized her father's voice.

The man who had been thrown out pulled himself up in a hurry, grabbed the door that Holm was trying to close, and yelled: "Yes, damn it! I want some more. I'll have as many glasses as I want as long as I pay you for them. You're probably afraid I don't have any money left—but you bet I do." He jingled the coins in his pocket. "I'm an honest worker, I am. You better believe it! I don't have to have your permission to drink a glass more than I need. By God, I don't. And who do you think you are? You're no better than a swine taking money out of the pockets of poor people. That's what you are." He hiccoughed again. "You think you're so much better than us simple laborers, but I would rather get myself drunk every night than be a saloonkeeper—a damned saloonkeeper!" He spit far out on the street.

"If you're not quiet, I'll call the police."

"The police? And why the hell should they help you? They should put you and people like you who won't do an honest day's work in the pen . . ."

Then a policeman came. Strangely enough, he came from their house, too. He took the man by the collar. "In the clink with you, old man!" He was conspicuously thick in his speech. "Come now, or . . ." He waved to a policeman who came sauntering along on the other side of the street. That one understood the situation at once, crossed the street, took the fellow by the other arm, and they both marched away with him in spite of his scolding and cursing.

Astrid lay with the upper part of her body entirely out of the window, looking and listening, her eyes wide. Suddenly it dawned on her. She moved away from the window, ran over to the farthest corner of the room, and put her hands in front of her face as if she wanted to hide. "Dear God, dear God," she moaned. "What shall I do? What shall I do? And to think that I'll have to go through this every day." She spoke like a whimpering child.

Finally she took her hands away from her face. She was petrified. Her eyes had an eerie expression, her fresh young lips were painfully distorted. "Saloonkeeper, saloonkeeper." She repeated the man's words mechanically, and, without realizing it, she wrung her hands and walked up and down the floor. "We sell liquor, and people come here to get drunk. That is what I have come to America for. It seems ridiculous." She twisted her mouth in an attempted laugh, but it would not come.

"Hush!" The hall door opened. "I cannot face him. Not tonight." She ran out of the living room into her own room, tore off her clothes, jumped into bed, and hid her head under the covers. Then she felt safe from him. She lay in bed as if in mortal fear. No tears came. She could not think either. How tired she was. Oh, so tired. "Mother! Mother!" She finally cried and burst into sobs. It made her feel better. She thought she could cry forever, and she did until she fell asleep.

It was indeed Holm who came up the stairs. He had been worried that Astrid had heard the racket down in the saloon, and had been restless until he could come up to see if Astrid was in the living room. At the same time he was nervous about meeting her there if she had heard it. "It will be unpleasant if she finds out about the situation here in that way."

It had not been as easy for Holm to make his way in America as he had thought it would be. His upbringing and talents were not at all appreciated. People only asked, "Can you work?" But that Mr. Holm could not do. The modest business ability he possessed was not of any use, for he could not speak English. The little bit of it he had learned at school he had forgotten entirely. He did not have the capital to begin any business of his own; fifty dollars was all he had when he arrived in Minneapolis. His only choice was manual labor or the saloon. The first he felt, and probably was, entirely unfit for, and so he ended up in the saloon, like thousands of others who came over with big dreams of carving out a brilliant future in America. It would be unfair to him, though, not to admit that the decision was not an easy one. It was very tough for him—not so much because of the ethics involved but because he felt it was a disgrace that he, a well-bred gentleman, the scion of an old patrician family, should sink so low as to become a dispenser of alcoholic beverages. But it looked to him as though he had no other choice. He took it as something he could begin with and hoped that in time he would be able to move up to the more fashionable part of the city and develop his present saloon into a wholesale business. The more he became aware of his situation, however, the more he realized that such hopes were farther and farther away in the blue. Yet he still felt a kind of comfort in clinging to such thoughts of a brighter future. At the same time he gradually grew less anxious about the unpleasantness of his present state of affairs and the need to move out of it. He thought that he had an advantage over the other simple saloonkeepers because he had only fallen back on this business in self-defense and would move out of it when the situation permitted. It was, at any rate, a comfort to him that none of his old acquaintances and friends saw him in these circumstances, and in America, of course, you had to take life as it came.

In the meantime he sought as far as possible to raise his saloon above the common run by making it a hangout for the dashing young men who had the urge to get together to chat over a glass of beer. In this endeavor he hoped to get much help from Astrid as a drawing card for these fine gentlemen. He would have to tolerate the simple customers, of course, for they were necessary if the business was to yield an adequate profit. So he would shrug his shoulders and talk about them as "a necessary evil" and "society's dregs" or observe that, "we who are well bred must try to keep our distance as well as we can." He sought to avoid vulgar incidents in his saloon and was very much annoyed when the inevitable sometimes occurred. He was especially irritated that something like this had happened the very evening Astrid had arrived since he had been anxious to give her the most favorable impression of the business from the beginning. He had written to her that he was in the wine business. In a way he was, and he had hoped that when she came over and saw the situation with her own eyes she would, little by little, learn to take the matter sensibly and put up with the inevitable.

He was, therefore, very uneasy until he knew for certain that Astrid had not heard the uproar. He was quite relieved when he found the living room empty. "She was tired and went to bed," he said to himself, "but I'd better speak with her in the morning and get her to see the matter from a sensible point of view. If only she hadn't had such fantastic notions from her mother. She has such damned annoying eyes."

{ 7 }

Astrid slept late the next morning. She felt as though the blanket of death lay over her and she could not shake it loose. Nor did she want to. It was just too horrible to wake up. All she wanted was to sleep.

Annie came in. "Miss Astrid, Miss Astrid, it's almost eight o'clock."

"Oh, Annie, let me sleep," mumbled Astrid. "I'm so tired."

An hour later Annie came in again. "Miss Astrid, your father is asking about you."

"Let me lie here. I'm so tired."

Annie shook her head. Something was wrong. The young Miss was always so sprightly in the morning.

Later in the morning Holm looked into the living room for the fifth or sixth time to see if she was there. He was uneasy about her late arising. "Of course, it's natural for her to be tired after the journey." He comforted himself with the thought as he stood by the window, looking out on the street while stroking his long mustache.

Then he heard a step. Was it Astrid? No, it was too heavy, almost shuffling. It must be Annie. The living room door opened. He turned, then jumped back alarmed. He forgot what he had intended to say. "Astrid, what's wrong. You look terrible!"

She cast a shy, nervous glance at him but said nothing. He understood at once that she had heard everything.

Astrid went over to the other window, sank down in a chair, and stared absentmindedly out on the street. He glanced furtively over at her from the side. What would become of her? It was as if all her youth had passed away in one night and all that was left was a hopeless, flat, despondent shadow. He was frightened. It was madness, of course, to take it so hard. No misfortune had occurred. Yet, it was impossible for him to scold her. All his usual platitudes failed him. A faint perception that he had ruined his daughter's life, that there was more at stake than he thought, dawned on him.

He began to pace the floor. Neither one said anything. Astrid continued to stare ahead of her. He was suddenly afraid that she was losing her mind. "Astrid," he said anxiously, suddenly stopping his walking, "just be sensible. Don't take it all so seriously."

She did not move. He was not at all sure she had heard him. "Hmm," he began again. Her lack of response angered him and this gave him more courage. "I'm very sorry about what happened last night. It was a distasteful affair, but now it's over and there is nothing to be done about it. And now you know the whole story. You must realize that it's not a pleasant business for me either, but what am I to do? We have to live. I don't know any other way out. It's essential for me to fall back on this temporarily, and you must not make my life more difficult than it already is over here. Do you understand?" It was good to hear himself talk. It gave him more courage, and he gradually regained his old poise. "You must realize that this thing isn't regarded the same way over here as it is in Norway. In the eyes of others over here, one man is as good as any other—no matter what kind of work he does—as long as he makes an honest living."

Astrid looked up at him. The drunk man's words, "a damned saloonkeeper," rang in her ears.

Holm dimly perceived what she was thinking. "Such incidents as the one last night hardly ever happen," he continued. "As a rule all is nice and orderly here. I do all I can to keep the drunk people away and never give them more than I see they can tolerate. We don't only serve strong drink here, but also lemonade, soda pop, and seltzer water—all kinds of cold drinks. For that matter you could just as well call it a café or restaurant or something like that, and many well-mannered young men patronize me, I can assure you. You should get acquainted with them, Astrid. You will find a friendly atmosphere and be entertained by their company. Of course, I can't keep all the rascals away. That's one of the burdens of these businesses here in a country overrun by riffraff, and no one feels that more than a man of my up-bringing and traditions. But," he shrugged, "we all have to have patience and learn to accept what we can't change anyway. One thing you can be sure of, Astrid, is that I won't stay one day longer in this business or in this district than absolutely necessary. As soon as I can, I'll move up to the most fashionable part of the city and begin a respectable wine business such as the best men have at home in Kristiania. So, you see," he added impatiently, "there is no reason to create such a hullabaloo and look as if your father had become a murderer or one of the rabble."

Astrid reluctantly turned her head toward him. "But I'm not saying anything," she said slowly. There was no intonation in her voice.

"No, that may be so, but on the other hand you look as if you were about to be hung. Now I hope you understand the situation better and that you will be a sensible girl. It cannot be otherwise." He looked at his watch, kissed her on the cheek, and went downstairs, relieved that this scene was now over.

"Now I hope you will be a sensible girl. It cannot be otherwise." Those were his very words the morning after her mother's funeral when he had forbidden her to follow her dream and her call. Now he used the same words to argue that the one right and sensible thing for him to do was to run a saloon. For her to be an actress was an impossibility and a disgrace, but this was not a disgrace. Did he understand how cruel he was to her, that in cold blood he had trampled on all her dreams and hopes? Was it not just because she was a woman that he dared to behave in this manner toward her? Would he have dared do it if she had been a man? A flush of anger colored her pale face, her lips trembled, and, as was her wont when emotions overpowered her, she stretched out her arms. Oh, if only she had been a boy! What right had they to tie her up and destroy her because she was not a man? She collapsed on the chair. She felt such nameless pity for herself that she could have screamed aloud. She was so infinitely lonely and forlorn in a foreign land without knowing a single person, not one to whom she could relate her unhappiness.

⌒

IT WAS A HOT SUMMER— OPPRESSIVELY SO IN THE CITY, especially in the poor areas where the houses were small and low and the streets, which were never sprayed, were baked by the sun all day long. Sprayed streets were a privilege of the wealthy, who had their costly homes nestled in nice gardens where the grass was like the softest velvet and tree-lined boulevards shaded them from the sun. Down here both the sun and the dust had free reign and if there should be a strong gust of wind to relieve the stuffy, oppressive heat, then the dust whirled and frolicked in the street and filled the eyes and mouths of the passers-by. A suffocating stench came from all the saloons. Every third or fourth building housed one and they were all bustling with customers, however empty the streets otherwise might be, for a dusty throat had to have a glass of beer.

Holm's saloon, too, was doing a good business. People came and went, but Astrid paid no attention. She acted as if she neither saw nor heard. Old Annie would often look at her with a worried look in her face and shake her head. She had her own thoughts about Astrid's shame and declining health. It just could not be right to make your living by selling beer and liquor to people. When she came in from the street and paused at the bottom of the stairs by the door leading into the saloon and heard people striking billiard balls, shouting and cursing, Annie would shake her head and sigh. "And he was from such a good family and thought so highly of himself! Who would have thought it? The poor children."

Astrid said nothing. She had become so withdrawn that she hardly looked at anyone, and dark rings had formed around her eyes. Holm did not bother her. He saw that it would do no good for him to try to talk sense into her. "It will probably pass by when she has pulled herself together and become used to it," he thought. He tried to take her mind off the situation by inviting some of the "handsome young men" upstairs for a glass of wine. But it did not help. Astrid found these "handsome men" dissipated and revolting, and they thought she looked damned stuck up. So no further closer acquaintance developed. She preferred to shut herself up in her room and sit in her rocking chair with a book, which she never read. She could not concentrate on reading. Or she would sit with her hands hanging limp as she rocked. She felt weighed down by a deadly numbness. At times she wondered if she was not going mad. She would look around the little room at the white, bare walls and the narrow window where the sun never entered. Perhaps she was already insane and had been put in her cell and everything was gone, and here she would sit until she died. At such times she could be so overwhelmed by self-pity that she sometimes burst out in hot, bitter tears that brought temporary release.

Sometimes Annie would open the door. "Won't the young Miss come out to help me a little?"

"Yes, right away," Astrid would answer, but she would remain sitting until she heard her father calling. Then she would jump up and pretend to be doing something over by the chest of drawers or would go to the kitchen.

During the day Astrid hardly ever went out. If she had to go on an errand, she would hurry as fast as she could to get home again. It was as if the strong, clear sunshine was too much for her. She also feared the swarm of strange people and was afraid to look them in the eyes. But in the evening when darkness closed in, the lamps were lit, and the boys were in bed, she often put on her hat, wrapped a black lace shawl around her neck, and sneaked out. She always wanted to know if the boys were in bed before she went out. She had an instinctive fear of them hanging around downstairs in the saloon in the evenings. She did not want her father to see her and ask where she was going. She always ran through the dimly-lit streets in her part of town. She was afraid someone would grab her. When she came into the more fashionable, better-lit part of the city, she slackened her pace. She walked past the wonderful shops on Nicollet Avenue where people were streaming up and down dressed in light colors and fashionable clothes. How wonderful it was to see them so happy! And they all had friends to talk to. Apparently they were able to follow their call and live to work and be happy. She alone slunk around forsaken and lonely without a person in the entire populous city who knew her or could help her in her distress. Often when she came so far uptown she turned into Seventh or Eighth Street where the electric lights, the lighted store windows, and the buzz of happy people ceased. Here were the homes of the successful and wealthy families. In the American custom they had lighted their gas lamps but had left their curtains withdrawn so that the bright light from their living room fell out on the street. There she could stand for a long time, leaning with her head in her hands on the graceful iron fences that surrounded the front yard. The odor of flowers drifted over to her while she listened to the refreshing trickle of a fountain. The soft, velvet-like grass and the trees glistened in the gleam of light from the house where happy people were sitting in comfortable, well-furnished homes. The thick curtains, the paintings on the walls, and, once in a while if the evening was a little chilly, a lighted fireplace were all so splendid and homelike. There they could talk together and laugh and be happy. She would stand there as if petrified until a door opened. Then she would run back into the darkness where she felt that she belonged.

Once in a while she would go down to Bridge Square and out on the suspension bridge and stare down at the Mississippi that ran there so wide and rapid until it fell into the broad and foaming St. Anthony Falls. She would stand and stare at the rows of lights on both sides of the river with the noise from the city buzzing in her ears. The fresh river breeze would cool her warm cheeks. Here was neither dust nor the smell of beer. Overhead were the dark blue heavens with their sparkling stars. Beneath her was the black water. She had recently heard of a young girl who had leaped from the bridge. What if she should do what the young girl had done? She had a sudden vision of the coal-black waters and towering mountains of Svartediket. She smiled bitterly at the thought that she once had been unable to understand that people could be so unhappy. And now she understood it all too well. She broke into tears. She was not yet nineteen years old.

{ 8 }

Autumn was well under way. Already the end of September had arrived. Days were still sunny and clear, and the sky a wonderful blue. Trees wore their colorful autumn foliage, and the air was fresh and easy to breathe. It seemed to Astrid that along with the oppressive, stifling summer heat a little of the suffocating weight, which had lain over her like a nightmare and had threatened to destroy her, was gone. Once more she felt the blood throb in her veins, and her desire to live was awakened. The blow had been so overwhelming that she had become passive and powerless, but now her strong character began to assert itself. Her sense of misfortune had not abated, but a growing need to fight against it awoke in her. She wanted to take forcibly what life did not offer her willingly. Complex and strong characters bend far more helplessly under adversity than others, but they recover more easily, having absorbed new courage from their misfortune. She began to consider what she should do. She had to do something. But what? To leave this place was impossible because of her brothers. She had not been of much help to them, and she thought with a bad conscience how completely she had been preoccupied with herself all this time. Yet, she could try to keep them away from the saloon and the street. Now they had begun school, and that was a big help. She could supervise them in their English lessons in the afternoon and keep an eye on them. Besides, where could she go? She did not know anyone. The only thing would be to go to a Yankee family as a hired girl. But she dreaded that. She remembered all her unsuccessful attempts in Aunt Stina's kitchen and realized how unsuited she was for such work. That would be to go from one miserable situation to another. Her old desire to become an actress again arose in her more intensely than ever before. But how was that to be done now that she was a stranger to the language and to the society? How would she make her way in anything here? Besides, there was her father and the home she was tied to.

One morning her father called to her from the living room. She was in her room and she hurried into the living room. There he stood with two young gentlemen. The one she knew. He had been upstairs with her father before. His name was Hanson. She liked him better than the others her father had dragged up. He appeared rather cheerful and merry. He was always somewhat casually dressed, but there was a kind of good-natured charm about him. He was dark in complexion and under his black mustache a red, fresh mouth laughed, showing a row of badly neglected teeth. The other gentleman she did not know. He was rather tall and blond, and—what struck her as something unusual—properly dressed, with a kind of dignity that impressed her. His nose was curved, his eyes were light blue, though somewhat lackluster, and he had thick, sensual lips.

"Mr. Meyer," Holm introduced him. "This is my daughter. You know Mr. Hanson, Astrid. I have invited these gentlemen up for breakfast. Yes, to be sure, gentlemen, you must take what the house has to offer."

"Naturally, naturally," was heard in a chorus from the two. "But aren't we making too much trouble for the young lady?" added Meyer, turning toward the door which Astrid had just opened.

"Not at all, not at all. It is a great pleasure for both of us," Holm quickly replied. Astrid was already in the kitchen.

Holm entertained the gentlemen until breakfast was ready. He noticed Meyer's surprised glance following Astrid while she served coffee and went back and forth from the kitchen. Holm looked at her himself and discovered with satisfaction that she now appeared well. There was more elasticity in her walk, more color in her cheeks and more life and vigor in her body than he had seen since her first day in America. "Ah-ha, we are over the worst part now," he thought. "Now things will improve."

"And you say you just came from Chicago on the morning train, Mr. Meyer?" asked Holm, turning to his guest.

"Yes, two hours ago. I went straight to my good friend Hanson and washed and dressed up a little. We were going out to look around the city, and Hanson suggested we should come to say hello to you. But it may be a little early in the day to go visiting."

"Not at all. You are heartily welcome. It makes me very happy to have refined young people around me. Another cup of coffee? No? Then I think we'll go in and have a cigar. You see," Holm continued as he struck a match and held it out to Meyer, "for a man of culture and education it isn't so pleasant to be in my present position, but"—he shrugged—"we have to live, of course, and as a temporary measure I must put up with it. Before long I hope to be able to disentangle myself."

"So you are thinking of quitting the business?" asked Meyer.

"Yes, as soon as I can I'll move up to Nicollet Avenue and open a wholesale business. Down here, of course, a refined man can't possibly endure in the long run. It's impossible to keep the riffraff at a distance."

Meyer, who had noticed that Astrid's cheeks had become blood-red when her father began to talk about his business, turned to her. "How do you like America, Miss Holm?"

"Oh," Holm interrupted, "my daughter is still so unfamiliar with life here and she is alone too much. If I could provide her with some refined acquaintances, then she would soon prosper."

"Yes, it isn't easy for refined people to make themselves at home in these western cities where all the dregs from the Old World are streaming in," said

Meyer superciliously. "In Chicago it is barely possible, for there are some people of culture gathered there. But Minneapolis is still disorganized and in its infancy. We educated persons have a mission here. We must all contribute our share to the improvement of society."

Astrid looked at him suddenly with wide open eyes.

"Yes, you look at me, Miss Holm, but you also have your mission here."

"I?" exclaimed Astrid astonished.

"Yes, you. Among the Scandinavians here there are so few refined young ladies. Most are hired girls—or came over as such. So ladies of culture are what are most needed. And, of course, you also have talents as an actress."

All the blood rushed to Astrid's cheeks. "How can you know?" she stammered.

"Well, that's a mystery," said Meyer, laughing.

"I had better explain it then," said Hanson. "One day not long ago I was visiting with your father and I started to talk about how splendid it would be if some of us young people could get together and form a private theater. Then your father said that you have both the inclination and the desire for the stage."

Astrid could not help looking at her father. Was it possible that he could speak that way to complete strangers—he who had said to her: "not even if you beg me on your knees will you get my permission."

Holm laughed and took his pipe out of his mouth. "Yes, she had some high-strung notions of going on the stage at home in Norway. I didn't want her to get involved in that. It's an entirely different matter, though, if such a private company is formed here. If you wish to join them, Astrid, I would be happy to give my permission."

"Yes, at home anyone from a good family would think twice before becoming an actress," said Meyer, fondling his knee with both hands. "But here it is precisely the better people who must get to work and show the less fortunate the value of true art. A small theater with good talents can have a strong educational influence on our poor countrymen here. Wouldn't such work attract you, Miss Holm?" He turned to Astrid.

"Are you sure there are others who would want to join?" she asked hesitantly.

"Of course I don't know Minneapolis very well, but I know a little about the situation here through my friend Hanson. Besides, I have quite a few friends here. I'm sure there are many who are interested, but the talent they could rally around has been wanting. Now it has come. Will you help us, Miss Holm?"

"How do you know I have talent?" asked Astrid lightheartedly. Her cheeks burned, and her big eyes sparkled.

"I understand a little bit about people," said Meyer with supreme confidence.

"I shall gladly try, but . . ."

"Hurrah," shouted Hanson. "Now it's settled. And do you know what, Miss Holm? You must permit me to bring my sister Marie here to call on you. She's a great girl. I'm sure that she would want to go along with our theater. You'll like her."

"That would be a great pleasure for my daughter," joined in Holm. "It is precisely female companions that my daughter lacks. If she could only find some then everything will be all right, as the Americans say. Have you thought of actually settling in this city, then, Mr. Meyer?" he continued, turning to Meyer.

"Yes, I have. I have never really liked Chicago. I believe that basically Minneapolis is a pleasant city. It's a young city, growing rapidly, and that alone is interesting to observe. I also believe I'll have a greater future here."

"What are you thinking of entering upon?"

"I have thought that at first I would enter a law office. I have always said that the study of law is the only way for an intelligent young man in this country. In that field a person can expect a great future here."

"Have you studied law for a long time?" asked Holm.

"Hmm, yes—that is to say, I have not been able to apply myself to it as completely as I have wished," answered Meyer, pulling on his small, imperceptible mustache. "One has to live, too, as you just very correctly remarked, but I hope that I can soon begin in earnest. In a couple of years I will be finished, and as a Scandinavian attorney in Minneapolis I'll be able to have an immense influence on my fellow countrymen."

"Yes, fortunate are those who have come here in their youth with an adequate foundation of knowledge," said Holm with a sigh.

"Yes, you can say that again, Mr. Holm," answered Meyer grandly. "But we can't sit here all day, Hanson. What time is it? Oh, that's right, my watch has stopped. What does yours show?"

When Hanson's watch was also found to be stopped, Holm's was checked and it showed eleven. "No, is it so late?" said Meyer, jumping up. "How fast time goes in pleasant company. But I must go uptown. There is a man I absolutely must meet before noon. Will you come, too, Hanson?"

"Yes, I'll follow you. Good-bye, Miss Holm. Will you be here tomorrow? May my sister come to meet you tomorrow afternoon?"

"Yes, I'm always at home," answered Astrid laughing.

"Well, I hope that's not true. If it is, we'll at least put a stop to it. Good-bye, Miss Holm. Good-bye, Mr. Holm."

"Good-bye, gentlemen. Thanks for the visit. Come back again soon."

Astrid was in a fever of excitement. Would she really get to act? Was it possible to find a mission here? Could she really participate in showing her countrymen something beautiful by helping them to understand what true art is? Would she? She clapped her hands. Oh, God, if that were possible she would begin to live again. She went into her room and looked around. It was as bare as ever and the sun shone in no more than before, but it was still considerably lighter. It was just as if sunshine were in the air. She sat in the rocking chair and rocked back and forth. She half closed her eyes.

How frightening it had been to see how Meyer looked at her all the time. No doubt he was a very gifted person with a great future in America. But not Hanson. She laughed. He looked as if all he wanted to do was to amuse himself and enjoy life. She wondered what Marie Hanson would be like. It would be wonderful to have someone to talk with. Would she like her? Would she really find a girlfriend and not always have to go around alone? She wondered what Marie would think of her father's liquor business. Her heart beat when she thought of it, but she pushed it aside. They were going to put on a play! But what should they begin with? *The Feast at Solhoug?* Oh, Lord God, would she finally get permission? She stared ahead of her while the chair rocked slowly in time with her dreams.

In the afternoon Astrid went out. It was impossible to stay in. How easy it was to walk today, and how friendly and cheerful all the people looked. The cloud she always imagined hanging over them was gone. When she turned a corner she ran right into Meyer.

"I declare! It's Miss Holm! What good luck. How wonderful you look."

"Do I?" she laughed. How good it was to laugh.

Meyer devoured her with his eyes. How beautiful she was as she stood there in full youth, her chin lifted, her long eyelashes falling on her cheeks, the blood pulsing warmly under the pale downy golden-brown skin, and the red mouth with full lips laughing and showing her healthy teeth. He let his glance glide down over her. She was terribly dressed—like an immigrant. The simple gray dress with the little black wool jacket that fit her erect body so tightly around the waist and the black straw hat without feathers or flowers. "Well, we'll soon get that straightened out," he thought.

"You're not at all like the description my friend Hanson gave of you," he said as they walked up the street.

"So what description did he give? I scarcely knew he was aware I existed."

"Oh, Hanson is one who knows people, but he said that you were so terribly serious and unapproachable."

Astrid fingered her gloves nervously. A little twitch came between her eyes. It hurt her to think back on that time. "I felt very unhappy then," she said half aloud, as if ashamed to have such things mentioned. "But let's not talk about it. Do you know Marie Hanson?"

"Yes, very well."

"How do you like her?"

"Oh, she's quite a lively girl. She's not so bad."

"Oh, how arrogantly you speak of her. I'm so happy I'll be able to meet her. I have no girlfriends here. Well, I didn't at home either," she continued, as if to herself, sighing involuntarily.

"Marie Hanson can't become your friend. You are much too superior. But you can find a little companionship with her and she can show you around more quickly. She doesn't play such bad comedy. She played quite often in Chicago."

They began to talk about the theater. For Astrid this was an inexhaustible subject, and Meyer was very eloquent. He accompanied her home and without further ado went upstairs with her. He was sitting there when Holm came up. Very much surprised to see that Astrid had such good company, he invited Meyer to tea.

"You just can't imagine," Meyer said with a deep sigh, as if from one who had finally found peace of mind, "how good it is, when one is accustomed to wandering about homeless, to come into a cultured and pleasant home. How much we single people miss having a home to take refuge in when we are tired of the everlasting mad rush and turmoil that one always experiences in this country."

Obviously moved, Holm looked at his guest. "I hope you will always regard this home as yours, Meyer."

"Thanks, thanks, Mr. Holm. That's all too kind of you. Most likely I shall take advantage of your offer. It's too tempting. Just so you don't become too tired of me," he added jokingly, looking at Astrid but talking to Holm.

"No, that will never happen. You can be sure that my home will always be open for you and your friends."

"Thanks. I won't forget it, Mr. Holm."

Holm was in superb humor. Finally things were beginning to go as he wished. Astrid was having a good time, and young refined people who had a great future ahead of them would regard his home as their home. "May I offer you a cigar, Mr. Meyer?" Holm asked after supper, obviously elated over his guest.

"Thanks, but doesn't the smoke bother your daughter?"

"Not at all," Holm hurried to say. Astrid shook her head.

Meyer sat leaning leisurely back on the sofa, letting the smoke puff in thick clouds around him. In between he sipped on a glass of punch that stood in front of him and, through half-closed eyes, enjoyed looking at Astrid, who sat with her needlework. He felt that he had arrived.

The next day Miss Hanson came up, followed by her brother. Astrid was a little taken aback and felt a secret disappointment when she saw her. Marie wore a blue wool dress of radiant color, a little velvet mantilla studded with pearls, and a hat with a gold and black fluttering feather. She had a lively little snub nose and small white cheeks. Her forehead was covered by a mass of curls. Her eyes, however, looked kind and friendly, and she greeted Astrid with such sincerity that Astrid got tears in her eyes. It was so unusual for her to be met with friendliness and she was still a little nervous after all she had gone through. Marie wanted Astrid to go out for a walk with her.

"Usually I am in the store all day and am free only in the evening, but this afternoon I took off work to be with you. So now you must go out with me. My brother has told me so much about you. And you look so sweet. We shall become really good friends."

How good it was. She felt like a child who has been sick and then is pampered and spoiled. They went out together. How much fun it was to have someone to walk with! And Marie knew so much and could tell her who this one or that one was. They often met her acquaintances, and she introduced Astrid to them. When they came up to Nicollet Avenue, Marie wanted to go in several stores, and when she saw something especially beautiful, she would say, "How attractive that would be on you, Astrid." She was already using the familiar pronoun. "Yes, yes, we shall get you dressed up and you'll be so charming."

In the evening Meyer and Hanson came up. Holm treated them to drinks. Marie emptied her glass and was in high spirits. She laughed at Astrid, who would barely sip hers. "What a sweet little goose you are," she said, kissing her.

Then they began to talk about their theater. Astrid listened with beaming eyes while the others talked about whom they should get to join them, where they should hold the tryouts, when they should have the first performance, and more. But when it came to what play they should select, Astrid, too, joined in. When Hanson suggested *Peter and Inger*, Astrid dismissed it with indignation. Was it not their intention to educate and refine the public? They would then have to select something that was both beautiful and serious. "We shall have Bjørnson and no one but Bjørnson," she said enthusiastically.

The others smiled at her naiveté, but they gave in when they realized that on this point her mind was made up. She suggested *Between the Battles*, but they rejected it because it would require strange costumes. Finally, it was decided that they would take *The Newlyweds*. To be sure, Meyer and Hanson shook their heads and said that she did not know the public, but they had to give in. It was precisely Meyer who had spoken so enthusiastically about educating the public. Astrid would be Laura and Marie would be Mathilda. "Miss Paulsen will make an outstanding wife of the county governor," said Marie, turning over the pages of the book that Astrid had brought in from her little library. "Yes, you don't know her, Astrid. She is a beautiful woman. I'm sure she will join us. She is old, between thirty and forty, so it will be just a perfect role for her."

It was midnight before they broke up. Astrid was in a daze when she went into her room. She hurried to bed and lay and thought about Laura. She felt she was already getting into her role. What if she would become frightened when she went on stage. What if she . . . Then she slept and dreamed that she was acting and the audience was clapping, but Meyer stood by her side and said: "Yes, for us refined and intelligent people this is, of course, not anything, but for the uneducated—God help us!"

⁌ 9 ⁌

It was between Christmas and New Year's. The new dramatic society was to make its first appearance with a performance of Bjørnstjerne Bjørnson's *The Newlyweds.* Outside the entrance of Turner Hall one sleigh after the other stopped to discharge its bundles. People were well wrapped up as protection against the thick falling snow. After shaking off the snow in the foyer, the spectators gradually began to fill the seats in the noisy hall. Fathers and mothers came with their children for a little Christmas excitement. Yes, even the babies had to be brought along to celebrate Christmas because most of the mothers were without hired girls and this was the only way they could get away. Afterwards there was to be a grand ball. Astrid had been indignant when she heard there was to be a ball after the performance, but Meyer and Hanson and Johnson had unanimously declared that otherwise they could just as well forget the play because no one would come to see it. "We'll have to proceed cautiously," Meyer had said. "First we have to get people to attend because of the ball. Later they will come for the sake of art." Astrid had to give in.

They had had many rehearsals and the others said it went well. Astrid played her role with all she had. Each time they rehearsed she felt she had a deeper understanding of the play. At the same time she also felt a secret disappointment every time they practiced, for there was always something she had seen but that she had been unable to express in her acting. Would she ever manage it? Or was it with her as it had been with her mother—

more feeling and imagination than real talent? She always felt a secret anxiety when she thought of her mother's words: "I am afraid it will be the same for you, Astrid." The closer the time of performance came, the more tense she became and the more often her mother's words came to mind. If she failed, what then would she do? She placed everything on this first attempt. If that failed—Oh! she dared not think about it. It had to be a success. For her it was also a tremendous burden because she thought that the others had an inferior understanding of their roles. They were of no help. Instead, they dragged her down to a lower level. Then, too, they were always fully satisfied with each other's performance, especially with hers. But she thought that sharp criticism was the only thing that could help her. Meyer did not have a role himself. He took the part of director. He was not an artist, he said smiling, just the artists' Maecenas.

The hall filled up quickly. At last it was so packed that every single place was taken, both sitting and standing. The audience was a motley group. There sat the common laborer with his thick woolen scarf around his neck and by his side his solidly built wife with bulging cheeks and curls over her forehead and a velvet hat with a deep red ribbon. Close by sat another woman with a little one in her arms. Her pale face and lackluster eyes told of days without rest and nights without sleep. The mother looked around furtively and anxiously whenever the baby cried and those around her looked back at her annoyed. She pulled her threadbare black woolen shawl around her to cover her shriveled-up breast with which she finally quieted the baby. Her husband sat beside her, fat and contented, with thick inflamed cheeks and moist eyes. It was easy to see who took the lion's share in that marriage. Nearer the stage sat some young girls around fourteen or fifteen years of age, overly dressed in silk and velvet, giggling and fooling around because a couple of young gentlemen with pompadours and starched shirt fronts were flirting with them, asking if the ladies preferred lemonade or beer. On another seat sat a lady with rouged cheeks wearing a blue velveteen dress on which butterflies were sewn in cheap beads. Her hair was curled like a poodle dog's. Her thick red hands and fat wrists, covered for the moment with imitation bracelets, showed that she was a hired girl. Her cavalier was a large robust fellow with a broad, happy smile. He seemed to believe that the chief purpose in going to the theater was to stamp one's feet and make all the noise possible.

Not far from them was a young lady who was out of her element. She certainly did not fit in. Dressed in a light blue silk dress and yellow gloves that reached up to her elbows, she nonchalantly carried a white swan's-down fan in her hands. Her thickly rouged cheeks and the sexually provocative glance she sent out under her long black eyelashes set her apart from the stolid and respectable ladies sitting around her. Those sitting nearest to her tried to distance themselves discreetly, but they still could not avoid looking at her from time to time.

On the floor on each side stood a row of small tables. Ladies and gentlemen sat at these, and waiters moved around them with baskets containing glasses filled with foaming beer. By one of these tables sat a group of lively young fellows exchanging stories. They were obviously modish young men, with their fine tailored clothes and dashing manners. On the benches along the rear wall little children lay sleeping, wrapped in shawls and coats, while their tired mothers sat beside them enjoying a momentary rest and looking around the hall. By one of the tables sat some older, stodgy fathers, some with ruddy faces, talking politics and discussing the financial prospects for the coming year. A little scatterbrained editor with gold-rimmed glasses and a goatee ran among them, paying compliments to the mothers for their beautiful babies and their own charming appearance. He whispered to a young lady that she was the queen of the evening and engaged another for the first fandango. Most of the time he hung around the worthy fathers, once knocking over a glass of beer that fell noisily to the floor with beer running out over the table. No one bothered to wipe it up. Then he sat down with a serious face to hold forth for the listening heads on the candidates that were running in the mayoral election and on what was in store for the city and state in the coming year.

Up in the corner nearest the stage, his eyes turned toward the audience, sat a young man with an intelligent face but an ironic smile playing in his eyes and around his lips. Crossing his arms and riding his chair, he looked out over the motley assembly. Now and then he cast a witty remark across to a young lady sitting on a nearby bench attempting to conceal her laughter behind her fan. Far back in the rear of the hall were several police officers—engaged to keep order. It appeared that they were needed back there, for the crowd was large and their faces became more and more vulgar and rudimentary the further you looked back in the hall. The room echoed with a noisy buzz. People were becoming impatient for the curtain to go up. The music, a deafening orchestra of wind instruments, had already stopped, and people began to stamp their feet. More and more people joined in until there was a terrible din.

Finally the curtain went up. A roar of applause greeted the actors. They began, but laughter and applause kept them from being heard. They began anew amid some laughter and applause and continued unconcerned. Those closest to the stage stood up in order to hear, and children and women stood on the tables in order to see over the shoulders of those standing in front. In between they cast angry glances at the disturbers of the peace in the rear of the hall. Finally it quieted down enough so that those closest could hear more or less continuously what was being said. It was time for Laura to come in. She had been waiting in the wings looking at the audience. Everything floated together for her into a bewildering mass—the many heads, the beer glasses, the stamping, the shouting, and the roaring.

"Now you enter." Meyer came over to her.

She looked at him, bewildered. "I'm not going in," she answered mechanically.

"What are you saying? Are you mad? You must go in." He ran over to a table and returned with a glass half full of port wine. "Drink!" he commanded.

She seized it and downed it with one gulp. She heard her cue, and then she stood on the stage. How she got there she did not know. A new roar of applause greeted her, and the unaccustomed drink gave her courage. Her blood rushed through her, a kind of desperate defiance seized her, and she acted. The audience was jubilant. "She plays damned well that girl," a crude voice was heard to shout during a moment's silence. She smiled bitterly. How could she play well?

The curtain was lowered at the end of the first act. The audience stamped their feet and roared ecstatically. "Bring them out! Out with the girls!" they shouted. The curtain went up. Marie pulled Astrid out on the stage with her. She struggled against it.

"Are you crazy? You must!"

The audience shouted and clapped, and the curtain went up and down several times. Finally the noise subsided.

"It went brilliantly," said Marie, turning to face Astrid. "But you see this play is too refined for this audience. They can't appreciate it. But now it's all the same. We benefited our cause and you acted splendidly."

"Do you think so?" asked Astrid in a daze, looking at her with a curious expression.

"How strange you look, Astrid! At least it seems so to me. But don't you now understand that we must select a different kind of play for this audience. It's not an easy crowd to educate, you'll see."

Astrid almost had to smile. God, how naive she had been. She was apparently the last one who could educate them. Suddenly she turned to Marie as if seized by a thought. "But they were drinking beer. While we were performing, people went around with baskets of beer. Where do they get them?"

"How should I know?" said Marie, shrugging her shoulders. "But I must hurry. We're soon to go on again."

A terrible fear gripped Astrid. She ran over to Meyer, who was setting up properties on the stage, and seized him firmly by the arm. "Tell me, Meyer, where are they getting the beer from down there?" She pointed to the audience.

"Well, you better ask your father about that, Miss Holm, if you really want to know," he answered a little sharply.

Astrid jumped back. So even here he was pursuing her. All at once she burst into an uproarious laughter. This was just too much of a farce! She had wanted to educate this audience and show them something fine and great. Meanwhile her father was serving beer—moving the saloon into the theater! She laughed and laughed.

"What's wrong with you?" shouted Meyer alarmed. "Have you gone crazy?"

"Not quite, but not so far from it either," she thought as she kept on laughing.

"Stop it at once! This is disgusting. Hurry up now. The music is almost over and you haven't even begun to change your costume."

"Yes, right away." She swallowed a full glass of water and ran into the little room that was assigned to the ladies as their dressing room. She came out a moment later dressed as Laura for the second act. She looked magnificent, but there was a wild defiance in her eyes. Meyer looked at her. She was beautiful—but terrifying.

The curtain went up. The same shouting and clapping greeted them along with hushes from others who wanted to hear. Then a voice was heard from the rear: "We can't understand a syllable of the whole thing!"

"Yes, but the women look beautiful," shouted another.

When Axel took Laura in his arms after they had finally come to an understanding, there was a "Wow! He likes it, he does!" followed by a universal roar of laughter. Finally the curtain went down. There were no curtain calls now, for the people sat impatiently waiting for the dance to begin. After all, that was what they had come for. Soon the hall was cleared. Chairs were thrown without consideration through the air onto the stage, and people began dancing as soon as a little space had been cleared. They were so crowded that they pushed and elbowed and shouted at each other, keeping on all the same as if duty bound, as the sweat poured from them.

Behind the stage there was confusion and changing of clothes and turmoil. Holm stood beaming, serving punch in some glasses and calling for order. "Ladies and gentlemen! I want to thank you one and all for the delightful evening you have given us. No doubt the audience could have been a more select group—at least, yes—how shall I put it—more tactful. But in America you have to take the situation as it comes. And you, ladies and gentlemen, you have done your duty. It is a proud occasion, and I congratulate the new dramatic society of Minneapolis for a brilliant beginning. Artists one and all—*skoal!*"

They raised their glasses, laughing and chatting with each other. Astrid emptied her glass and laughed loudest of them all. Holm looked at her with fatherly pride.

"You are in high spirits this evening, Astrid. That's the way I like to see you."

"Yes, isn't it true! Now you have me as you want me, Father." Holm was too happy to detect the scornful note in her voice. He was too busy calculating how much beer would be sold and how much money he would make. He rubbed his hands in satisfaction. "Isn't it grand, even in such an outpost of the earth where we have been thrown, to be able to have a little green oasis in the desert where culture and intelligence may thrive and feel at home," he said with emotion, clinking Meyer's glass. "*Skoal,* young man!" Meyer clinked glasses with him.

Hanson turned to Astrid. "May I dare hope for a dance, Miss Holm?"

"Yes, of course," said Astrid enthusiastically. "I want to do everything."

"Oh, is it possible?" he shouted, enchanted. "And here I thought you were opposed to having the dance here this evening."

"Yes, before, yes. But now I have become wiser. It's incredible how much a person can learn in one evening."

"Well, then I'll ask for the first dance. Will you do me the honor?"

"Yes, yes. Come, Marie. Let's go in and dance."

The other young gentlemen followed along, and soon most of them were on the floor. Hanson danced splendidly. Astrid was so easy to lead that they managed more or less all the roadblocks others were encountering. Anyway, the hall was not so full any more. Many had left in desperation because of the crowded conditions. The wine and the dance intoxicated Astrid—and she wanted to be intoxicated.

"Come, Meyer, aren't you going to dance, too?" she said, out of breath when Hanson set her down.

"Yes," said Meyer, flattered by her courtesy. He bent over her: "With you I will dance, Astrid. But with no one else. But you must rest first," he continued when she stood up right away.

"Oh, that's not necessary. Just come."

In the middle of the dance she was overcome by a strange limpness as she felt Meyer's warm breath up against her own mouth. How closely he held her! Suddenly she became white. "Oh, stop a little," she finally mumbled. It was as if everything was whirling around her.

"Are you sick? I told you that you should rest a while. Shall I get some water?"

"No, not at all. It's over already. I was just a little dizzy."

Peterson came over and asked for a dance. She stood up.

"Just wait a little," said Meyer, standing close by her and laughing as if she was his possession.

"No, I'm quite well now," she said, dancing away.

A while later Meyer came over to her. She had been dancing constantly. "You should go home, Astrid," he said with authority.

She arose passively. She had not noticed that he had called her Astrid. How pale and fatigued she looked! He assisted her with her coat, which he had fetched from the dressing room, and helped her put on her white hat with the swan's-down brim. Without further delay he placed her arm in his and led her through the crowd out into the street. She breathed the fresh air deeply when she came out. How strangely wonderful the fresh night air was to breathe after the disgusting smell of alcohol and the stuffiness and the choking fumes she had experienced in the hall. The sound of music reached them. The dance was going on merrily within, and no one thought of leaving. It had stopped snowing. The sky was decked with sparkling stars and the air was light and clear.

"A walk will do you good," Meyer said. He had had quite a lot to drink and the cold night air chilled him, too.

Astrid said nothing. She walked down the street with him. All at once she felt overcome by a deadly weariness. The ground seemed to sway under her. She would have collapsed had he not held her up. He threw his arms around her. "Just lean on me," he whispered, pulling her toward him.

She did not hear what he said. Nor did she notice that he took her hand and placed it on his chest. She heard him say something about his loving her. "Am I now going to marry Mr. Meyer, then?" she thought listlessly. She did not know how they made it to the door of her house, but they were there. He opened the door and helped her up the stairs. In the living room two lamps were burning, and the coal stove was glowing. Holm had given Annie orders to light the lamps and make it cozy when she went home with the small boys after the play was over. He had thought it possible that Astrid would go home at once and that the others would go with her.

Astrid looked around in despair in the strong light.

Meyer lifted her coat from her shoulders with trembling hands and took off her hat after saying that it suited her enchantingly. Astrid sank down on a chair and closed her eyes. Suddenly she felt something warm on her hands. She opened her eyes. It was Meyer on his knees in front of her, kissing them. He came closer and closer. Her eyes became fixed and large. Then she felt an arm around her body, pulling her forward forcefully, and a burning whisky-stenched breath touched her. She saw two lustful, bleary eyes and two thick lips that groped for hers.

She came to suddenly. With a loud cry she jumped up. "You disgusting beast!"

Meyer tumbled back from a hard blow on the ear. He got up in a rage. There stood Astrid gasping, her head lifted, nostrils quivering, and eyes flashing. She had all at once got the upper hand. He was all the more furious because she stood there so beautiful but, for him, unattainable. He moved toward her, then stopped suddenly as if he had thought it over. His face became red, and his eyes stood out of their sockets as if they would explode. Then he grabbed her hand and flung it away as if crazed. "You will pay for this, you saloonkeeper's wench," he hissed between his teeth. He grabbed his hat and went out.

When Holm came home happy and satisfied an hour later, Astrid lay unconscious on the floor. Terribly alarmed, he ran to get Annie, who wrung her hands in fright at seeing her dear Miss Astrid lying there like a corpse. They carried her to her bed. Then Astrid opened her eyes and saw Annie standing with anxious fear as she bathed her temples with water. Her father appeared, but when she caught sight of him, her expression turned to one of such loathing and abomination that even Holm's not very clear eyes could see it. He remained standing dumbfounded and looked quite bewildered at Annie. She led him out the door and closed it well after him, while she said to him: "Just go and lie down. I'll take care of her." Then she went back to Astrid, who lay and looked at her with large, shining eyes.

"Has he gone?" she whispered. When Annie nodded, she turned, comforted, toward the wall, mumbling something about her hand hurting. When Annie looked at it she saw that her right wrist was quite swollen and red. It had hit the edge of the table when Meyer had flung it away from him. Annie placed wet bandages on it. Astrid looked at her so pathetically grateful but at the same time so helplessly desperate that the tears ran down over Annie's wrinkled cheeks. "Oh, God, that's just the way her mother looked at me several times the first year. Is he going to kill this one as well?" She placed a cloth on Astrid's warm forehead, moved the lamp behind the bed, and turned it down so there was only a dim light in the room. Then she moved the armchair over by the bed and went after cold water for the bandages, mumbling, "I knew it would never go well with all this hullabaloo and play acting. She is not of the same stuff as those darned fellows who run after her here."

Suddenly Astrid sat up in bed. "Ugh! He was going to kiss me. Look, Annie, at the one over there in the corner. Ugh, those eyes," she mumbled and sank down again on the pillow. "Saloonkeeper's wench—that's what he said. Look, they are drinking beer over there and father is treating." She began to laugh. Then she said suddenly with a movingly unhappy expression: "It is all gone—everything!" Long afterwards came: "Oh, that beautiful garden! Mother!" She smiled in her dream as if she saw something beautiful, then fell soundly asleep. Annie sat hour after hour at her patient night watch while Holm's habitual snores could be heard from the room across the hall.

{ 10 }

When Meyer left Astrid he returned to the ball, sat down in a little room behind the stage where he found a bottle of whisky and drank like a sponge. At three in the morning he went home to his boarding house—or, more correctly, to his friend Pettersen's boarding house. Up to this time Meyer had preferred to make use of Pettersen's room instead of getting one for himself. Pettersen, who had not known Meyer until he met him up at Hanson's the day after Meyer had come to Minneapolis, had been greatly impressed by Meyer's dignified and self-important appearance and his bright future. Happy to have such a cultured and intelligent person's company, he had invited Meyer up to his room.

Meyer had been so kind as to accept the invitation and found himself so comfortable up there that he had done Pettersen the honor of sharing his bed with him until the present time. "Yes, yes, Pettersen, when I become a lawyer, then you can move into my elegant modern facilities," said Meyer in between his jesting and slapping Pettersen on the shoulder. That they should also share the bed was taken for granted. It appeared that Meyer regarded it as settled that until the time when he would have his own place it would be Pettersen's duty to provide whatever he needed. "Oh, that's right, Pettersen, do you have a dollar today?" he would remark casually. "By God, my pocketbook is quite empty, and I'll have to borrow my way until a better future arrives." Since Pettersen worked in a large store and had a good salary, he could easily procure what they both needed, especially since Meyer did not have a very great need for cash. Coffee he got in the mornings together with Pettersen for an insignificant addition to the rent. At noon and in the evening he ate at Holm's or, occasionally, at the home of another family whose acquaintance he had been happy to make. His pocket money went chiefly for cigars, which he always had to have in his mouth, or for boots since, unfortunately, Pettersen's boots were too small for his big feet. With this exception, Pettersen was in the fortunate situation of having all his clothes fit Meyer very well, so Meyer did not have to pay for any clothes.

All this was very good and Meyer was well pleased with the arrangement and saw no reason why Pettersen should not be satisfied, too. But strangely enough, to Meyer's utter astonishment, Pettersen did not always seem happy about it. What in the world could be better than this? This Pettersen must be a highly demanding and dissatisfied man, he thought. Content after a cozy evening with the Holms, where he had enjoyed the happiness of family life, followed by "looking around town a little," Meyer would come home in good spirits with a cigar in his mouth. There he would find Pettersen lying in bed, silently mulling over whether he had received the short end of their partnership.

To be sure, it was a big thing to have such a cultured and learned associate, but he could not say that he personally had such great benefit from it since Meyer was always sleeping when Pettersen went to work, and in sleep he was at least no more intelligent than other mortals. When Pettersen came home tired in the evening and yearned for a little pleasant company, Meyer had always gone out and did not come home until Pettersen was asleep and no longer in the mood for listening to Meyer's facetious remarks. Sunday morning was about the only time he was able to enjoy the benefit of Meyer's brilliance. Then, however, he was in such a melancholy mood because of the lamentable state of his wardrobe that he could not get himself to appreciate it. In his chest of drawers everything lay helter-skelter, dirty and clean clothes all mixed up. And he was always so proud of his white linen! His light Sunday tie that he had purchased last Saturday was dirty, and on his best black overcoat that hung in the closet were large stains of grease and mixed drinks.

One evening there was a Scandinavian festival in the city, and Pettersen took off work an hour early to have time to get dressed for it. He came home singing, happy at the prospect of an entertaining evening. Usually he stood in that damned store until almost nine every single evening except Sunday. He began to change clothes in good humor. Then he opened his closet to take out his best black trousers. He could not find them. He looked and looked, becoming more and more furious. Finally he threw all the clothes in the closet on the floor, but still no black trousers were to be found. It was obvious that Meyer had taken them. A suspicion seized him. He ran over to the chest of drawers and pulled out the top drawer. Just as he thought! His new white silk tie was gone, the one he had been so rash as to bring home with him the day before because of the festival. He had placed it, still in its carton, in the innermost corner of the drawer. Everything had now gone entirely too far! Worn out, Pettersen sat down on a chair clad only in his shorts, and that was as far as he got that evening. He had other trousers, to be sure, and he could most likely have purchased a new tie before the stores closed, but his jolly mood was gone. He went to bed and drew the featherbed over his head and lay there mumbling and spitting out his frustration. His clothes would be at the festival, but not on him. Then, when Meyer came cheerfully home late that night, puffing on his cigar, enraptured over the unusually pleasant evening and exclaiming many times about the pretty ladies he had been introduced to and the many new influential acquaintances it had been his good fortune to make, then it was impossible for poor Pettersen to join in Meyer's happiness. He stubbornly remained quiet, burying his head in his pillow. Meyer looked at him a little surprised, shook his head, and fell asleep content.

Of course, when Pettersen mulled over all this and weighed the pros and cons, he had to consider that one day the relationship would be turned around and he would be living in Meyer's elegant abode, getting money from Meyer's pocket, and walking around in Meyer's clothes. Then it would be Meyer's turn to sit at home. But strangely enough he found no solace in the thought. It seemed a long way off, and he was not by nature an optimist. "One doesn't become a lawyer by sleeping and going out and talking nonsense either," he thought. As this was to be Meyer's vocation, he found the prospects bleak.

Meyer actually spent some hours of the day at an attorney's office, and Pettersen had a nagging suspicion that there he had to cast off his dignity and take on a very menial position, like sweeping the floor, tending the stove, or running errands. The greater part of the day, though, Meyer compensated for this debasing insult to his dignity. While Pettersen fully accepted Meyer's right to do so, however, he was also aware that it did not bring him any higher up the ladder, on top of which waited the prize of a lawyer's profession. In return for his services at the office, when there were no errands to run, he was given permission to sit in a corner and read in Blackstone.

Meyer felt like a real student when he got that huge venerated tome in his hands, but it was strange how sleepy he became when he tried to read in it. His usually slightly ruddy face became redder and redder, and his otherwise intelligent eyes became hazy. "I'm going to a meeting this evening together with the other students," he said once to Pettersen with great self-importance, but Pettersen was never really clear about what kind of students they were. Yet it seemed to Pettersen that if you could lead such an easy and carefree life as a student, then everyone should take up such a business. Now and then Meyer made a miserable attempt to study at home when he didn't feel just right or had had too much to drink the night before or some other equally good reason kept him at home. Then he would lie comfortably in bed with his thick Webster and his Blackstone and, yes, damn it, he also had to have a cigar or two so he could really study. A different kind of peace was found here than in the office. First he had to smoke a little to gather strength. Finally, he would take up a book, but his eyes would become smaller and smaller until the book fell on the floor, and he would be sound asleep. The difference between his studies at home and those at the office was only that at the office he dozed, but at home he could sleep soundly and undisturbed. Around noon he would awake invigorated but hungry. He would dress himself with utmost care, pulling out drawers and throwing around the clothes. This was how Pettersen always found them when he came home in the evening. That was because Meyer never had time to tidy up. He had to arrive at Holm's in time for dinner and he always brought along an excellent appetite. "It's remarkable how much food one requires when he consumes so much brain power," he would then remark in utter amazement over this phenomenon.

～

THE MORNING AFTER THE EVENTFUL THEATER EVENING Meyer was lying in Pettersen's bed. He didn't go to the office, nor did he even try to study at home. The morning coffee stood cold on the table, the slices of bread beside it. His head hammered and pounded, and he was angry and upset. With sadness he thought about Holm's good meals with beer and an occasional glass of Curacao with the coffee. And then there were the nice evenings sitting on the sofa with a glass of punch and cigars. Now all that was gone. "Why in hell couldn't I restrain myself yesterday? But those devilish eyes and that red mouth burned like fire in my blood. And I was so sure I had her, the flirtatious hussy. But she'll be paid back. She can depend on it. It'll be worse for her." A malicious twitch appeared on his lips.

"Actually, it is probably better for me that it went as it went," he said to himself a while later, his face lighting up. He reached for a cigar that lay on the chest of drawers, lit it, and began to puff out clouds of smoke while he continued his meditation. "It's high time that I really get to work and show some persistence in winning the respect of acquaintances with influence who can help me get some sort of lucrative position. Pettersen is not to be depended on lately. He seems to be scheming about something. There's no pride in any of these despicable mercenary souls," he yelled contemptuously, sticking one foot out of bed. "But what can you expect when you wallow with such pigs. No manners. No culture." He shook his head. "Take courage, Adolf. The time will come when you won't need to deal with them." Pulling on his trousers, he pictured in his mind the golden age when they would read the reports from city hall in the *Minneapolis Tribune* or the *Pioneer Press:* "Yesterday, as usual, the well-known attorney, Adolf Meyer won a glittering victory in court. The whole room shook with applause."

"Adolf Meyer," he thought, "an aristocratic name. No one would doubt that he was a gentleman when he heard that name." Completely reconciled with himself and his destiny, he drank the coffee and gobbled down one slice of bread after the other, pacing the floor amid bright dreams of the future.

A couple of hours later Pettersen was surprised to see Meyer come over to the counter behind which he stood. "Have you had lunch?" asked Meyer.

"No. I'm going in ten minutes."

"Well, then I'll wait for you and we'll go together to Mrs. Rasmussen's. Are you still eating there?"

"Aren't you going to Holm's today?"

"No. To hell with them. I'm fed up with that saloon traffic," answered Meyer. "A person has to have a little dignity."

"What makes you come to that conclusion all of a sudden," asked Pettersen ironically.

Meyer laughed as if he did not hear him. Then he settled down comfortably in a chair, looking out into space and toying with the cigar he held in his hand. Pettersen looked at him anxiously. He knew why he wanted to go with him to Mrs. Rasmussen's. Meyer couldn't go there unless Pettersen or, more correctly, his purse went along.

"Listen, do you know what?" Meyer remarked suddenly. "Today I've been a lucky devil. When I walked up Washington Avenue, I met John Larsen walking with Fischer. You know who he is. People think Fischer will push forward at the next election for mayor. I went over to Larsen and got him to introduce me. I had a long conversation with Fischer and got a chance to tell him who I was, about my family, what I've been doing here, and my views on the future. I said I was expecting to make a career here, and then I added candidly that I needed men of influence to be interested in me. He promised that I could certainly rely on his support, and we parted on friendly terms."

"But how many do you think he has promised the same thing?" asked Pettersen, arranging some clothes on the counter.

"Oh, not so many intelligent men with real knowledge," Meyer remarked casually. "I think he recognizes refined people when he sees them. I'll go right up to his office this afternoon and offer him my assistance in the coming election on the condition that he promises me a position when he becomes mayor."

"Will you give up your studies, then?" asked Pettersen.

"Not for anything in the world. But you know I have to see about finding something to live on, so I'll quit at the office and study on my own from now on."

"Is that why you're so dressed up?" asked Pettersen, casting a glance at the freshly ironed shirt that he just yesterday got back from the laundry and his Sunday tie that sparkled on Meyer's chest.

"No, I didn't think anything about it when I went out," Meyer answered frankly, meeting Pettersen's look without blushing. "But I had thought of making some other visits today. That little Mrs. Hammer, whom I was introduced to at the last festival at Norden's Hall, is a damned sweet lady, and her husband has great influence here. I think he knows Fischer, and through her I'm sure to get him to put in a good word for me. Are you ready to go now?"

⟨ II ⟩

The day was cold and clear. It was the middle of January. Blue and numb with cold, streetcar conductors waved their arms wildly to keep life in their stiff limbs. Pedestrians walked rapidly along the sidewalk, their hats pulled down over their ears and cheeks, constantly checking if the tips of their noses were frozen. Ladies walked in furs or warm velvet coats, their heads wrapped in a thick shawl. A miserable wretch hurried by in a thin calico dress and an old woolen shawl that she pulled over her breast to try to keep out the cold. She was so used to toil in all kinds of weather that she had grown accustomed to the bitter cold, less affected by it than the well-clothed ladies in furs and flannel. Besides, she had to hurry because her three young ones were home alone. She had put them all in bed before she went out because their older siblings were in school. In that way she didn't have to put more fuel in the stove. But now the three would be awaiting their mother. She hurried home, all the time wondering if her husband had received a little work or if it would be like the other evenings, when he had returned home dejected, throwing aside the sawhorse he had had on his back all day. "Everywhere I went," he mumbled, "they had already chopped their wood. Or else they now use steam to heat their homes. So we will have to go without work and both starve and freeze."

In Mrs. Hammer's pleasant rooms, though, it was not necessary to freeze. Huge logs of oak and maple burned merrily in the open fireplace surrounded by a low, shining brass grate. A wolf skin was stretched in front to warm the cold feet. The entire house was kept comfortably warm by the great steam apparatus in the cellar, which sent its warm pipes to all the floors. Hers was a rich, elegant house.

Mr. Hammer's business was prospering, and his wife knew how to spend the money. She loved splendor around her and on her, and her home was always open to guests. Three large rooms were joined together by open archways on which hung thick draperies in Turkish fabrics. One of them opened into a glass-enclosed recess filled with colorful, blooming plants—calla lilies and hyacinths. They looked lovely when one came in from the white, colorless winter into this subdued light where the flames from the fireplaces blended with the rich colors of the rooms. Brussels carpets with flower designs covered the floors and muffled all harsh and grating noises, and light gold lace curtains hung in front of the wide bay windows. The rich furniture, apparently placed at random, produced a jarring, thought-provoking impression. On the fireplace mantels stood a quantity of bric-a-brac, Japanese objects, Chinese porcelain, and costly vases. Albums and photographs were casually placed on the tables. On the walls hung many oil paintings in costly frames, including one whose fiery red colors and wild rock formations showed that it was from "The Land of the Midnight Sun," where a ship was struggling in the churning waves. Mrs. Hammer was Swedish, but her husband was Norwegian. She had come to America as a child, and as a young girl she had acquired a position in merchant Hammer's store. He was twenty years her senior, but he fell in love with the attractive, lively young girl and married her.

Today was the day she received guests. Several ladies sat in the deep easy chairs, enjoying rest and comfort after the cold walk in the biting wind. "Sit here, Julia," said Mrs. Hammer, moving a chair closer to the fireplace. "You look as if you're still freezing."

The lady called Julia was pale and delicate, with large, shining eyes and a languishing expression. "It was really cold," she said, lifting her black silk dress a little in order to place her feet on the brass grate and warm them better.

"I was really afraid that none of you would show up today," continued Mrs. Hammer. "A cup of coffee for you, Mrs. Falanger?"

"Thanks. Just half." A lady with sharp features and thin lips reached her cup out to have it filled.

"How did you enjoy the banquet in St. Paul, Hanna?" Julia asked Mrs. Hammer.

"Oh, splendid. We sat at the table for two or three hours, and afterwards we danced until three in the morning. Why didn't you come, Julia? I was so sure I would find you there."

"Oh, I was really upset, as you can well believe. I had such a furious desire to go, but Mr. Hjorth didn't want me to buy a new dress. He said that he absolutely could not afford it right now. Well, it was impossible for me to go in any of my old ones. What dress did you wear?"

"A new wine-red satin trimmed in white lace. Mrs. Haslund sewed it. I paid a total of twenty-five dollars to the dressmaker."

"Oh, let us see it," several women shouted eagerly.

"Oh, Annie," she said to the maid who was carrying the coffee around, "run up after my new red silk dress."

"Look here," she said when the maid had returned with the dress. She held it up for them. "Isn't it sweet?"

"Oh, how charming! My, what dainty lace," said Julia.

"Have you heard that Robert Ingersoll has come to St. Paul? He'll give a lecture there tomorrow," said a young lady in a tightly fitting silk flannel dress that set off her firm shape. Her face was half covered by dark curls, and her cheeks were lightly powdered.

"He can lecture for all I care. I won't hear him," said Mrs. Falanger scornfully. "It's remarkable that in a Christian society a person can be allowed to say such terrible things as this Bob does."

"Oh, yes," said Julia, leaning back proudly. "It's because the mob is allowed to rule in this country. Oh, Emilie, pass me the cake platter."

"But have you heard the latest news, then?" asked another lady, who had just dipped her fingers in one of the colored glass bowls that stood on the table filled with water.

"No, what is it?" asked Mrs. Hammer with curiosity.

"Have you really not heard it? Oh, it's a terrible scandal. The beautiful Mrs. Hale—you know her—who is married to the rich banker Hale, who has that large elegant house up on Hennepin, has run away from her husband to New York with a lover!"

"Is it possible?" shouted the others, thunderstruck.

"Yes, there's no doubt about it."

"But doesn't her husband drink?" asked Mrs. Hammer.

"Yes, but that's really no excuse for her," put in Mrs. Falanger sharply.

"She has always looked to me like a flirt. Oh, the poor children!" she added with a pitying sigh, her eyes raised to heaven.

"Her husband is said to be beside himself in desperation," continued the first lady.

"The story isn't entirely as you tell it, Mrs. Nichol," said a serious voice behind them. All turned and looked toward the door, where a lady, about thirty-five, stood. She had rather plain features, but her large serious eyes were very attractive. Her brown shiny hair was worn plain and put up in a large bun on her neck. Her simple black woolen dress had a plain white collar around the neck.

"Oh, dear, is it you, Helene!" shouted Mrs. Hammer, surprised. "We sat so absorbed that we neither heard nor saw you. What way did you come in?"

"Through the back door. I knew you had company."

"Yes, come now and have a cup of coffee. You know all the ladies here."

"Yes, no doubt we have all had the pleasure of knowing Doctor Nielsen," said Mrs. Falanger a little sarcastically, puckering her lips while she exchanged a knowing look with Julia. Helene pretended not to hear her, turning instead to the lady she had first addressed.

"As it happens, I am very well acquainted with the situation in the family you talked about, Mrs. Nichol, and I know that Mrs. Hale has not run away to New York with a lover. She simply went back to her family in the East because she couldn't stand being with her husband any longer."

"And why can't she stand to be with him?" asked Mrs. Nichol, half insulted at seeing her interesting story lose all its spice.

"Because he's a brute and abuses her. He also drinks too much."

"Oh, if she was as innocent as you make her out to be, Dr. Nielsen, then she would have found some other way than to forsake her husband and children," said Mrs. Hjorth.

"She took her children with her. On the other hand, though, you can't mean that a woman should endure any indignity offered her, can you, Mrs. Hjorth?"

Julia shrugged her shoulders. "We apparently have different opinions on that matter, Dr. Nielsen," she remarked casually in a light, haughty tone. "Apropos, Hanna," she said, turning to Mrs. Hammer, "you have of course seen that Mr. Tobiesen is filing for divorce now?"

"I have heard rumors of it. Is it really true?"

"Yes, the case will come up next week. It's a terrible story. He is suing her for adultery, and one of his office clerks is supposed to be her lover. He had been suspicious for a long time. Then one day he came home from a trip earlier than he had said he would, and he found the fellow at home with his wife. That I know is true," she said with a defiant glance toward the corner where Helene sat, "because my Karen heard it herself from the maid in the house. There was a huge uproar. He was furious and she was howling."

"Then it's a shame," said Mrs. Hammer sympathetically. "Just think, I thought she looked so innocent."

"I don't think so at all. She is said to have had a questionable past over in the Old Country." She leaned over and whispered something in the ear of the lady sitting beside her.

Mrs. Hammer went over and sat down on the sofa beside Helene, who was talking seriously with a young girl with a friendly, pale childish face. "What are you talking about? You look so serious."

"Oh, Helene is telling such a sad story," said the young girl, her voice full of emotion.

"Yes, that's why I dropped in today—to hear if you could help a little," said Helene. "I just came from a terribly unfortunate family. The mother has consumption, and her husband is laid up with a broken leg. He fell fourteen days ago while laying bricks. They have six little ones and no food in the house, no firewood—you know how biting cold it is."

"But don't they get help? Doesn't the city take care of them?"

"They haven't been here long enough to get help from the city. I just received some free medicine for him. Then I got a little money from a private society for the poor. I was able to buy a little wood and flour for them today, but what help will that be? You can't imagine any greater squalor."

"Oh, how terrible that some people must suffer so," said Mrs. Hammer, deeply moved. "We must all help. I think I can contribute a dollar." She took up her purse and began to count. "Look here, now. I have no more than half a dollar here, I see, but I'll look to see if I don't have some old clothes of Marie's that you can have for the children."

"Thanks. I'm glad for everything I can get," said Helene, looking at her seriously.

"But now let's have something to cheer us up after the sad news. Oh, Mrs. Falanger, play a little for us."

Mrs. Falanger sat down at the piano and played a thundering waltz. Mrs. Hammer playfully took a few dance steps out on the floor. The doorbell rang, and she stopped suddenly. "Oh, Annie, run out to see who's ringing," she called to the maid.

Two men came in. The one was Meyer. The other was a muscular man around thirty. His black hair was curled tightly at his powerful neck. His full, red lips could barely be seen under his black beard, and his eyes seemed to burn anyone he talked to. He would have been handsome had he not conveyed such a strong expression of raw sensuality and animal strength. Life was his, and he wanted to enjoy it. Otherwise, "to hell with it all." He was a capable lawyer who had just recently come to town. He and Meyer had met just as they both were about to enter the garden gate. They had been introduced to each other earlier and Meyer seemed quite delighted with this chance meeting. Actually, he felt a hidden resentment toward Smith just as one feels toward a person who steals the march and reaps the laurels that were waiting for him. However, he found it prudent to seek out Smith's friendship.

"Oh, it's you, Mr. Smith. How nice of you to come visit us." Mrs. Hammer held out her hand with a smile. "Hello, Mr. Meyer." She nodded familiarly to Meyer as to one she saw often.

"I don't know if you both are acquainted with all the ladies here." She turned again to Smith. "Mr. Smith, Mr. Meyer, Mrs. Falanger, Mrs. . . . ."

"Yes, I think I have the pleasure of knowing most of the ladies here," interrupted Smith, "even if I am a new resident of Minneapolis. I have a wide acquaintanceship. I hope we are not disturbing the ladies."

"No, not at all."

"I am delighted to see you again, Mrs. Rask. I haven't had time to visit your place. You live so far out." Smith turned to Mrs. Rask, seated himself in the empty chair beside her, and began a lively discussion.

The young lady who had sat with Helene—who had quietly disappeared when the gentlemen came in—called over to Meyer, who sat chatting with Mrs. Hjorth. "Mr. Meyer, I think I was introduced to you earlier by Marie Hanson."

"Yes, I have had the honor," he nodded, pleased to be shown some attention.

"You were walking together with her and the charming Miss Holm."

"Who?" asked Mrs. Hammer, pricking up her ears.

"Miss Holm, the one who played in the comedy at Turner Hall at Christmas time. I see her every once in a while on the street. I like her very much."

Mrs. Hammer and Meyer exchanged an understanding glance.

"I think, though, I would advise you not to become too friendly with Miss Holm," said Meyer, smiling suggestively.

"Why? Is she so dangerous?"

"There are some people whose company one does not willingly seek, Miss Larsen."

"But you were walking with her yourself then."

"How shall I put it? Gentlemen often seek company that is not appropriate for young ladies. But, I don't think you will find anyone who has seen me with Miss Holm for the last five weeks."

"Dear Fanny, you must be a little careful of the company you keep," said Julia. She looked over at her niece with a worried look. "In this city, where the whole world is streaming in, you really have to select your friends with care." She herself, the daughter of a demented clergyman, had come over as a child and had been forced to put up with a little of everything. Now she was especially proud of her husband's respectable family.

"That's right, Mrs. Hjorth. One certainly can't be careful enough." Meyer turned to Mrs. Hjorth. "The young lady actually appeared to be very sweet, as Miss Larsen says. Well, I paid her a little attention. She was, of course, a stranger here. But I pulled away as soon as possible when I became better acquainted with the circumstances."

"Oh, listen, Fanny. Even a young gentleman does not want to keep her company, so you had better break it off before it goes too far."

"Yes, she is obviously no company for Fanny," said Mrs. Hammer, unusually sharp, whispering something in Julia's ear. Julia raised her eyes and looked appalled.

"But Marie Hanson keeps company with her," broke in Fanny weakly.

"Yes, but then she's rather vulgar, I should think. She isn't particularly careful," said Mrs. Falanger, breaking out in a peal of laughter. "But tell me," she turned to Meyer, "is this little lady you talk of the daughter of the saloonkeeper Holm?"

"Yes," answered Meyer.

"Then I will gladly believe there is something questionable about her. Her father is said to entice all the world's young men by treating them with wine in order to get them to drink later."

"Yes, and to use his pretty daughter as a drawing card." He shrugged his shoulders. "She's a smart girl. That's certainly a point in her favor. She knows what the score is."

"Oh, how brazen!" chimed in several of the ladies.

"May I ask what it is that is so brazen?" asked Smith. He had been chatting so ardently with Mrs. Rask that he had not heard what they had been talking about.

"We are talking about a young lady," answered Meyer a little sharply.

"May I ask her name?"

"It's the daughter of the saloonkeeper Holm down in south Minneapolis," said Mrs. Falanger.

"What? The pretty little actress? Good Lord, what is so brazen about her? I thought she was a damned sweet young girl. Yes, I beg your pardon, my ladies, if I swear." He turned to the ladies with a bow.

"May I ask if the attorney knows her?" asked Meyer sarcastically.

"I saw her at Turner Hall the day after I arrived here, and naturally I fell in love with her. Fire and blood were in her, which is just what I like. I think I'll go up to pay her a visit when I have more time."

"I dare promise you an extraordinarily pleasant meeting," said Meyer sarcastically, smiling contemptuously.

"All the better. It's frightful, though, how prudish you have become all of a sudden, Meyer. My God, we're all human."

"No, Mr. Smith. Here I must permit myself to take Mr. Meyer's side," broke in Mrs. Falanger. "A young girl cannot be too careful about her reputation."

"Why a young girl more than a young man, Madame?"

"Gentlemen—well, after all, they have the privilege nowadays to be . . ."

"Swine?" laughed Smith. "Thanks, Madame. We shall know how to make use of our rights."

"Would the gentlemen like to come in to see my flowers?" interrupted Mrs. Hammer, who thought the conversation had taken a less pleasant turn. She went into the other room toward the greenhouse.

"It would give me a great pleasure," said Meyer, standing up at once and following her.

"What an unusually nice young man," said Julia to Mrs. Falanger. "It's so seldom you meet a young man with such firm moral principles. You can see that he comes from a good family back home in the Old Country."

In the meantime, Smith had stood up and was saying good-bye to the other ladies. "Adieu, Madame!" he called out to Mrs. Hammer.

She turned. "Are you going already? Won't you wait to say hello to my husband?"

"Thanks, Madame. My time is too short today. I ask you to greet him."

When Meyer had marveled at the flowers, he said with a smile, "I think I can congratulate you, Madame, that your husband's elevation to alderman at the next election seems almost certain. I have been sampling opinions and everywhere I've found them in favor of him. That is to say," he added superciliously, "it is not quite definite yet, but in a couple of months of persistent work from us, his friends, we'll most certainly get the results we want. But, then, I have a favor to ask of you, Madame," he continued.

"What is it?" she asked in a friendly voice.

"Right now I am applying for a position at the city hall that is exactly suitable for me since there is such a good salary and relatively easy work there. If I could get such a position I would have plenty of time to resume my studies. But it is important to have the application accompanied by the strong recommendations of influential men. I already have two good names. If you could prevail upon your husband to put in a good word for me with the judge of probate, then I would be quite certain of my job."

"To be sure. I have no doubt my husband will do it," promised Mrs. Hammer.

"A thousand thanks. I can't thank you enough, Madame, for your kindness. You have no idea how good it is of you to extend a hand to a friend when he stands alone in a strange land and has only himself and his skills to rely on," said Meyer, moved. "But now, Madame, I will no longer take up any more of your valuable time. The ladies are anxiously awaiting their gracious hostess."

"Won't you stay for the evening and take tea with us?"

"Thanks, not this evening," answered Meyer, who already had decided that it would be more sensible to decline the evening meal and allow the pretty lady to try to persuade her husband privately, without the embarrassment of his presence. "Tomorrow afternoon, if I may, I would like to get Mr. Hammer's recommendation—if he is so kind as to give me one. Now I must go home to my solitary little room and do some work."

As Meyer walked down the street, pulling his coat tightly around him, he smiled. All went well. He could now be sure of the job, and then he could say adieu to Pettersen and all the others. As for Astrid, yes, she would find out what it was to have him as an enemy. "I think, by God, I'll go to Lundberg's and have a glass."

"What happened to Helene?" asked Mrs. Hammer when she came in.

"Oh, that's right. She asked me to say good-bye. She had to leave," said Fanny Larsen, "but she didn't want to disturb you."

"My dear, how does it happen that this Miss Nielsen comes here to you?" asked Mrs. Falanger sharply.

"Oh, she's Hammer's cousin, and he has known her many years. Poor Helene! She's very kind, but she is, of course, so strange. And she has such peculiar notions."

"I wonder if she has any kind of practice as a doctor," said Julia.

"Doctor!" said Mrs. Falanger contemptuously.

§ 12 §

When Astrid awoke the morning after the performance at Turner Hall, the fever had left her, but she felt indescribably weak.

"You must stay in bed today, Miss," said Annie when she came in after fixing breakfast and getting the boys off to school. "You are as white as a sheet."

"What would I do without you, Annie?" said Astrid, looking thankfully at her as she puttered around her and straightened up in the room.

"Oh, Miss, you would manage. But I won't leave you and the boys as long as you need me. That I promised myself when the blessed angel passed away."

Annie went out for some tea. Astrid looked at her hand. The swelling was gone. It was just a little red and stiff. She lay and stared at it. It had come to the point where they dared to treat her in this manner! She felt strangely weak, almost indifferent. She looked at herself as if she were looking at a stranger. She wondered what would come of her in the end. When she thought about the day before, she shuddered. She, too, was not an actress. That, too, had been a dream, an illusion that she had built her entire life around. But what if she had played under other circumstances, a little more reasonable and not quite so stifling, maybe then . . . But, no, that would be of no help either. She would never be able to have a great career. All she had was feeling and imagination. These frightening words had also become the simple truth. She lacked the creative spark, the wonderful gift one calls talent. In despair she turned over in bed, burying her head in her pillow. Oh, what would become of her.

Annie came in with the tea. "Your father is asking about you, Miss."

Astrid was startled. "Oh, no, Annie, not now," she groaned. "Not now. I'm so tired. I just want to sleep, Annie. Say I'm well, but very tired."

"Just sleep, Miss. That's the best thing you can do. You can rest assured that I'll not let happen to you what happened to your mother."

Astrid actually dozed off. She thought she was back home, up in the old attic again. But it was not she. It was a little girl with sparkling eyes and a joyful smile. The cobwebs hung like dense curtains. The rats stood with large shining eyes looking at the little girl in the light blue silk coat with a lace kerchief over her black hair. The afternoon sun fell in through the little cracked window and cast its flushed reflection over her, filling the whole room with its radiance so that the dust trembled like a golden cloud. When it grew dark she crept on tiptoe to her beloved mother and sat on a footstool by her bed while the fire from the stove shone in the room and her mother's delicate fingers played gently with her hair. When Astrid left to go to bed, her mother took her head and looked at her with beautiful eyes while she whispered: "God bless my little girl!" Who could be happier than that little girl? The tears ran slowly down Astrid's cheeks while she once more lay dreaming and rocking her sick soul to sleep with happy memories. She sat again on the shore of Sognefjord, listening to the splashing of the waves on the rocks. The strip of gold was quivering on the surface of the sea, and above all towered the white-clad giants in their eternal majesty. She ran around in the garden and bathed her cheeks in the fresh night air. She sang with joy. How beautiful it was to be alive. And from the sea came sighs of a dreaming desire. Life itself beckoned her, calling and filling her with dreams of unending happiness. Oh, how good it was to lie there and dream and listen and never more have to wake up to the stinging pain.

When Astrid got out of bed the day after, she was well again. Anyone looking at her closely, though, would have noticed that those two days had brought about a great change. Something cold, almost stony, had come over her. Her blood-red mouth now had a firm and determined look. She had buried her childhood with its happy memories, her bright youth with its jubilant premonitions, dreams and hopes. Now she was determined to live life in all its dreadful reality, taking things as they came. She was a saloonkeeper's daughter, neither more nor less, and would never be anything else. "A saloon wench"—that's what Meyer had called her. Her mouth curled contemptuously when she thought of him. That's the way it was, then, with everything. The platitudes about culture, knowledge, and intellect that came so easily to her father and Meyer—oh, how she hated it all. She had all of a sudden become so terribly enlightened, she thought.

Her father looked at her sharply when she came to the dinner table. "How are you, Astrid?" he asked.

"Thanks, well," she said curtly. "I'm quite well now."

There was something in her voice that struck him. It was so dry and sharp. "You overexerted yourself that evening when you danced so intensely. You'll have to take a little better care of yourself," he said in an irritated manner.

Astrid's large eyes met his with a cold stare. It was probably his imagination, but he thought he saw hate in them.

He did not say another word but hurried downstairs as soon as he had eaten his food. When he came to the stairs he mumbled, "I think the devil has taken possession of my daughter. I'm getting fed up with this business. If it keeps on, I'll have to put a stop to it one way or another."

Later in the afternoon Astrid sat in the living room by the window looking out on the street lethargically. It was dark in the room, but the outdoor gaslights had been lit. She heard the door to the saloon open and shut, and vulgar oaths or words of abuse would come up to her from the street. Every now and then a fellow staggered out from the saloon over to the other side of the street. It was the Christmas season and, of course, people had to celebrate and be happy. She thought of the first evening she sat by this window and made the terrible discovery about their situation. It seemed ages ago. She smiled in pity at herself and her own innocence.

Hurried steps came up the stairs, and the door opened. "Are you sitting here as usual? I suspected that," Marie Hanson called out. "But now you're going with me. I'm not working, and I want to enjoy my time off. I quit my old job, and after Christmas I'll begin to work for Thomas & Hale. I'll get better pay and shorter hours. I came by yesterday to tell you, but Annie said you were sick. She guarded the door to your room like an old dragon."

"I wasn't feeling so well, but now it's over."

"Well, then hurry up and put something on. The air is so fresh. It's not at all cold. It's New Year's Eve, you know. There's always so much life in the streets then."

"That's true, it's New Year's Eve—my first in America!" She stopped suddenly as she was about to get her clothes. The boys! Shouldn't she stay home with them?

"Phooey on the boys. I saw them down on the street together with some other boys having fun with a drunk man. They won't miss you."

Her brothers making fun of a drunk man! Oh, there was no help for it. They'll be just like all the others. She might just as well resign herself to that, too.

"I'm ready now," she said, coming dressed in a little jacket trimmed in fur and the little Pennsylvania fur hat that Marie had helped her select just before Christmas, declaring that it was so attractive on her.

They walked up the street. How easy it was to walk on the white packed snow and so good to fill her lungs with the fresh air. Marie looked admiringly at her red cheeks.

"How good it is for you to come out in the air. Now you look so radiant. When I came, you looked as if you were going to a funeral. It doesn't pay to take the world so seriously, Astrid. Do as I do and take it as it comes."

"Yes, that's surely the most sensible thing to do," answered Astrid with a short, bitter laugh. "You'll see, I'll learn to do it little by little."

When they turned on Nicollet Avenue they met Hanson, Marie's brother. He was walking with a few of the kind that Holm called handsome young men.

"Hello and good evening," said Hanson gaily. "May I ask where the ladies are headed?"

"Oh, we're just going for a little stroll to look at all the people," answered Marie.

"Well, then, I hope you will allow us to accompany you. We're out on the same errand."

"But my dear Karl, I thought you had found work. Haven't you begun in the music store?" Marie asked her brother apprehensively as they walked up the street together.

"Yes, but you can't really expect that a person should slave away continuously. Anyway, we must take time off on New Year's Eve," he answered nonchalantly.

"Well, at least it's not likely that you will overexert yourself."

"No. Why should I want to do that?" he laughed good-naturedly. "Now, Miss Holm," he said, turning to Astrid, "how has it been going since the theater evening? It went brilliantly."

Astrid only nodded. She couldn't stand any reference to that event.

"Yes, but now let's talk about something else," she said with forced cheerfulness. "Do you know the lady coming there? I've seen her often. Isn't she attractive?"

They walked on, joking and laughing, up through the brightly lit Nicollet Avenue. People streamed in and out of the stores. After all, it was New Year's Eve. Hanson was inexhaustibly merry. Astrid surrendered completely and joined the others in their laughter, but her own laughs occasionally frightened her. They were so strange and so cold.

"There comes Meyer," said Hanson. "Who is the fine lady he now has laid hands on?"

Astrid felt herself blush. She started to chat eagerly, laughing loudly at a dumb witticism of one of the men. She saw Meyer whisper something to his lady friend, who then looked searchingly at them all, at last letting her glance rest on Astrid in half pitiful, half worried contempt. Meyer walked by jauntily, lifting his hand up to his hat without tipping it and smiling with an ironic arrogance. Astrid did not look at him. She saw only the glance of the woman. What did it mean? That kind of look one saw only on . . . Like a flash it went through her. This was his revenge. Oh, God, this was all that was lacking. She braced herself against Marie, feeling herself so strangely dizzy.

"I'll be damned how dashing Meyer looked today," she heard Hanson say. "Soon he'll get such uppity friends that he won't have anything to do with us poor devils."

"Aren't you feeling well, Astrid?" asked Marie when she felt her leaning so heavily against her.

"Yes, absolutely," said Astrid, straightening up proudly, her dark eyes sparkling like stars in the light of the street lamps and her red mouth laughing contemptuously. She was white as a sheet.

"Oh," broke out Marie spontaneously, "you know, sometimes you can be so strange, Astrid."

"Really?" said Astrid, laughing shrilly.

⁓

WHEN HOLM CAME UP LATE IN THE EVENING he found Astrid still up. She stood by the coal stove, preparing it for the night. She did not turn when he came in. He walked up and down the floor, then casually remarked in a light tone, "What's happened to Meyer? He never comes around anymore. Before he was here as certain as the day itself."

Astrid did not answer.

"Has something come between you?" Holm asked, irritated at her silence.

Still Astrid did not answer.

"Yes, because . . . " he continued, "I hope, then, you have the sense not thoughtlessly to reject a young cultured man with a promising future."

Astrid laughed loudly.

Holm turned to her. "It's a strange and distasteful laugh you have acquired recently, Astrid!" he said furiously.

Astrid became suddenly serious. She looked at him again with the frightening look that he had noticed that morning. Then she turned around and stirred the glowing coals and said in a low, hard voice: "Well, it's better than crying the way I used to."

Holm suddenly stopped pacing. Bewildered, he looked at her stupidly. "I think you're going mad," he said angrily, banging the door after him as he went to his room.

Hour after hour Astrid remained sitting by the stove. She folded her hands over her knees, staring intently at the glowing white heap of ashes that trembled like vibrating burning leaves.

How tired and old was the young face that stared into the fire. There was something in her expression that reminded one of the look of a hunted animal. The clock struck twelve hollow strokes. It was the old year's farewell to her. What a year! And the one she was now entering? She looked around in despair, put her head down on her knees, and whispered to herself, "Oh, God help me!"

⊱{ 13 }⊰

One afternoon in the beginning of February Astrid put on her coat and went out. She had not been out for several days because she was afraid of meeting someone. She was now certain of her situation. Time after time she had met those contemptuous disdainful glances cast on her. It was as if each time they burned into her soul like a hot iron. How clever Meyer was! He could not have gotten at her more effectively in his revenge.

But today there was almost a little spring in the air. The severe cold had suddenly stopped. Snow dripped from the roofs in the warm sunlight and the icicles that had been formed during the night hung in rainbow-colored crystals from the eaves. Astrid felt a little more lighthearted than she had been for a long time. She just had to get out no matter what happened. How beautiful it was, and how good it was to feel a little less bitterness and coldness in her heart.

Up on Washington Avenue she saw little Miss Larsen coming down the street toward her. She became quite happy when she saw her. She thought well of her. Maybe it was a good sign that she should meet her today. She would stop and talk with her.

All at once she saw Miss Larsen turn blushing red. She saw her stand still a few seconds as if terrified and then suddenly cross over to the other side of the street as fast as if she had burned herself. Astrid felt all the blood stream from her cheeks. She had to lean against the side of the building for a moment. So she, too . . . All the gentleness and mildness left her. She clenched her fists.

"Well, isn't it Miss Holm?" she heard a strong, clear voice say. "But aren't you well?"

She looked up. A husky man with black curly hair and beard and two burning black eyes stood beside her. She thought she had seen him before.

"Let me introduce myself since you apparently have forgotten that I earlier had the pleasure. Mr. Smith, attorney at law. I had the pleasure of seeing and admiring you when you acted at Turner Hall during the Christmas season, and afterwards I also had the honor of dancing with you. But you're so pale. You don't seem to be well."

"Oh, it was just a momentary dizziness. But now it is all gone."

"It's this sudden change in the weather. The climate here is severe for newcomers. You must allow me to accompany you home."

"No, that isn't necessary," she said eagerly.

He laughed at her enthusiasm. "You have, then, no desire for my company, but I must nevertheless burden you with it. It was fortunate that we had this chance meeting, for I have long wondered whether I dared pay you a visit. Now coincidence has provided me with the best of opportunities."

She looked critically at him from the side while they walked down the street. Did he act like this toward her because he, like the others, despised her and believed he could treat her as he wanted? It didn't seem so. They met a lady whom he knew. He greeted her in the same generous and straightforward manner.

"Do you know that I have recently acted as your knight, Miss Holm?" he asked jokingly.

"No, really? That is more than I could expect," and she laughed a little forced laugh while she felt as if her heart stood still.

"Of me? Now you are really being polite."

"I didn't mean it to be that way," she said confusedly, "but you don't know me at all."

"Bah! I always defend beauty. But what have you done to the poor young man?"

"I don't know what you mean."

"Pardon me, I was about to say that you lie. Your cheeks betray you, Miss Holm. And besides, when a young man like that Meyer behaves like the insulted, virtuous one, then . . ." He shrugged. "So, yes, I know what's going on."

"You are very clever, Mr. Smith!"

"I had better be, or I wouldn't be the well-known lawyer," he answered jokingly. "But this is where you live."

"Do you know that, too?" asked Astrid, her cheeks burning. So he, too, knew that she was a saloonkeeper's daughter.

"Yes, naturally I know it. But you must allow me to accompany you upstairs and pay the visit I have long thought about making."

Astrid showed him up the stairs. Oh, how humiliating it was to smell the odor from the saloon when they passed the door. He laughed as if nothing was wrong and took the steep steps two and three at a time. Astrid sent downstairs for her father to come up. Holm came up and was introduced to Smith.

"You must forgive me that I, an ardent admirer of your daughter since the theater evening at Turner Hall during the Christmas season, pay a visit to your home," said Smith.

Holm expressed his great pleasure at the honor shown him and his daughter, and his beaming face showed that he meant what he said. To Astrid's annoyance he offered Smith some wine. That did not appear to bother Mr. Smith at all. He seated himself and chatted cheerfully, enjoying the wine and smoking the cigar that Holm offered him with the assurance that cigar smoke did not bother his daughter.

An hour later Smith looked at his watch. "But I am forgetting everything," he said, looking at Astrid with his intense eyes. Astrid blushed. "At two o'clock I have a case coming up at city hall, and here I sit instead of making my preparations. I hope to have your permission to return."

"That would be a great pleasure for me and my daughter," said Holm enthusiastically.

After many bows and assurances that his house always stood open to the

lawyer, Holm walked with him down the steps. He remained standing in the
door looking after him. At last he mumbled to himself, "It probably wasn't
so stupid of her to give Meyer the cold shoulder. She's smarter than I am."

Lately Holm had felt that he no longer had any power over Astrid. Hearing the contempt in her laughter and seeing the hate in her eyes, his cowardly nature began to fear her. Ever since the evening when he had asked
her about Meyer, they had had a sort of tacit agreement to stay clear of each
other and to exchange only the most necessary words. After Smith's visit
Holm suddenly changed his conduct toward her. Respect and courtesy came
into his manner of behavior—a humble recognition that she was the
stronger. Astrid saw this and understood the reason. She smiled even more
contemptuously as she became aware of a deeper insight into her situation.

Smith returned many times. He was amusing and entertaining and often
told stories about his work as a trial lawyer and his early experiences in the
United States. He was so clever and witty that all had to laugh. In spite of
his coarseness there was something rather good-natured about him, and for
Astrid this interruption of her terrible loneliness was a relief. Still, she became more and more aware of his coarseness. Once in a while, when he
looked at her with his intense, sensual gaze as if he would devour her, her
cheeks would burn. She would get up, ready to leave the room, then stay.
"Good Lord, they're all the same. At least he was open about it, though, and
did not pretend to be something other than he was." At the same time she
felt that he was not that way toward her because he despised her—as the
others did. No, he treated her with the same measured respect he would have
shown any other beautiful woman he encountered. Yes, perhaps even a little
more because she impressed him with her proud reticence.

One day Smith invited her to go with him to the theater. She excused
herself. She feared going out with him alone. She felt instinctively that it
would be the beginning of something more. But the next time he invited
her she accepted. That same day she had met Miss Larsen and another lady
in the street. Miss Larsen had blushed and tried to let on as if she did not
see her, while the other lady looked at her with a questioning, withering contempt. It was Mrs. Hjorth.

A wild defiance seized Astrid, and when Smith came that evening and
invited her to the theater, she said yes. She would defy them all and show
them that she laughed at their scorn, and besides—why should she deny

herself every pleasure that was offered her? She would not gain anything by doing that.

She was gorgeously beautiful that evening. Smith noted it with great pleasure and introduced her with pride to the ladies of his acquaintance they met at the theater. Astrid felt their astonished, reserved gaze but she triumphed. Now they were forced to greet her, yes, even to talk with her.

One who recently had passed her coldly on the street, pretending not to know her, was exaggerated in her politeness this evening. Astrid smiled and returned her politeness with her lips curled scornfully. Now that she appeared in the company of a man whose mere presence she felt to be an insult to the purest and most feminine in her character, they all greeted her profusely. In his company she was safe from their contempt. What kind of society was she living in? A man could be whatever he wanted, and he was still accepted. No matter how immoral his talk or tactless his behavior, he was always tolerated, while a poor, defenseless girl who had done nothing wrong was despised and shunned until she came under the man's protection. Well, if that was the way it was, then she would simply adjust. And that is precisely what she did.

She now went out with Smith whenever he invited her to a concert or to the theater. Occasionally he also took Marie along, but most often they went alone. When she sat in the theater and saw something beautiful, she could forget herself for a while. Then Smith and all the others were far away, and she sat with large eyes looking into a beautiful world that had the power to enchant her. But it was as different from the real world as heaven from earth, and this was the one she had to live in. The other was closed to her.

When the curtain went down she returned to reality with a deep sigh. But then came her moment of triumph when she met the outstretched hands, the ready smiles, and the open welcome to homes that had been sealed from her. She rode home with Smith with a mixed feeling of gratitude for him and the deepest scorn for herself. She trembled in fright when she thought about the way she was going. She accepted the love of a man whose look burned her and whose animal desire made her tremble. Still, she had, of course, no other way to go. Life's icy, cruel hand worked its way with her.

One morning Marie came up to see her. Over her face she had a dark veil that she pushed back when she came in, and Astrid saw at once that she had been crying.

"Marie, dear, what is it?" she asked, taken by surprise. She laid down the book she held in her hand.

Marie sat in the rocking chair and began to sob loudly.

Astrid looked at her inquiringly.

"Oh, Astrid, what a disgrace and scandal."

"What?" asked Astrid calmly. She seemed so accustomed to disgrace and scandal.

"My brother Karl has been arrested."

"Why?"

"Yes, why? You know he is so terribly lazy. All he cares about is having fun. He isn't bad. Really, he is very good."

"Yes, but that isn't why he was arrested," said Astrid. She could not help smiling.

"No, naturally not. But I'm so upset that I don't know what I'm saying," said Marie, wiping her eyes. "But listen. You know I was so happy because he finally had found a place at the piano factory. You know he is musical and I thought this would interest him a little. And it was an excellent position, with sixty dollars a month. But it went as usual. Fourteen days later he was fired. He was, of course, so lazy that they wouldn't have him. Since then he has gone without work, and that's now over three months. He has been living with an old lady who has been very fond of him. You know how cheerful and good-natured he always is. She treated him like a prince the whole winter without getting a cent of pay. She is so odd, for her greatest delight is to keep such unemployed young men."

"Yes, but the arrest. She didn't go and get him arrested, did she?" asked Astrid a little impatiently.

"Oh, far from it. She would gladly have walked many miles on her knees just to get him out. No, it was a clothing merchant on Nicollet Avenue to whom he owed so much money. He had recently ordered a new suit of clothes. Then he went in and asked to try on the coat. And just think, after he had it on he told them that just that very day his monthly pay check at the factory was due and he would go right up there to get it. So it really wasn't necessary for him to take off the coat for such a short time. What do you think of such impudence?"

"So?"

"So the man believed him and let him go, but Karl never returned. He had, of course, no wages coming, poor fellow. And then when the man saw that he wasn't coming back with the money, he went to the factory and learned that Karl had been fired three months ago. And now he has had Karl arrested. What should I do? How shall I get him out again?" Then Marie began to sob.

Astrid looked at her almost with envy. How lucky Marie was that she could cry.

"What? How strange you are. Here I am telling you that Karl is sitting under lock and key, and you look as if you haven't heard one word I'm saying."

"Of course I've heard, and I'm terribly sad about it. But what can I do?"

"Well, you can help me, and no one else can."

"I? Marie! What do you mean?"

"Well, I know no one else, you see. Almost all my friends are poor creatures like me who live from hand to mouth. But if you would ask Mr. Smith to use his influence on Karl's behalf . . ."

"Mr. Smith!" exclaimed Astrid, turning blood red.

"Yes, is that so strange? He's so much in love with you that he would take the moon down from the heavens if you only asked him to do it."

"But my dear . . ."

"Oh, God bless you, Astrid. Help me. Imagine that your only brother sat in jail. Wouldn't I do all I could to help you? Don't you think so?"

"Yes, that I believe, but . . ."

"Oh, no more buts. Just promise me that you'll ask Mr. Smith to take care of Karl's case, and I'll be forever grateful to you, Astrid."

Marie looked so entreating and unhappy, and Astrid was moved when she thought that Marie had after all been the only woman who had shown her a little friendliness and loyalty since she came to this country.

She kissed her, saying, "I shall ask Mr. Smith for your sake, Marie, but don't depend too much on what he may be able to do."

"Oh, thank you ever so much, dearest Astrid," shouted Marie happily, and her tears were as if brushed away. "He can do it, he can. That's for sure. Lawyers can do everything in this country. But now I must hurry as fast as I can to the store. I sneaked out in order to come to you." She looked at the clock, dried her eyes, poked a little at her curls in front of the mirror, then kissed Astrid quickly and ran down the stairs with the veil on her arm. She smiled and waved with it up to Astrid as she hurried up the street.

Astrid stood by the window looking after her. How quickly her tears had dried up. Forgotten were the shame and disgrace that she had just sobbed about. Now she was all full of life and hope. She pressed her cold forehead against the windowpane. Oh, if she could only cry over her shame and disgrace. Not in a lifetime could it all be cried away.

In the afternoon she was sitting by the window with her sewing looking thoughtlessly down on the street. Suddenly she turned red. There came Smith merrily swinging his hat up at her. He held something in his hand. Oh, now she would have to ask him for a favor. How embarrassing. Almost before she had completed the thought he was standing in the room.

"Hello, Miss Holm! Do you see what I'm bringing? The first violets. Isn't that unusually early? If I would now be really sentimental, then I would claim that I been out in the spring sun and picked them myself. But that would have been a lie because I've been in the city hall just about the whole day, and God knows violets don't grow there."

He sat down on the sofa while Astrid took the violets and smelled them. How wonderful they smelled! She unconsciously closed her eyes, and a host of happy childhood memories swarmed forth at the odor of these small blue flowers. How often as a child she had run joyously in the green hills outside the city looking for violets. The newborn spring with its lush, dripping green, its sprouting leaf buds, and its wonderful smell had filled her with such delight that she often threw herself down flat in the grass, wishing that she had dared to shout out loud for joy. Of course she could not do it, for someone always came walking stodgily by down on the road. Someone else would look up curiously to see why a silly little foolish girl would be lying there and rolling around in the grass. She remembered how her mother's pale cheeks had reddened and how eagerly she had breathed the first bouquet of violets that Astrid had picked for her.

"Well, whenever you are finished smelling those trifles that I, to speak quite frankly, can't get interested in, then come and sit down here and be a little cheerful." Smith's voice startled her. She found a glass of water for the violets and sat down obediently.

"Tomorrow you must go with me to the theater. Keene is going to play Othello. You probably haven't seen that one before, have you?"

"No, I've actually seen very little."

"All the better. The more pleasure it is for me to show you everything.

And Keene is magnificent. Even I must admit that—I who otherwise can't stand Shakespeare. Would you like to bring your girlfriend along? I can't really say I'm crazy about her company, but if you would like to, then of course you may."

Astrid's heart pounded. Now it had to be done. He himself had brought Marie into their conversation.

"I'm afraid that Marie is not in a very good mood for entertainment right now," she began a little hesitantly.

"Well, what's the matter with her? Usually she seems to be in the mood for entertainment. She's not like you."

"Her brother," interrupted Astrid, who preferred to keep the conversation away from herself, "has been arrested."

"Damn it, I know that, of course," exclaimed Smith, hitting himself on the forehead, "but I didn't remember that it was her brother. Yes, he's one of those Norwegian scoundrels that we have such a confounded overabundance of here in America. They want to live but they don't want to work."

"He has, basically, such a good heart."

"Yes, they all do. And they all want to live at someone else's expense."

"Marie is terribly grieved," continued Astrid without paying attention to him.

"Yes, poor thing. It's a pity for his sister. She is apparently a good young lady even though she has so damned little beauty."

"You couldn't, well help him out of this, could you? You would do me a great favor, Mr. Smith," said Astrid bravely, looking at him. "Marie is my only girlfriend here, and they are both so alone and friendless," she added as an explanation.

Smith got up, went over and lit himself a cigar, and puffed a little while as he paced the floor. Finally he turned to Astrid. "I shall do it. I'll see about helping the fellow out of this pinch. But it will be just as well to get him out of the city at the same time, for here he has made himself entirely impossible. If he gets out of this spot, he'll soon be in another one. We can see about getting him out West or some other place where we'll hear no more of his follies." He walked right over to her and looked at her with one of those expressions that Astrid always vaguely feared. "But it's only for your sake, Miss Holm. I most likely wouldn't lift a finger to help the lazy scoundrel if you hadn't asked me."

Astrid had become a blushing red. She was now angry with herself for having made herself obliged to him and shown him that she relied on his influence.

"I am extremely grateful to you, Mr. Smith," she said in a whisper, but she would not look at him.

"Damned if you are," he said, laughing good-naturedly. "Then you wouldn't have said it in that tone and then not given me so much as a glance from your beautiful eyes. Well, then, when the time comes, so will the opportunity, as one says. But come now," he continued, "I've been kind to you, and now you should be kind to me and go for a stroll."

Astrid looked at the clock. "Isn't it too late?" she asked, looking for an excuse.

"Late? Bah! Just come. Hurry up."

Soon they were out on the street. It was one of the first days of April. There was a somewhat sharp north wind and the streets were almost dry after the awful spring slush. On Second Avenue the trees stood bursting full of buds and the front lawns were a lush green. Elegant light carriages rolled by at high speed, drawn by powerful horses. Silk-clothed ladies and playing children dressed in their finery filled the sidewalks. Astrid herself became affected by all the budding and teaming life, natural and human.

"Marie is apparently right. I take life too seriously. I might as well do as the others and enjoy life whenever possible and take things as they come." She laughed and chatted with Smith. As they were turning into another street, they bumped right into Meyer, who turned the corner deep in a serious conversation with two ladies. His ironic, haughty greeting did not disturb her in the least. She met it with a cold glance and lifted her head.

"Poor devil," said Smith when they had passed. "He's in a pinch now. He doesn't dare be rude to me even if it means his life. So he'll have to keep his remarks to himself until he's so far away from us that we can't hear them. Besides, he has almost played himself out in fine society so far as I have been able to determine."

⌇

THE NEXT DAY THERE WAS A LETTER FOR ASTRID along with a nice bouquet of flowers. "Your friend is free," it said. "I am sending him out West this evening and hope that this will ease your heart. At seven o'clock I will arrive with a carriage outside your door to drive you to the theater. I hope to get at least a friendly smile in return for my labors. Your respectful Knight."

⊰ 14 ⊱

I t was a Sunday in the middle of July out by the shores of Lake Minnetonka. The charming lake, with its rich, lush banks on which the white tents of the Indians had shone in the sun thirty years earlier, lay rocking gently in the bright sunshine. One little wave after another flowed on toward the shore, casting small pearls of foam on the rocks. The lake lay there as if dreaming—just as blue as it was thirty years ago. Gone, however, were the white tents from which the smoke rose like light clouds in the clear air. Gone were the brown faces and the light canoes that shot like arrows over the surface of the water. On the densely wooded banks no mysterious hunter darted out on quick feet with his quiver of arrows on his back. No young men in love—decorated with feathers in their long black hair, their cheeks painted in red and blue, and pearls in their ears and on their hands— sneaked to a meeting with a loved one, the one who would be his squaw, move into his father's tent, and bear his children whenever the "Great Spirit" granted them fortune.

Where are they now? They have all gone. The white man has chased them away from their paradise, for the white man's God is a mighty God, a terrifying God. The Indian fled, trembling before his face, farther and farther away. At last he could do nothing but lie down like a wounded animal on the narrow strip of land that still was granted him, and slowly bleed to death. He was superfluous. The earth had no more use for him.

How different the picture on the lake was now. Pleasure boats glided past with banners flying from the masts. The decks were filled with happy people who came out from Minneapolis on the morning train to throw off the week's wear and tear for a little while. They wanted to leave behind the toil and the oppressive stuffy air of the shops and offices to breathe in the fresh air on Minnetonka's charming blue water. The large attractive sailboats glistened in the sun, their white sails still hanging somewhat slack because there was only a faint breeze. That did not in any way hinder the elegant people who filled the boats from being cheerful and enjoying the moment's indescribable beauty. Along the shore small villas and graceful summer homes had been built. Among the trees one could glimpse ladies dressed in white and small children playing. In the bay of the lake one saw the towers of Park Hotel peek forth from the forest. Over there in the bay lay the austere St. Louis, and far away on the top of a hill was the enormous Hotel Lafayette with its verandas and covered balconies and its colossal ballrooms. There wealthy families from the South took refuge when summer became too hot for them under their burning sun. On dark summer evenings lights shone out from the open windows and one could see figures clothed in silk and velvet and lace glide back and forth. The dance was in progress on those polished floors while the music sent its vibrating sounds out over the quiet lake that lay there dreaming in the summer night, responding with one or another quiet sigh that it cast in on the beach. The lake alone remembered the old days. It alone could not forget. Civilization had made its entry. It had come with its all-ruling, all-crushing power, and it had been in a hurry because all this had been done in thirty years. What did it care about what it had crushed under its feet or that blood and tears sprouted in the path of its victorious progress! Thirty years! How much had changed! A long time, and yet only a drop in the larger stream of evolution.

~

"WHAT ARE YOU SITTING THERE AND DREAMING ABOUT, Miss Holm? You look as if you are in another world. Be so kind as to come back to us simple mortals," shouted a strong voice that sat by the helm in an attractive white sailboat. On the boat's prow, painted in large gilt letters, was the name *Astrid.*

The person speaking was Smith, who had invited a little group out with him for a tour on Minnetonka. There he had overwhelmed them with his new sailboat that lay in the bay when they came, shining white, the seats covered with red cushions, ready to receive its namesake. Astrid had blushed deeply when she discovered the name and had scowled. Mrs. Rask and her husband and Mrs. Hammer were part of the group. They were all sitting in lively conversation when Smith shouted over to Astrid.

Astrid sat staring listlessly in front of her, her one hand, from which she had removed her glove, hanging and playing down in the rippling surface of the water. She pulled herself together when her name was called. "I was thinking about the poor Indians," she said. "It's a hard fate they have endured."

"Damned if they were worth any better. They're nothing but scoundrels and thieves—the whole lot of them. Just don't worry your little head over them. Bring out the champagne basket, Thompson. A person gets terribly dry in the throat lying and splashing out here. There in the other basket beside you are the glasses. Now we'll drink a toast to the new *Astrid*. Wasn't that a nice surprise, Miss Holm?"

"Yes, it was totally unexpected."

"See, that's all the gratitude I get," he said as he turned toward the others. "You can depend upon it—she's not too generous with her praises. Well, let's toast to both the new and the old Astrid then," he said, lifting the foaming glass which the young man responding to the name Thompson handed him.

Mrs. Rask looked over at her husband, twitching her mouth a little. This was too much honor being shown to a saloonkeeper's daughter whose reputation, moreover, was more than questionable. But they were Smith's guests and had to play along. Moreover, in all likelihood she would soon become Mrs. Smith. That Smith was madly in love with her was, of course, clear, and she naturally held on with both hands—the poor girl. Meyer had been right when he said she was smart. Just look how she sat there so shyly, looking so innocent. She knew very well that this was just how she had aroused Smith and driven him to take the affair more seriously than he otherwise was known to have done on such occasions. Mrs. Rask raised her glass together with the others.

The toast was drunk with much enthusiasm. Mrs. Hammer, who appreciated everything beautiful and had already fallen in love with Astrid, said good-naturedly, "You must really come out to visit me, Miss Holm. Take her along one evening, Mr. Smith. Then maybe we may also have the pleasure of seeing you for once. It happens so seldom these days."

Take her along. So it had come to that. Without further ado they now asked Smith to take her with him—as if she were already his possession. She opened her mouth in order to give an angry reply, but closed it again and forcefully bit her teeth together. It was, of course, her own fault. What else could she expect? She had given them every right to talk that way by always accepting everything from him. Her sitting there at that moment was witness enough against her. They were right. There was no way back. Where could she go? Now, at least, they opened their gilded halls to her, she thought with a bitter smile.

Smith seemed to find Mrs. Hammer's words quite as they should be and replied undisturbed, "Thanks, Madame. That I shall do. But it was really a pity that you couldn't get your husband along today. He works too much."

"Yes, Nils never has time. Both Sundays and weekdays he works at the office. It's too much of a good thing. And now since he has become an alderman, it's worse than before."

"But then there is all the honor it brings, Madame. It is so fair a fruit, you know. Oh, look! Here we are at Big Island, the most romantic of all the islands in the world. I propose we go up there for a while before we go over to the hotel for dinner. Let's take the sails down now. There's no wind here anyway."

His suggestion was unanimously approved, and the boat glided right below the island's steep cliff. The water was shallow, but the ladies could not easily come ashore without getting their thin shoes dirty.

"We shall carry the ladies across. Watch out, Miss Holm. You'll get your white dress dirty," he shouted to Astrid, who, just as he was about to take hold of her, scurried away from him light as a bird and a moment later was over on the island.

She ran up the slope and stood at the top, while laughter and little shrieks from the other ladies sounded up to her. From there she could see out over the entire Minnetonka, which lay there smiling and rocking gently in the sun.

She walked from the cliff into the forest. Oh, how beautiful it was there! She took off her hat and let the cool breeze cool her warm cheeks.

Civilization had not forced its way into the forest. One almost expected to see an Indian peek out from behind one of the enormous moss-covered tree trunks. These monstrous old trees almost shut out the sky. One saw only a few deep-blue flashes up above. The sun trembled on the tree tops and sent white-gold stripes down among the trees, which shook mysteriously and enticingly out over the dark forest ground. She walked softly on her toes. A bird struck a clear warble. The dead leaves rustled under her feet. Otherwise, all was still—nature's eternal, solemn stillness. She sat down with her back against a fallen old giant and half closed her eyes. How good this quietness was! Why did human beings have to torment each other with their endless turmoil and fuss?

"Miss Holm! See, there she is. Leaned up against an old venerable gray-beard that the storm has knocked down. Just stay seated. You look right at home there."

"Just like one of the Dryads of the past," said Rask smiling. "Just so she doesn't vanish when we get closer to her domain."

Astrid blushed at seeing them all staring at her. She stood up quickly, reluctant because they had broken into her sanctuary and disturbed it. She brushed back her hair, the unruly hair that was always in the way.

"Isn't it beautiful here?" she asked, just to have something to say.

"Well, I'm not so crazy about the gloomy atmosphere. I desire the full light of day. But if the ladies want to sit and get carried away a little while, we have plaids. Thompson, get the shawls." Thompson spread out the shawls for the ladies to sit on. He worked in Smith's office and was taken along today like an obedient servant to help Smith wait on the ladies.

"What is actually so wonderfully beautiful here, Miss Holm?" Smith turned to Astrid. "To tell the truth, I see nothing but some old trees and some black dirt with dead leaves and a few poor lonely blades of grass."

"I don't know," replied Astrid hesitatingly, "just what it is. I think it must have something to do with the feeling one gets on coming in here that no human foot has been here before. It's as if one is the only living creature in this mysterious world."

"Well, if that's so indescribably beautiful, then you must have a high opinion of us human beings, it would seem. Now we can understand why she always runs away from us," he said, turning to Mrs. Hammer, who sat a little uneasily, smoothing the folds in her chamois-colored silk dress.

"Oh, just so there aren't any snakes here," shouted Mrs. Rask, glancing nervously around her. "I don't think it's wise to sit here."

"Oh, Thompson will be your knight," said Smith nonchalantly. He lay stretched out on his stomach in front of Astrid's feet, looking at her while he talked. "Thompson, see that no snake comes to bite Mrs. Rask."

Mrs. Rask scowled. Her cheeks burned in spite of the powder. That was going too far, indeed.

Astrid felt disagreeably uncomfortable. She suggested that they get up. Then, after walking around the island, they went down to the lake again. When Astrid wanted to jump over into the boat, she was seized by Smith, who lifted her high in his arms while he shouted, "There, I caught you Miss Holm. Run away from me now if you can."

"Let me go," she shouted angrily, casting an angry look at him. But then she laughed afterwards in order to conceal her anger. He carried her first and then helped Thompson with getting the other ladies into the boat. They rowed across the lake to the little private hotel that lay there on the bay, half hidden by trees. There dinner awaited them.

Later in the afternoon, while they all took a little siesta after the good dinner, Mrs. Rask and Mrs. Hammer walked under the birch trees. Smith came walking toward them. "Where is Miss Holm?"

"Indeed, I don't know. I thought she was with you," said Mrs. Rask sarcastically.

"No, by God, she isn't, Mrs. Rask. Miss Holm! See, there she is lying in the hammock between the trees."

Astrid lay there motionless, looking at the light summer clouds floating across the deep blue up above. It was as if she could hear her own heart beat; such an anxiety had come over her. She felt in Smith's whole manner—in his look, in his voice, in everything—that it would come today. Of course, she had realized that it would come one day, and yet she shook in fear at the thought that it finally was there. Could she still retreat? No, she did not even want to do it.

Jumping up when her name was called, she saw Smith coming over toward her. She was standing on the grassy green bank when he arrived.

"Well, have you had a nap? We are waiting for you."

She followed Smith to the veranda, where those who had spread out in groups now were assembling.

"He neither hears nor sees anyone but her," whispered Mrs. Rask angrily, pointing with her lace-edged parasol at Astrid.

"I don't wonder that he is in love. She is really sweet," said Mrs. Hammer. "And God only knows how much truth there is in what Meyer says."

Since a fine little breeze had come up, Smith suggested that they should try *Astrid* one more time with all the sails up. The suggestion was received with applause as Mrs. Rask remarked anxiously, "If only it isn't dangerous." Thompson received the order again to watch out for Mrs. Rask so she would not drown, and laughing they all proceeded on board. *Astrid* moved away like an arrow with great speed. The ladies let out the prescribed little shrieks when the boat listed a little, and Smith, who sat at the helm, laughed. Astrid would have rejoiced if she had been able to be alone and dip her hands and face in the pearly foam. Now Smith's eyes followed her in all her movements, and she felt as uneasy as before a thunderstorm.

They were out as long as they dared. Then, panting and hurrying, they arrived breathless at the railroad station. They were just in time because the locomotive was already puffing in the forest and turning the bend. A moment later they sat squeezed in the crowded car and were on their way to Minneapolis.

When they came to the city, it was already dark, but the moon had come up and cast its white beams on the platform when they stepped out of the compartment. A couple of steps away from the station stood a closed carriage with a team of white horses.

"It is good you are so prompt," said Smith in English to the coachman. "May I have the pleasure of taking all of you home?"

Mr. and Mrs. Rask thanked him but declined the offer. They lived in an entirely different section of the city from the others, and the streetcar went right to their house.

"Well, I still accept with thanks," said Mrs. Hammer, who had been looking around carefully. "I don't see Nils anywhere even though he promised faithfully to pick me up. As usual he has not had the time." She jumped into the carriage.

Smith, who had kept his eyes on Astrid so she would not slip away from him in the crowd, said: "Then you sit up by Mrs. Hammer, and we'll drive her home first, then you."

"Oh, but I live in a completely different area," she stammered, "and the streetcar . . ."

"Oh, come now. Just sit up there." There was something commanding in his voice. Astrid felt a kind of weakness come over her. There was no avoiding her fate. Smith sat directly opposite them on the front seat. The carriage doors were slammed shut, and they rolled in full speed down Washington Avenue.

"It has been a beautiful day," said Mrs. Hammer, leaning back in the carriage.

"That makes me happy, Mrs. Hammer. I really think it was successful, too. And you, Miss Holm, what do you think?"

"Yes, it has been very pleasant," came from Astrid as if she had to force the words out.

They all drifted off into their own thoughts until the carriage stopped outside Mrs. Hammer's door. "Good night, good night. It has been such a wonderful day. Come to visit me, Miss Holm. Don't forget, Mr. Smith, you promised me you would bring her out for a visit."

"Rest assured we shall come, Madame." How this "we" fell naturally from his lips as if there were no disputing the matter. The two of them belonged together!

"Well, thank God," said Smith when the street door had closed behind Mrs. Hammer. He gave the coachman directions and with a sigh seated himself on the back seat by Astrid. Astrid crept involuntarily closer into her corner. How fast her heart beat. It was as if she would suffocate.

"Well, thank God," he repeated. "Now we can have a little peace. This time you can't avoid me, Astrid," he said a little later, leaning forward and looking her right in the eyes. "You have managed to slip out of my hands all day, but now I have you. You see, that's why I didn't invite your girlfriend today. When she is along, it's impossible for me to have you to myself for one moment."

So that's how it was then. Her hunch had been right. A ray of the moon fell right on Astrid. Smith, too, was anxious at that moment. His natural self-assurance failed him.

He stopped a little. Astrid answered nothing. She thought she would not be able to open her mouth even if her life depended on it.

"Now you must promise me that you will be my wife, Astrid. This evening I want the matter settled. That I have promised myself. Will you?" he whispered, taking her hand. It was clammy and ice cold. Astrid bent her head a trifle. It was impossible to speak. He held her close to him in a passionate embrace, and Astrid felt his kisses burning her mouth, face, and throat. She tried in fright to tear herself loose, but he held her tightly in his strong arms. Then a strange faintness overcame her, and her eyes closed shut. She still felt his kisses, but it was as if she were far away. They no longer burned. Her ears rang as if from many bells. Then she knew nothing more. Her head sank down on his shoulder. She had fainted. The excitement and anxiety and now his intense passion had become too much for her, and she collapsed.

Smith was so thrilled with finally being able to hold her in his arms that at first he did not notice. It seemed to him that he had never been in love before. There had been something about her that had always kept him at his distance. He felt that a tactless word would have lost her for him forever. But this had stirred his infatuation all the more. Never before did he have to restrain himself in his passion. And now he could finally give it free rein.

"You are beautiful, and I love you," he whispered as if intoxicated. Astrid's hat had slid off her head, and her black curls fell in disarray down over her face and out over his shoulder. He kissed them and buried his ardent face in this profusion of hair. Then he pulled her still more closely to him and let kisses rain over her face.

Suddenly the cold listlessness struck him as unnatural. He lifted her head and looked at her. How chalk white the fine face lay there on his arm in the moonlight.

"Astrid!" he whispered anxiously. She did not move. "Astrid!" he shouted louder. She raised her eyelids, but they closed together right away. He finally realized that she had fainted.

"It seems as though . . ." he mumbled anxiously. At once he became more sober. He looked out the window. They were almost at Astrid's house. Then they rolled up in front of the door.

He glanced up. It was dark. Only the moonbeams played on the window panes. Within the saloon burned a low light. Apparently Papa Holm had guests there who had taken refuge in the back room since it was Sunday. "Thank God," he thought. "Then we can get her upstairs without more trouble." He lay Astrid's head back on the carriage seat, went out first by himself, ordered the driver to wait, and then took her in his arms and carried her up the stairs as easily as if she were a child. He opened the door to the living room. No one was there. He carried her over to the sofa and placed her on it. Then he looked around searchingly. He found a bottle on a little table and smelled it. It was "Bouquet," something he had sent her. He held it under her nose and then moistened her temples with it. She opened her eyes and first looked around confused, but then it all came back to her. She put her hands over her breast dismayed. He was fumbling with her dress to open it up so she could breathe more easily. She whispered as if in her soul's distress, "Go! Just go! I am quite well again."

"How you frightened me. Are you sure you're all right?"

"Yes, yes. But go now." She raised herself.

He took her firmly around the head and kissed her many times.

"Go! Go!" Astrid whispered, drowning under his kisses.

"You little fool! Why do you want to chase me away? You are mine now."

"Yes, yes, but go now. No more this evening. I can't . . ."

"Yes, I'll go now, but tomorrow I won't let myself be chased away. You can be sure of that," he said jokingly. He took her once more passionately in his arms and kissed her one, two, three times. "So, goodnight my beautiful one. Now you are mine!" And he was gone. A moment later she heard the carriage rumble down the street.

Astrid stood in the middle of the room. The moon cast a broad silver strip through the open window out over the floor. It fell right on her figure. She stood with her head bent as if listening. Her hair fell down over her white dress and over her throat and breast. When she heard the carriage roll away, she lifted her head and breathed deeply. Now it had been done. But had she known it would be so terrible, then she would never have agreed to it. She would rather have gone begging from door to door. Had she really sold herself? She touched her throat at the place he had last kissed her, rubbing it unconsciously. She touched her lips and looked at her arms. Everywhere she looked she thought his kisses had defiled her. "Oh, God, how I despise myself," she whispered, raising her arms and striking her hands together above her head in silent desperation.

The door downstairs slammed. It was her father, and she could not look at him. She ran into her room, closed the door quietly, and threw herself on her bed. She heard him walk up the steps and into the living room. He had probably heard them come and was surprised to find no one there. He went out in the hall, stopping there in front of her door. "Astrid," he said softly. She almost stopped breathing. She could not answer him. He mumbled something to himself and went down the stairs again. She remembered that first evening she had come to Minneapolis, when she also lay there fearful of seeing him. How long ago it was! Then she was still an innocent child who could cry over her broken dreams, and now, what had she become in this one year? A tearless woman who with a bitter smile walked toward her humiliation. And the worst of all was that she hated the man who had destroyed her mother, who had destroyed her own youth and innocence and her faith in mankind. And that man was her own father. She buried her face in the pillow and moaned loudly from pain. Thus she remained lying hour after hour, quietly, as if petrified.

She heard her brothers come up the stairs, laughing and chatting. She heard the voices of Annie and her father among theirs. Someone opened the door to her room but closed it again. At last all became quiet.

Late in the night she awoke from her daze. She got up, slowly brushed the hair from her face and put it up for the night, took off her clothes one by one, and went to bed. Her face was calm and cold. She had spent herself. Tomorrow she would receive her betrothed.

{ 15 }

When Astrid came into the living room the next morning, Holm was standing by the window. It was evident that he had been waiting for her. He turned when she came in. "It looks as if the country air has affected you. You usually don't sleep so late."

"Yes, I have overslept," Astrid answered indifferently as she began to straighten up the room a little.

"Well, how was it yesterday? A fine trip?" He looked at her uneasily, carefully observing her.

"Oh, very nice."

"Where did you go last evening? I heard you come home. I was sure Smith was with you, but when I came up no one was here."

"I was tired."

"A very satisfactory answer," thought Holm, tapping violently on the window pane and looking out on the street. Something had happened. That was obvious. But then why had Smith left? "Has she given this one the cold shoulder, too? I'll be damned . . ."

Suddenly he heard Astrid say in a clear voice: "I might as well tell you right away, father. I have become engaged to Mr. Smith!"

He turned as if shot out of a cannon. He was fiery red in his face.

"My dear child, what is this you are saying? How you take me by surprise," he blurted out emotionally, going over to her with outstretched arms. But his arms went limp, and he involuntarily stepped back a step when his glance met hers. She stood there intense and pale, her head erect, with an accusing glance.

"Does it really surprise you, father? I thought you had been waiting for it for a long time."

This time he could not avoid hearing the scornful ring in her voice. "Astrid, you are hard on me," he stammered. "I just want you to be happy, my child, and then I want to share your happiness with you."

On Astrid's mouth appeared a bitter smile, but she did not reply. She took up some needlework and sat down. Holm picked up courage then, went over to her, and kissed her on the cheek. "God bless you, my child," he said pompously, putting his handkerchief up to his eyes. He then quickly left the room.

Later that morning the doorbell rang. A young man stood outside. He held in his hands a small package and a flower basket filled with yellow and dark red roses.

"Miss Holm?" Astrid nodded. "From Mr. Smith. He will be here at five this afternoon." He handed the basket and package to Astrid and ran down the steps.

Astrid went into the living room. She loved flowers, especially roses, and these were unusually beautiful. She sniffed them ardently. How beautiful they were, these roses, half open and expanding as they bent the slender stalks. There was a Mediterranean beauty about them. Life's own flaming rich glow was over them. Here was the beauty that she was searching for but could never attain. Around her were only dust and dirt and the stench of whisky, and she herself now seemed the dirtiest and the ugliest of all. She carefully filled the basin in the basket with water. Even if they could bloom only a short time, she could still forget herself and her poverty as long as they lasted.

Finally her eyes fell on the package. She picked it up, and once again the hard look came to her face. She opened it. It was a small deep-red velvet case. She pressed the lock. There lay a precious diamond ring. She took it out, placing it slowly on her finger. How it sparkled in the sunshine. As she sat there looking at the glittering ring that shone in rainbow colors from her white hand, a verse came to mind. How was it now? She could not get hold of it right away. Then all at once the old attic came to mind. She saw herself in the black velvet dress in which she always played Dame Margit. That was it then:

> *Red-gold ring, surrounding my life,*
> *With gold did the Mountain King secure his wife.*

She said it once half aloud, then again, very slowly. She wanted to pull the ring off her finger quickly, but it seemed to close firmly around her pale white skin and glow with a demonic luster. She let it stay, hiding her face in her hands. What is done cannot be undone. She had wanted to play Dame Margit, but that had been denied her. But to live her—that she was allowed to do. Her dream had become bitter reality, the play most horribly serious.

❧ 16 ❧

The summer went by, and Astrid was always occupied. Smith wanted her to accompany him around to meet all his acquaintances to whom he introduced his fiancée with great pride. Everywhere she was received with open arms and a friendly smile. The past no longer existed. All were delighted to see the "sweet Miss Holm." When the sun went down in the evening and the oppressive heat had given way to a pleasant temperature, Smith would most often stop outside the door with a carriage.

Astrid threw a light summer shawl over her shoulders, and soon they drove in the city's best sections past the elegant houses and the delightful lakes on the modern boulevards, where light vehicles drawn by stately horses rolled by, the one faster than the other. In the carriages white-clothed ladies leaned back against the soft cushions and enjoyed the evening's coolness half hidden behind fans edged in swan feathers.

As the carriage bearing Astrid and Smith rolled along, Astrid thought about how the summer before she had sneaked like a thief outside these elegant houses and with despair in her heart had peeked in at the fortunate people who sat there. Now she was one of them. Was she more happy? Well, she had been attracted by a certain numbing sense of comfort. She was fond of wealth and being beautifully clothed in rich fabrics. She loved life, color, beauty. Yet she thought with a mixed feeling of pity and sadness of the little dark figure that had crept so extremely lonesome and unhappy through these same streets. Yet, that dark figure possessed something that the Astrid who sat here in the elegant carriage did not have. And she leaned back in the carriage with a sigh, pressed the gorgeous bouquet of flowers that she held in her hands up to her face, and intoxicated herself with the fragrance—all in order to forget.

On Sundays Smith would have a party out by Lake Minnetonka, and *Astrid* would spread its white sails in the sunshine while they sailed easily over the blue water and the champagne flowed.

Holm was enchanted. This went beyond his wildest dreams. He treated Astrid like a queen. Now everything had to revolve around her. The young boys shouted with joy when they occasionally got to sit in the driver's seat or come along out to Minnetonka and help Smith hoist and lower the sails. How they would swim and romp on the fine beach and shout loudly with joy! This was something quite different from being confined to the smelly, dusty street they lived on and were accustomed to, and Astrid was happy just to see their excitement.

Marie was always embracing Astrid: "Oh, Astrid, how happy I am for you. Aren't you very happy?" Then she would look into Astrid's thoughtful eyes.

"Yes, naturally. Why shouldn't I be?"

"Because you're so strange. You're not like the others."

Astrid, however, thought that she was just like all the others. She had done what thousands had done before her and thousands would do after her, and she sighed involuntarily while she thought that life really was a strange comedy.

Smith was passionately in love. For her the time of agony was when he caressed her—the price for all the magnificence he so generously bestowed on her. Yet, little by little, she grew listless even then, and his kisses no longer burned her like fire. They became for her a necessary nuisance that she finally was able to be patient about. Every once in a while, when he was more violent than usual, she would move back involuntarily and some of her old anxiety would come over her. Then he only laughed at her. "What a little fool you are!" he would say, pulling her still closer to him.

It never occurred to him to think about whether she loved him. She was beautiful, and she would be his possession, and he would shower her with gold and jewels and flowers. That was all. For her not to be happy was ridiculous.

Autumn came with its cooler days, its clear air, and its golden splendor—finally also with dead leaves, rain, and slush. Their trips to Lake Minnetonka were over. She missed them. It had been so delightful to lie and float in the water and look at the deep blue heavens arched above and feel the fresh breeze on her cheeks. Now they were restricted to the nauseating, unpleasant city again.

Smith wanted to set the date for the wedding, but Astrid always delayed it. "Just a little while longer. Then I'll be a little more used to him and it will be easier," she thought, while her heart trembled. She knew that soon it could no longer be postponed.

Throughout the fall Smith had to make several business trips out East and was, therefore, not able to put such great pressure on her, but when he was finished with these trips he did not want to wait any longer. He said so one day in the beginning of November, more seriously than usual.

"Sometime in January, then," she said hesitantly.

He seized it eagerly. "Yes, yes. We'll set the date for January 20th. That's my birthday."

She nodded. It was therefore decided.

One day in the beginning of December, Smith came to her. He had just returned home from a trip and was to leave again the next day. "Have you heard the big news? Bjørnstjerne Bjørnson is coming to town," he said after he had seated himself on the sofa and pulled her down on his lap.

The blood rushed to Astrid's head. "Is it possible?" she blurted out. "I didn't think he would come so far west." Her eyes shone.

"Look here," he laughed. "Now she comes to life. You should always look like this, Astrid. Now you are radiantly beautiful." He wanted to draw her to him again.

"No, no!" She held back. "Tell me all you know. When is he coming here? Most likely he'll give a lecture here, won't he?"

"Yes, of course. That's why he's coming. Most likely it will be around Christmas time. That will be fun. I know him from the time I was a young student in Kristiania before I came over here. Have you never heard him?"

"No, never," answered Astrid, staring engrossed into space.

"Listen. You'd better not look like that—as if there were no one else in the world but Bjørnson. I'll soon be jealous."

He laughed at his own wit and pulled her to him with force, and this time she did not escape.

"Shouldn't we go out soon to look for a house?" he asked after a little while. "They are building one up on Hennepin now that will be utterly charming, but I don't want to decide on it until you have seen it."

Astrid had gone over to the window, where she remained looking out.

"Now, what do you say?" he asked a little impatiently. "This doesn't seem to interest you as much as Bjørnson does."

"Yes, I'll be happy to look at it whenever you want," she answered, turning toward him.

"Well, right now I don't have time, for I have to leave tomorrow. But when I come back next week we'll look at it together. If you like it as well as I do, then, maybe I'll buy it."

He left soon after, but he was to return in a few hours and they would go together to the theater.

Astrid sat by the window long after he had gone, looking out. It had begun to snow softly in thick wet flakes. It was the first snow of the winter.

Darkness fell over the room. She still sat there. She could not understand why it was, but it was as if everything was torn up in her again just at hearing that Bjørnson was coming to town. At first she felt happiness, but now that was gone. How strange that he should come just now! Just now when she was so busy sinking comfortably into apathy and taking everything that was offered. But now he was coming—that miraculous man who from her childhood had stood in her imagination as the greatest and the grandest. Now, in her hour of humiliation, when she had given up everything, he was coming. What should that mean? If he had only come a year earlier, then, perhaps, he could have saved her. Now it was too late. Unconsciously, she squeezed her hands together, and the diamond ring shone with a merciless brilliance in the glow of the gas light. But the snow fell thicker and thicker, clean and soft. It spread its white shroud over her.

{ 17 }

Bjørnson had come. He was to give a lecture in the evening at Market Hall. People were streaming up the steps. Smith and Astrid were among those who pushed forward in order to get a good seat. She was decked out in a fur-lined silk coat, a Christmas gift from her father. She was pale from excitement, but her eyes beamed feverishly. She was tired. After she had heard that Bjørnson would come it was impossible for her to calm down again. Her old feeling of despair overwhelmed her, and she often lay awake at night and tossed. During the day she was nervous and restless and it was difficult to conceal her agony when Smith caressed her. As a rule he did not notice it, taken up as he was by his own infatuation, but a couple of times she could not help pulling away. His touch was repulsive to her. Once he had become annoyed and said to her: "What the hell, Astrid. You have become so prudish again now. It's a good thing this won't last much longer. Otherwise I would become fed up with it," he added roughly.

They found good seats not far from the rostrum. The huge room filled up quickly. Far out in the vestibule it was full of people. When Bjørnson appeared on the stage, there was a tremendous uproar, clapping, and shouts of "Bravo!" Astrid sat with open mouth, her head bent forward. She heard none of the commotion around her. So that was the way he looked! He was almost as she had imagined him. She stared up in amazement at that strapping figure who stood on the middle of the stage with his proud head cast back, determination and courage expressed in every feature. So there were still such men to be found in the world! She had almost forgotten it. A nameless joy broke through her pain from a new sense of the infinite distance between herself and the world. It was the joy of a new sense of faith, faith in mankind, a faith that there was still something in life worth fighting for. She absorbed each word he said as a dried up, scorched field soaks up the merciful rain which finally comes. Redeeming tears ran slowly down her cheeks as she sat quietly and listened.

He talked about Grundtvig, picturing the mighty reformer for them in words so vivid, so full of power, wit, humor, and gentleness that they touched hidden heartstrings and caused minds that never rose above material concerns to soar in rapture. It was the spirit's triumph over matter, enthusiasm's victory over apathy.

She sat motionless, his voice still ringing in her ears, when Smith took her by the arm and said in a whisper, "Come, let's go up to greet him. I'll introduce you."

"No, no," she said fearfully. She had a feeling that Bjørnson would see right through her. Oh, God, how he would despise her!

"Why not? I know him, you know."

"Not this evening," she said imploringly. "Another time. You see, there are so many around him."

"Well it doesn't really matter, I guess. We'll see him tomorrow evening at the Hammers'. Come then, let's go."

That night after she went to bed Astrid lay weeping for several hours. She sobbed as she did after her mother's death, only much more bitterly and painfully. It was impossible for her to be saved, of course, but it was beautiful to know that there was something in the world worth admiring and that there were people who would suffer and fight for it—give their life for it. How fortunate these people were!

The next evening at seven o'clock she sat in her room. A lamp burned on the little table in front of the mirror. On the bed lay a little silk dress trimmed with lace. It had just come from the dressmaker, and the basket it had come in was still on the floor. On the table was an attractive necklace of corals with a bracelet to match. Smith had purchased it at great cost when he was in the East. He thought that the blood-red stones would perfectly accentuate Astrid's slim neck and emphasize her golden complexion and gray-blue eyes. He had insisted that she wear it this evening. She put down the comb and placed the red coral pin in her hair. She looked at herself in the mirror. It was as if drops of blood hung in her hair. She saw that she was beautiful, yet there were still some fine blue shadows under her eyes. She smiled painfully. Now the sacrificial lamb was to be adorned.

This evening she would meet Bjørnson. It could not be avoided. She took one of the bracelets and placed it on her naked white arm lying on the table as she stared absentmindedly in front of her. What if he would see through her—see how despicable and contemptible she was?

The door opened and August came in. "I have such a sore throat, Astrid," he said whimpering.

"Do you?" she said without turning around. She scarcely heard what he said. "Ask Annie to wrap something warm around your throat."

He went, letting the door stand ajar. Not noticing it, Astrid sat in further meditation. I wonder if he, that great strong man, could imagine such a painful, miserable person's life? Well, he was a poet and should be able to understand the most miserable human life better than others. But think of speaking with him! Oh, no, what would become of it? She would be ruined. There was no way out for her. In utter desperation she took the bracelet and fastened it on her wrist. Again the same verses came to her:

> *Red-gold ring, surrounding my life,*
> *With gold did the Mountain King secure his wife.*

Suddenly two arms locked her tightly in embrace and lifted her up from the chair. A burning breath touched her, and she felt hot kisses raining on her throat, her naked arm, and her half-exposed breast. She let out a shriek and tried to free herself, but Smith's dark eyes laughed above her while he held her closely in ardent desire. "Now I have you, you wild bird," he whispered, again covering her breast and neck with kisses. Desperation gave her strength, and she tore herself loose.

"Go, or I shall scream loudly," she whispered hoarsely.

Smith laughed. "My God, how seriously you take it. Have you forgotten that in ten days the pastor will declare you to be my lovely possession, and then," he added triumphantly, pulling her to him again, "no shout will help you."

Astrid said nothing. His last words stunned her.

"I'll go now," he continued, releasing her. "But you must hurry. The carriage will be here in a quarter of an hour." He went, but turned in the doorway. "If you don't want any visitors when you're getting dressed, you shouldn't let the door stand open while you sit in such deep thought that people can come right up to you without being noticed." He laughed, slammed the door shut, and went into the living room.

Astrid stood as if stunned. She braced her arms on the table and looked toward the door that he had just gone out of. "In ten days you will be my lovely possession, and then no shout will help you," rang in her ears whatever way she turned. She looked around confused. Where could she go?

For the first time she fully realized where she was heading.

"I am no better than the prostitute on the street," she mumbled appalled. She looked at her breast and her neck. The skin was still red after the passionate kisses. An indescribable feeling of disgust at herself came over her. She went quickly over to the washstand and rinsed her throat, arms and breast with clean water. That felt good. She had to hurry. That was the best thing to do right now. She dared not think any further. She put on the silk dress in feverish haste. The shiny sleek fabric fit snugly on her. The red jewelry looked splendid against the pale background of silk and lace. She looked at herself in the mirror. She was very beautiful. No one would see her shame. If it only would go away!

When she came into the living room, a lovely corsage of rosebuds lay on the table. "Here are some flowers for you, Astrid," said Smith. He stood by the window watching for the carriage, which just then rolled up in front. "It's best you fasten them on when you get there. The carriage is already here."

He turned. Astrid stood pulling on her light gloves. "Come now," he said, throwing her coat over her shoulders and going quickly down the stairs.

Astrid looked back. She went over and bent over the roses. It was impossible for her to fasten them on her breast which had so recently been branded. The purity of the flowers did not suit her. She kissed them and hurried down the stairs.

Mrs. Hammer's drawing room was glittering with light. Cozy fires burned in the fireplaces, and green plants and flowers decorated all the rooms. When Astrid came down from the dressing room, she was almost blinded by all the light. Velvet dresses in dark colors, soft satins, and rustling silk swished around each other. From the various groups came high and lively conversation.

Mrs. Hammer met her at the door. "Oh, there you are, Miss Holm. Welcome! How marvelously beautiful you are this evening!"

Smith came over to her. "Come, I'll introduce you to Bjørnson. I've already met him and he remembered me. But where are the flowers?" he asked, casting a scrutinizing glance over her.

"I forgot them," she said. She blushed deeply.

"Forgot them?" he repeated angrily. "I must say there is real pleasure in giving you things. Well, come now."

Bjørnson stood with his back to them, speaking to an older gentleman, but he turned around when Smith seized him by the arm. "Let me introduce my fiancée, Miss Holm, to you, Bjørnson."

Bjørnson held out his hand and said, looking at her sharply, "So this is your beloved, Smith." To Astrid he said, "I knew your fiancé in the old days and had least expected to meet this wild man again here. Now you'll have to try to make a well-behaved husband of him, Miss Holm," he added jokingly. "If I know him right, then it is not the easiest job you are taking on."

Smith laughed loudly. He put his arm around Astrid and said, "Yes, what do you think, Astrid? Do you think you'll be successful?"

Astrid stood as if on pins and needles. She had unconsciously lowered her eyes when Bjørnson fastened his sharp glance on her. Now she raised them a moment. It was barely a second, but Bjørnson caught her expression. The joke he had on his lips suddenly disappeared. He looked seriously and critically at her.

"You must have given my betrothed a terrible fright, Bjørnson," laughed Smith. "Of all things, I believe your arm is trembling, Astrid."

Bjørnson said nothing. He looked absentmindedly at Smith. "How long has your fiancée been here?" he asked suddenly.

"I don't really know. How long have you been here, Astrid? It's just a year ago that I saw her for the first time. And then, I'll have you know, she was playing the part of Laura in your *The Newlyweds.*"

Bjørnson turned quickly toward her. "Have you performed that comedy here—*The Newlyweds*?"

Astrid fumbled nervously with her handkerchief. Would this suffering never end? "An unsuccessful venture," she forced herself to say with an assumed air of nonchalance.

"Unsuccessful?" Smith butted in. "No, by God, it certainly wasn't. She was the most charming little Laura you can imagine."

Bjørnson pretended not to hear what Smith said. He nodded as if in thought. Then he said, attaching great importance to his words, "Yes, it would have to be unsuccessful here. It couldn't be otherwise."

"Now, Mr. Smith, you and your beloved don't have permission to monopolize Bjørnson the whole evening." Mrs. Hammer's happy, laughing voice was heard suddenly behind them. "Now you must let the rest of us poor creatures have a chance. Bjørnson, may I have the pleasure of introducing these ladies to you?"

Astrid moved as quickly as she could into a corner of the room. She thought she would sink through the floor in shame when he looked at her with his strange look that appeared as if he could read right through her.

Smith had gone into another room where he could smoke and have a gentlemanly chat, while all the women were so preoccupied this evening that they did not take any notice of her. Here in the corner she could sit undisturbed, and that was good, for she felt that she had no control over herself. She stared toward the corner of the room where Bjørnson stood surrounded by a circle of women. How proud he was. How different from all the others she had seen. And then that enormous head of hair! "A King's head," she thought.

"How are you this evening, Miss Holm?" a soft voice said, and two serious eyes looked sympathetically into hers. They were Helene Nielsen's.

After Astrid had become engaged she had been together with Helene several times at the Hammers'. She had felt attracted to her, and yet she had misgivings about her. There had been something sorrowful in her look whenever she looked at Astrid, and Astrid had felt it each time and tried to avoid it. Now it came over her again, that same sorrowful look. This evening, however, it was almost more than Astrid could bear. She had a burning urge to throw herself on her knees in front of Helene, lay her head on her lap, and sob. How infinitely lonesome she was.

"You don't look very happy," Helene ventured.

The muscles around Astrid's mouth began to tremble. "Yes, thank you, all is well," she finally got out. It took much effort to speak.

Helene saw that Astrid couldn't take any more. She sat down so that she shielded Astrid a little from the others and began to small-talk about trivial matters, just as if she were talking a sick child to sleep. Astrid only nodded here and there. She understood Helene's intention. That mutual understanding did her good.

Ice cream, fruit, and all kinds of refreshments were served. Champagne bubbled in the glasses, and Mr. Hammer delivered a toast to the honored guest.

He was no speaker, he stammered. He only wanted to express his happiness over seeing the world-renowned poet and popular *skald* in his home. He hoped that Bjørnson would not take home with him too cold an impression of the West's snow-covered prairies, but that he would remember the many warm hearts that were so happy to see him and overjoyed at getting a greeting from their old country through its most prominent son. He hoped that they would have a stronger effect on Bjørnson than the cold and snow and dominate his memories of his visit to America when he returned to his dear fatherland. Then he asked that all present drink a toast to Bjørnstjerne Bjørnson! It was done amid a storm of applause.

Bjørnson proposed a toast to the homeland—"That great home which we each have in ourselves." He had never known until now, he said, quietly and seriously, what power the homeland had over a person's mind. Now that he himself had the great ocean between himself and his home, he could see how finely spun were the heartstrings that bound people to their homes.

Then he went on to speak about Norway and gave a short description of the political work for freedom that was being done and expressed gratitude to the country that had dared to go in the lead and show people the way, the free American republic. "Much needs to be done yet at home," he added, "but it is still wonderful to be alive in the spring time of a new age. All the old petrified conservative concepts are being washed overboard by the swelling new demands for truth, for equality for all, and the right for all men and women to think for themselves and to create their own destinies. It is wonderful," he continued, "to live at such a time, and to add one stone to this work. I am certain that we shall succeed at home, that we may live to see the dawning of a new day in Norway. Let us drink to that," he said, visibly moved, and raised his glass.

A more serious conversation developed. Everyone gathered attentively around Bjørnson, who told about affairs at home, about the Ninth of June resolution, about the Norwegian parliament's difficult but courageous opposition to the cabinet. At times they would all sit breathless and attentive. Then they would break into laughter when he let his generous humor come to play. Astrid almost forgot herself for a while. She looked around. What power genius has, she thought. There sat all these people whose thoughts usually never stirred from dresses, society, town gossip, day to day politics, and material concerns. Now they sat completely transformed, breathing in every word he said. A gentleness came over them, a sense of community that otherwise was quite strange to them.

"Give us some music," Bjørnson said once during a pause, and he looked around the room. At Mrs. Hammer's request a young girl went to the piano and played a few pieces. She had much dexterity, but she evidently was a stranger to the music's soul.

Bjørnson sat in deep thought. It looked as if he were far away. "Does anyone know anything about Wagner here?" he asked when she stopped. Without waiting for a reply, he stood up, walked a few steps up and down, and said: "He is a colossus! What a genius! One doesn't know music if he doesn't know Wagner. One of my most memorable experiences was when I heard *Tannhäuser* for the first time in Munich," he continued while he stopped by the table and placed one hand forcefully on the tabletop. Then he depicted in stirring colors the marvelous legend about the unhappy knight who spent seven years on Mount Venus and, in the goddess's arms, forgot heaven and earth and his innocent betrothed. It was as if they could hear the music, at times sensuous and voluptuous as it enticed Tannhäuser to forgetfulness and sin, at times rising to the sublime and pure, awakening in him more noble memories and longings that finally drove him to flee from Venus and sin.

Astrid sat in a corner behind the piano, breathless and spellbound. She forgot everything and everyone around her, seeing only that mighty figure, who had never seemed to her so powerful as when Bjørnson stood there with his head lifted, visibly affected by the images he created for them. She saw before her the musical procession in Wartburg, when all ran away in fear from the unhappy Tannhäuser. She thought she could weep blood for him when he went with the pilgrims to Rome. The music interpreted his suffering on his pilgrimage. At last it changed to a shrieking scream of terror when the Pope threw out his curses on him and, lifting his staff in the air, cried to the terror-stricken crowd that this dry staff would bear fresh flowers before Tannhäuser's terrible sin could be forgiven him.

Astrid was chalk-white. Her eyes stood wide open while her hands tensely clenched the back of the chair in front of her. She thought that the thundering curse had been pointed directly at her. She, too, was bewitched—taken underground by the Mountain King. She had sold herself for the red gold. She bit her handkerchief into shreds in order not to cry aloud. For her Bjørnson became a figure of terror, taking the form of an accusing angel. Then, all at once, it was as if the air exploded with praise and resounding hallelujahs. The pilgrims now came singing their delightful hymn with its token of forgiveness for Tannhäuser, who, bewildered by his fear, had fled back and lay dying in a German forest. The miracle had happened. The withered staff bore white, fragrant almond blossoms. Tannhäuser's sin was forgiven! God's love was greater than man's.

Someone grabbed her shoulder. It was Smith. As if bitten by a snake, she leaped up, freeing herself from his hand. "What's wrong with you, Astrid? Have you gone crazy? Why do you look like this?" he continued, alarmed. "I think Tannhäuser has scared the wits out of you?"

She tried to pull herself together. "I'm not really well," she said. "Should we go?"

"Yes, indeed, we should. Bjørnson has gone, and most of the guests as well. Our carriage has come. I have been running around looking for you in all the rooms. Who would have thought that you would hide yourself here in this corner?"

She did not answer him but followed him mechanically. Stiff as a statue, she went over and said goodnight. Mrs. Hammer stood surrounded by departing guests. "Goodnight!" "Goodnight!" "What a delightful evening!" "Yes, isn't it true!" "But we can thank Bjørnson for that." The voices were buzzing around her. "How pale you are, Miss Holm. You must be very tired." How strangely far away all the voices sounded—as if they were lost in a fog.

Finally they sat in their carriage. Smith talked the whole time. He had drunk too much wine and was in high spirits. "An excellent evening," he said as he lit a cigar. "Didn't you think so?"

"Yes," said Astrid.

Smith puffed on happily. "You know, it's a pleasure to be together with such people! It's a shame that it happens so seldom. It's so damn annoying that I most likely can't get back to Minneapolis again in time to hear Bjørnson's lecture on Friday."

"Are you going away?" asked Astrid when she heard this.

"Yes. Don't you remember I told you that early tomorrow morning I must take a quick trip to Eau Claire. Most likely I won't be finished there before Friday noon, so I won't be able to get back here until after eight."

"So, then, three days," she thought. She didn't know just what she meant.

"Do you know what, Astrid? If Bjørnson is still going to be here, then I'm going to invite him to our wedding," continued Smith cheerfully. "Wouldn't that be exciting for you?"

Not on your life! Invite him along to witness her disgrace? She seized Smith by the arm. She wanted to cry, "No! No!" But she could not get a sound out.

"What's wrong with you?" asked Smith unconcerned. "Are you cold? Bundle up well." He put her fur-lined coat more firmly around her. Astrid sank back in the carriage.

"Yes, we'll do it," he said. "Listen. While I'm away you must really go up to the new house and see if the carpenters will soon be finished. There is no time to be lost if everything is to be in order by the twentieth. It will be quite magnificent up there, let me tell you. What did Mrs. Haslund say about the material for the bridal gown? It was the nicest in the whole store. Tell her she should make a long train on the dress and get it elegant. I shall certainly pay her if only she gets it beautiful. Lace and such things you must select while I'm away, but pick out the best you can find. I insist on having you spectacular as my bride."

No, she would never be able to endure this. Couldn't she just run away? She looked desperately out the window. The carriage stopped.

"Now we're here," he said. "Come. I'll do as I did the evening we were engaged and carry you up the stairs." Before she could refuse he had taken her in his arms and carried her up. When he put her down on the highest step, the door opened and old Annie's worried face peeked out.

"Oh, my God, is it you, Miss?"

"What is it, Annie? Is there something wrong?" asked Astrid frightened.

"Yes, August is not at all well, Miss. I'm really afraid for him. He has such a pain in his throat. I put him in your room, I did, Miss. I didn't dare let him lie with Harald. I thought I could take better care of him there until you came."

In fear Astrid started to run in, but Smith held her back.

"I must go in to August," she said quickly, her face turned away from Smith. He wanted to pull her to him, but she tore herself violently away.

"I have to go in right away," she whispered. She could not kiss him if her life depended on it. She ran quickly into her room and closed the door after her.

Smith stood there in the hall and watched her disappear. He stamped his foot on the floor in anger. "No, I'll be damned if I'll tolerate this any longer. What a prudish woman! The more you keep giving the best you can imagine, the worse she becomes." He ran down the steps and slammed the door after him so the whole house vibrated.

When Astrid came into her room, she saw August lying on the bed with his eyes closed, flushed with fever and tossing restlessly back and forth. It cut her to the heart to see him there. It was only a few hours since he had come to her and complained about his distress, and she had barely listened to him. Annie was much more like a mother to the boys than she was—she, who thought only about herself. She knelt down by the bed.

"Dear August, how are you?" she asked, gently stroking the yellow locks away from his burning face.

He opened his eyes and closed them again. "Good," he said weakly. Then he turned away from her and dozed off.

Astrid stood up. "You go to bed now, Annie," she said in a determined voice. "I shall watch over August."

"But you're tired, Miss, aren't you?"

"No, not the least, but you are very tired, I think. Go now and lie down."

When Astrid was alone, she quickly took off the necklace and placed it in its velvet case. She would never again open it—that much she knew. But that was also all she knew. She almost ripped off the silk dress. Ugh! How slowly it went with all these buttons. There, now it was off. She breathed a little more freely when she got all that finery off and put on her soft wool robe. She looked over at August. He lay and tossed. She arranged his bed as well as she could. Finally, he fell into a kind of restless sleep again. She walked up and down the floor while he slept. Her soft felt shoes gave no sound on the carpet. It was impossible for her to think of sleeping. She was wide awake. She had not been so wide awake for a year. What had she been thinking all this time? How miserable she had been! She heard again in her mind his words: "In ten days you will be my lovely possession, and then no shout will help you." She could still feel his burning breath. She shuddered. Suddenly she stopped walking. Could she yet be saved? Was life still so precious that she should attempt to live it right? Could she, who was so soiled and unclean, hope for forgiveness and still expect something of life? The pilgrims had come with the staff covered in white almond blossoms. Even a Tannhäuser's sin was forgiven. Could she not then also have hope? Her pale cheeks colored suddenly as she lifted her head and whispered: "I'll try one more time."

Quickly she got out a pen and paper and wrote in feverish speed:

I will never be your wife. Your behavior and words to me this evening showed me what I have to do. I have committed a great sin in ever thinking of becoming your bride when I did not love you. My lonely, unhappy position when you came to me is my only excuse. I beg you sincerely to forgive me.

Astrid Holm

Now it was written. She read it over, placed it in an envelope, and wrote the address on it.

She took the diamond ring off and put it on the table. She gathered all the things she had received from him. It all had to go away—all of it. Before that was done she would not have made a clean break. She thought about the princess in the fairy tale who had been enchanted and taken into the mountain by the troll people and she felt as if the spell was suddenly lifted. She would come out from inside the mountain, out from the shining and glittering halls where everything had seemed stark and cold and where the river of life trickled in hollow, empty drops. She would come out into the full daylight and return to life again with all its suffering and pain, but also with its delights.

"Oh, God," Astrid moaned as she got down on her knees by the bed and buried her head in her hands. "Let me suffer. Let me suffer. Only never force me to go through this again. It has been worse than death!"

August called her, and she took care of him. She was as gentle as the most loving mother and the child looked thankfully at her. She thought about her own mother—something she had not been able to do all this time. Like a little child she began to sob: "Mother, now you must help me. Now your little girl is yours again."

Toward morning she slept briefly with her face on the edge of the bed, and around her mouth was the gentle expression of a child that had been so long gone from her face. She jumped up. August was calling her: "Oh, give me a little water, Astrid." The gray daylight was coming in the window and the lamp was still burning feebly on the table. She looked around confused. There lay the letter, and she remembered what had happened. She gave August water and he became quiet again.

She sneaked quietly out of the room into the living room and looked out the window. How strangely dreary everything looked in the dull morning light. Down in the street a drowsy vehicle rumbled, and below her window a pitiful wretch sneaked by. How shabby and miserable he looked. God only knew how he had spent the night. She heard the young men quarreling down in the saloon as they cleaned up and aired out the evening's carousing and sins. Yes, her father. Her heart pounded and she felt an indescribable weakness come over her. It was as if all the old malice stretched its thousand clammy fingers after her to suck the heart's blood from her newborn resolution. She was not afraid of Smith's anger. Her lips curled. No, she still dared to face him. To live forever amid all this evil and crudeness, however, would be her death. Then she would become evil herself, worse than ever— she was sure of this—should she now backslide. Then she would be destroyed forever. It was now or never. It was a matter of life and death.

Someone came in the door. It was Holm. "Are you here already, Astrid?" he asked. "How is it with August?"

"He has a high fever. I'm afraid he is very sick. We must get a doctor as soon as possible," replied Astrid. She turned to go in to August, but when she saw her father go out the door, she stopped. He came back quickly.

"He is sleeping now. It isn't anything to get excited about, but I'll see about getting a doctor before noon."

After breakfast Annie came in to sit with August. "Miss, now you go to sleep for a while. Lie on the boys' bed. I'll see that nothing disturbs you."

"Annie," said Astrid suddenly as she got up, "will you watch August while I go out a little? And even if I'm gone for a while, I know I can depend on you." She looked affectionately into Annie's eyes.

"Yes, you can depend on me, Miss," answered Annie, taken aback and visibly moved. "But won't you sleep first?"

"I'm not at all sleepy, Annie, and there is someone I must talk to. Don't say anything to father about my leaving."

"Don't worry, Miss. I'll tell him you are sleeping."

Astrid didn't answer. She had her coat on and she covered her face with a heavy veil. Then she slipped quietly down the stairs and was soon up the street.

She would go to Bjørnson. He had to tell her what she must do to keep from destroying herself. How fortunate that Smith had chanced to name the hotel he was staying at. She walked quickly—so quickly that people turned around and stared after the well-dressed figure hurrying up the street without looking right or left as if it were a matter of life or death.

Her knees shook when she stood in the hotel lobby and asked the bell-hop if Bjørnson was in. When he came back and asked her to follow him, it was as if her breath failed her. Would she find the courage to face him? Weak and pale she followed the bellhop.

Bjørnson sat writing at a table with his back half toward the door. "Wait a moment," he said without looking up. "Just sit down."

She sat down. It was good to have a little time before she faced him. Her courage came back slowly as she sat and looked at him. There was something about the strong, self-assured person that captured her. The harmonious peace and order in the room gave her composure. A lively fire burned in the fireplace. The bed stood in an alcove. All was neat and in place for the day. It showed a man who was up early and who did not tolerate anything that disturbed his sense of order and beauty.

"There," said Bjørnson cheerfully. "I'm finished." He stood up as easily and briskly as a young boy and threw down his pen. Astrid had stood up and pushed her veil aside. Bjørnson, who was nearsighted, came over to her without at first recognizing her. His cheerful expression suddenly changed when he saw the pale trembling girl in front of him. He was immediately sympathetic and worried.

"What? Is it you? Sit down, sit down." He moved a chair near the fireplace and had her sit there.

Astrid gained courage. She unconsciously folded her hands over her knees and looked at him as would a child. She forgot everything except that she was in need and here was her savior. "I come to ask you for help," she said slowly.

The glance from those large, gray-blue eyes that met his and the helpless desperation that emanated from the trembling figure sitting in front of him deeply affected Bjørnson. His eyes became filled with tears. "What is it?" he said softly, taking her hand. "Tell, tell, my friend!"

"I was almost lost when you came," she said at last, half aloud, without moving. "I was about to sell myself. I had given up faith in all good in life. I didn't think there was anything more to fight for, and then you came. When I heard you speak, I began to believe that maybe I could still be saved. And now during the night I have put it all behind me, broken all ties. But I'll fall back if I don't get help. This is why I come to you."

"I had a suspicion there was something wrong when I saw you yesterday evening. How did you come to be engaged to that man?"

"I was harassed and despondent. Everyone avoided me. I had lost all hope and thought nothing was worth anything any more and decided that one misery was no greater than the other."

"Tell me everything," he said firmly. "Tell it all."

"Back in Norway I dreamed about becoming an actress. I believed I had a call, and I was so happy. I thought it was the highest goal in life to have a call and to be able to follow it. But then my father forbade me to pursue that call, and I had to promise my mother on her death bed that I would not become an actress without my father's permission. Then father went to America. We were to follow and I thought of America as the land of freedom where something must be waiting for me. When we children came over and I discovered that father was running a saloon, I almost thought that I would lose my mind. Father and I don't understand each other in the least, and there was not a single person I knew or could talk with. I was so ashamed of my situation here that I preferred to hide and be by myself. Then that autumn I became acquainted with some young people who acted as if there was nothing wrong with my situation. So I began to think that it was just me who was stupid and took life too seriously. They suggested that we should perform a comedy, and they talked in such a way that I finally imagined that I had a mission here, that I could show my countrymen in America something beautiful. I received new courage, and then I also got permission from father. So we performed *The Newlyweds*. But, my God, I'll never forget that night. There was such noise and coarseness. I thought the entire audience was like a many-headed monster. And father sold beer at the event. I just gave up and became miserable. I felt that I had deceived myself, that I hadn't the talent for being an actress, that I was just a saloonkeeper's wench—as one man called me—and would never be anything else. A young man, whom I slapped in the face when he thought he could handle me any way he wanted, went out and spread rumors about me. No one would say hello to me after that. Everyone looked at me as if I were a woman of the streets. One acquaintance, when she saw me coming down the street, crossed to the other side to avoid meeting me."

"Detestable! Revolting!" mumbled Bjørnson, half to himself.

"Yes, it certainly was. Aren't people cruel to one another? They stab one another until the blood flows. Then came Smith," she continued. "He wasn't afraid of me, and when I went with him, all the faces smiled gently at me, and everyone wanted to know me. I knew it was a sin, but I couldn't fight against the temptation. I couldn't bring myself to stand alone any longer. So I accepted everything from him, slid more and more into it, and, when he asked me if I would become his wife, I answered yes. At first it was terrible. Then I became accustomed to it. I was dead. But then you came and I suffered and struggled again. I had forgotten that there was something called truth and that life was more than just a terrible comedy. Last evening, when you talked about Tannhäuser, I thought you were talking about me. And last night it dawned on me that maybe I could still be saved, that there was still hope. I wrote to Smith that I would never become his wife." She said the last almost in a whisper. Memories of all she had suffered had taken her strength and chased all blood from her cheeks.

Bjørnson had sat quietly, listening. He held her hand and caressed it slowly as if to soothe her. "Yes, it is not only possible that you may be saved, but it must and shall happen," he said gently and firmly.

Astrid looked up. "Do you think so?" she sobbed. "But then you must find a mission for me." She spoke strongly: "If I am to be able to live I will have to have something that fills my life. I know that I'll have strength. I know that. I feel it. Give me something! Oh, isn't it terrible to be a woman?" she burst out.

"A woman in our day has no excuse if she gives up," said Bjørnson firmly. "God forbid! That time is past, especially here in America. Here a defeated woman does not have to take her own life or give herself in an immoral marriage that is no better than another form of prostitution. That is the history of barbaric ages and it has demanded millions of sacrifices. Now that must come to an end."

"I know. I feel you are right. But how?"

"How? Yes, I'll tell you how. By women ceasing to regard themselves as subordinates. By women demanding full individual freedom and, with the strength of this freedom, by setting themselves higher standards by acquiring a full sense of responsibility. An individual is not first a woman or a man but a human being. And as a human being one has to take one's place."

"Yes, that is just my problem. I have had this pressing demand to be a complete person, but then I've always been made to feel that I was only a weak woman."

"Yes, the curse still remains with us," replied Bjørnson seriously, almost painfully. "We have come no further yet, but"—he stood up proudly—"but, by the living God it shall be otherwise!" Light shone under those bushy eyebrows. "It is this generation's next task. But you are also to blame." Then he turned around suddenly to face Astrid. "You are still too humble. Your perspective is too narrow. For example, just now you have gone on and on, around and around, all about yourself, about your own little I. Nothing beyond that. Nothing beyond yourself to include the entire humankind of which you are only a tiny link."

"Yes, that is certainly true," replied Astrid, hurt to the quick. "I know I have been terribly self-occupied and egotistic, but I have stood so alone. Where can I find help?"

"Help? If nothing else, you can read. You need to gather knowledge. You must discover what those great spirits in the vanguard of mankind's history have to tell you. Have you read much?"

"No, very little. And, unfortunately, it has been so sporadic."

"Yes, that's what I thought. Take now, for example, Stuart Mill's works, or Herbert Spencer's. Read them seriously. You'll see that you will come to a clearer understanding. It won't be just a vague longing for a mission. Instead, you will at last find out where your own capabilities and talents lie. You will better understand, not only yourself, but all of life around you. And you will find your place in it. Keep yourself informed about everything—about what is stirring around you. Be a part of the great, pulsing human life.

Life will then no longer be a morbid concern for your own mood changes, your own misfortunes. You will learn to hold your own and conquer life inch by inch in spite of all that stands in your way."

There was such an assured strength in him, such powerful defiance, that Astrid felt as if her blood flowed more forcefully. She began to realize that there were greater horizons than those she had been aware of. Her expression said: "Continue. Give me more. It is food and drink for my soul to listen to you talk." But she said nothing.

Bjørnson continued. "It's this lack of a broad vision, a common sin in human beings, that is our curse. It makes us narrow and egotistical and ties up our hearts so that they do not open freely and fully to each other as in one large brotherhood. And Christianity, as it is proclaimed at home, does its part to obstruct us. It says, 'Think about yourself. See to it that you are saved, that you rescue your little soul. Then the others don't matter.' And so they allow life to go its crooked way while they sing 'How blessed is the little flock.' That thousands of lives are wasted doesn't bother them. All they care about is to have people in their last moment to swear upon Pontoppidan's explanation of Luther's catechism. And this leads to prostitution, beastly marriages, war, falsehoods, and lies in all situations in life. Does a single one of these Christian servants lift his voice against all this? No! It is beyond their concern. Instead of being guardians of morality and apostles of human love in our country, they have become appointed servants in the state church, which every Sunday consigns those to hell who do not swear by the Trinity or on God's need for blood for redemption."

He paced quickly up and down the floor. He was so taken up by these thoughts that came rolling over him that she thought he had forgotten her. Suddenly he stopped in front of Astrid. "Why don't you become a minister?"

"I?" she replied, astonished.

"Yes, a minister. I mean, naturally, not like those I just spoke about, but a minister like those found here in America—gentle, loving men and women who proclaim peace on earth, who do not believe that people are little devils created for hell's fire. Instead, they have a glowing faith in the victory of goodness in the world and in perpetual progress. They don't stress faith, but life—the way ministers of a liberal persuasion do."

When Astrid didn't reply, he continued, "I believe that would be something for you to consider. You have what it requires—a strong capacity for enthusiasm. You will never become an actress. You need life itself—not its reflection. You can love art, but you can't be an artist yourself."

"I know you are right there. I have felt it myself," she replied thoughtfully.

"Yes, think about it. Or else, be something that is equally substantial and good. I just came from the East. There I met so many noble women who boldly stood up beside the men and proclaimed their views just as skillfully and with just as convincing arguments, and I am more assured in my mind than ever that women's capabilities are equal to men's. It is only the terribly unjust circumstances of society that have intimidated women and held them down. Therefore, you women who now begin to see clearly have a double responsibility: first, to save your own lives, and afterwards by your example to save those of the thousands of women who follow you. You have no excuse if you allow intimidation and oppressive circumstances to place themselves as obstacles in your way. You must and you shall overcome them. For," he continued gravely, "every woman who works faithfully with this vision before her eyes to develop her own individuality and to sacrifice it for her suffering sisters adds a little stone to the building which one day, so help me God, shall arise proudly toward heaven, a community of brothers and sisters where injustice and oppression are gone and the stronger individual supports and helps the weaker and does not, as now, oppress them."

Astrid looked up at him. Her eyes shone and her lips trembled. "I shall try," she whispered. When she held out her hand to him to leave, she said only "Thank you," but her eyes said much more.

Bjørnson took her hand in both of his. "Now don't disappoint me," he said cheerfully, and the moist eyes under the heavy eyebrows looked so gently at her that Astrid's heart overflowed. "You made a beginning last night by breaking off a disgusting relationship," he said in a low voice. "That was the thing to do. Now go further and do not stop until you have arrived."

Astrid walked home as if in a dream. She had to hurry. August needed her. Before her she still saw Bjørnson's strong figure, and his words rang in her ears like a work song. "You must take charge of your life. You have no excuse," he had said. No, after this she had no excuse if she did not do it. But how? She had yet to find out. She knew only one thing—that she would do it.

What a joy it was to want to do something again, to believe in something once more. God, was it actually she, Astrid, who just yesterday was so miserable? She went home with her heart bursting as if a thousand spring flowers had blossomed in her. So at least they were not dead. They had only stagnated under their winter cloak. The gentle love had moistened them and melted the crust of ice.

When she arrived home she took off her coat in the living room. She did not want to go in to August with it on. She heard footsteps in the hallway, and Holm came in with a stranger whom she understood to be the doctor. Her father seemed pale and worried. He looked surprised at Astrid and said, "Have you been out during this time? Annie told me that you were sleeping." Without waiting for an answer, he turned toward the doctor. "This is my daughter, Dr. Tibbitts. Unfortunately, the doctor has some sad news for us, Astrid. August has caught diphtheria."

Astrid grew pale. She looked inquiringly at the doctor, who said, "I hope it won't be too bad. It is still impossible to know how it will turn out. I have given your father the necessary instructions. I'll come up again this afternoon." He took farewell and left. Holm followed him out.

Astrid hurried in to August. Annie stood and took care of him with a troubled face. He was noticeably worse. Astrid kneeled beside him. "Now I'll stay with you, August, and never leave you until you are well."

She kept her word. Night and day she sat by his bed and slept only a few moments when he was more quiet than usual. She never felt tired. Two days later Harald also came down with the disease. She went from one bed to the other during the long nights and tried to ease their pain as much as she could. Her eyes became large and sunken from the night watch and her cheeks grew pale. Nevertheless, in spite of the pain she felt for her suffering brother, she had not for a long time been as happy as she now was. She felt that she had to atone for her neglect of her brothers. Harald was not so severely affected by the illness, and he soon came around, but August became worse. Astrid was always with him while Annie took care of Harald. Holm didn't dare to appear upstairs. He walked back and forth in the saloon, which now had no guests, as one outlawed from the rest of the house. He was afraid of contagion and, though worried about the boys, he did not dare look at their suffering—coward that he was. So he fled from it all as well as he could.

The tenth day after August had become ill Astrid sat by his bed and watched her brother fight his last battle. The doctor had said there was nothing more to be done. The fever seemed to have fled from August as he lay there on his pillow, so pale and white, his eyes closed. Astrid just sat and stared at him. This was to have been her wedding day! The dense snow fell quietly outside. Soon August would lie under that white blanket. She sat with folded hands as large tears ran heavily down her cheeks. And still there was only gratitude in her heart. It was a holy day for her soul. She had cast all the old evil, wickedness, and self-love away at her brother's bedside, and she vowed to herself in this hour to find a new life—not the joyous, wonderful life of success she had dreamed of when she was seventeen years old, but a life dedicated to others in serious work and self-sacrifice.

Now it was no longer a burden to be a woman. Now it was twice as wonderful because she was in the company of the suffering and downtrodden, and this made her task greater and nobler.

Her brother looked up. His eyes were already dimmed. A convulsion went through his limbs, a weak rattle was heard, and all was over. Sobbing, Astrid closed his eyes. She knew she should go out, but she could not leave him. She continued to sit and look at him. The expression of pain had left him. He lay there so peacefully, half smiling as if in a happy dream. His yellow locks lay around his face like a shining halo. How painful it was to see a young, blossoming life broken before it had actually begun. Why? Suddenly she was seized by her realization of life's unsolved mysteries. The air around her was strangely mysterious. She felt as invaded by spirits, each sound coming back to her with a strange, vibrating, solemn resonance. Before death's nameless and indescribable mystery all human hearts stand quietly, in holy terror.

❧ 18 ❧

When Smith returned from Eau Claire and came up to his rooms, he found a letter and a large package lying on the table. He picked up the letter, wondering who it was from. Usually his mail was sent to his office. Recognizing Astrid's handwriting, he tore it open and read: "I will never be your wife."

"What the devil is this?" "I have committed a great sin in ever thinking of becoming your bride when I did not love you." "I believe the devil rides her." He threw the letter in the far corner of the room and began pacing up and down the floor. At last he went over to the table where the package lay, tore it open furiously, and, sure enough, it was what he thought. There was the jewelry case he knew so well, with the coral beads, the diamond ring, the gold bracelets, and everything else. He was about to throw it angrily on the floor, but he stopped suddenly. This was a serious matter. Has she gone crazy? Or what the hell is going on? He let the jewelry case lie on the table, took his hat, and ran down the stairs and out on the street.

He would go to see her and talk a little sense into her. "Anyway, there's been something damned high-strung about her lately, so disgustingly straight-laced. If it continues, there won't be much pleasure in her. But she would have to give that up as soon as they were married. Has the woman lost her mind? How could she cast him off in this way! It can't be very comfortable for her down there. By God, I thought she was as tormented as hell itself, for she is proud as can be." Again he saw before him Astrid's brilliant eyes and red, luxuriant lips—just as he had seen them that last evening when she had said he should go or she would scream. "Proud as the devil. But what a breast and what a throat!" He virtually drooled. "If I just had her here now I would clasp her to me and no shrieks would help her." He stamped his feet angrily on the street. "This was certainly a pleasant homecoming one week before the wedding!" He came to the saloon. He was about to run up the stairs when he saw a green placard nailed to the wall by the entrance. The light fell right on it. "Diphtheria," he read.

He tumbled backwards as if struck by a blow. What was this? He was suddenly very sober. "Diphtheria! So she's got that now. I'll be damned if I'll go up there." No, life was too precious for that. He had only this one life to live. So there would be an end to it all, he thought angrily, walking down the street without thinking where he was going. Now she will no doubt kick the bucket. It never dawned on him that anyone other than Astrid had gotten diphtheria. He did not remember the boys. "I can give her up for lost, the way things are going now."

He actually felt much more unhappy than he would admit to himself, for he had been more seriously in love than ever before. She had, after all, brought out the best in his nature. He loved not only her beauty but also her pride. At the same time he longed to get that pride in his clutches so he could break it to pieces bit by bit in his beast-of-prey claws. But now that was over. A feeling that she was too pure and proud for him overwhelmed him.

He looked around. Where had he walked? He was on the dark streets in one of the worst districts of Minneapolis. It was down by the river. He recognized where he was. He had been there only twice after he had become engaged. His blood burned like fire. He had to do something. He looked at his watch by a single light that stood flickering in the snow. It was almost nine. Should he go to hear Bjørnson? Bah! Anyway it was too late. Without thinking, he turned the corner past a few buildings and entered a tumbling-down wood-frame house. He went up the dark steep stairs, knocked at the door, and went straight in.

It was a large room, but terribly messy. A lamp stood smoking on the table together with an artificial flower, dirty gloves, and make-up jars. On one chair was thrown a bright red skirt, on another a black flannel bodice. In the middle of the floor was a worn-out slipper.

On the bed lay a young girl, half asleep. Her long golden hair hung loosely around her. She wore a light gold Mother Hubbard without a belt around the waist and open at the breast. When he came in, she raised herself up on her elbows with a half-drowsy, half-annoyed expression in her large shiny eyes. When she saw who it was, her expression quickly changed.

She let out a shout of joy, jumped out of bed, and threw her arms around his neck.

"Is it you? Oh, is it you? I never thought you would come back again!" She dragged him and got him over in a deep armchair with tattered upholstery that stood by the table. Then she crawled up on his lap and lay on his chest as cuddly and ingratiatingly as a pussy cat.

"Where have you been so long?" She pinched him on the ear until it became quite red. "Why haven't you been to see me? Have you loved someone else? You don't have permission, you see, because I don't care more about the others than *that*," she said, snapping her fingers. "But you . . ." She fell all over him, almost smothering him with caresses.

She twisted her long golden hair around him, while she gave him her red mouth for a kiss and whispered, "I love you. You are so big and handsome. Now you must not love anyone but me."

She cuddled up to him seductively, exuding only love and sensuality. He let himself be caressed. This was something better than those prudish women. He had been a big fool, he thought, and he hugged her in his arms.

"Now I shall love only you," he said. But all the while he was thinking of Astrid. Her proud figure had never been as alluring to him as just then. In a rage he pressed the little one lying on his chest to him. "Now you shall be with me. We shall travel together. Come, let's go to Chicago."

She clapped her hands in ecstasy.

"We shall be there a long time," he continued, "and you shall be dressed like the finest ladies, and we shall go to the theater together and to the finest hotels and drink champagne, and we'll call ourselves Mr. & Mrs. Smith."

She was speechless for joy. She bit him on the cheek and then kissed it again and again.

"And at home I have a gold bracelet for you and coral beads that you can hang around your white neck." He covered it with kisses but at the same time thought of the neck he had last kissed. "We'll leave tomorrow evening. Not a day later. Otherwise just forget it," he said brutally, shoving her aside. He got up and paced the floor. He kicked the slipper so it flew against the wall.

He stopped when he saw her standing with open mouth staring at him—terrified. He broke into a boisterous laughter. "Oh, I'm a big fool," he said, pulling her down with him on the bed.

Later, when Smith was walking quickly toward his home between twelve and one, he bumped into a man who came around the corner in just as much of a hurry. "Oh, excuse me," said Smith.

"Oh, never mind," said the other, and Smith recognized him as Meyer. He had not seen him for a long time. Meyer had played himself out in the fine society circles. The men of the house had begun to understand that he was a gossipy freeloader who wanted to live on their wives' good hearts and get ahead by their husbands' letters of recommendation. So they had warned their wives of him. The ladies had become more and more reserved and when Meyer did not even then seem to understand but kept coming on his visits as a familiar friend of the family, they managed never to be at home. If he tried to start a conversation when he met them on the street, their coldness was so obvious that at last he had to give it up. He saw that he would again have to rely on his old simple acquaintances and tried to pick up things there where he had left them as though nothing had happened. But it did not go there either. They would have nothing to do with him. He could no longer impress them.

So for some time he had been going around like an outcast, seeking out those saloonkeepers who still considered him to be the impressive gentleman.

When Smith saw Meyer, all the hidden anger that he had been holding back broke loose in him again. That he should meet him just now! He could not even bear to look at him. He raised his already clenched fist to give him a cuff on the ear, but when he saw how miserable and threadbare Meyer looked, he let it fall. Meyer moved away a little frightened, but he tried to make the best of the meeting.

"Good evening, good evening, Mr. Smith. It is an unexpected pleasure to see you at this time," he said smiling, using his most elegant tone.

"Think so?" muttered Smith between his teeth. "Well, I think there is cursed little joy in meeting you," he said a little angrily. "Get out of the way, or . . ."

"Good heavens, the lawyer is evidently not in good humor this evening," Meyer hurried to say, moving quickly out of the way. "Farewell."

Smith walked on. He was furious.

The next day he left on the evening train for Chicago—alone.

{ 19 }

Several days had passed since August's funeral. His body had been driven quietly out to the cemetery, and now he was sleeping peacefully in his cold bed.

All began to settle back into the old ruts. Harald was well again, but he was still too weak to go back to school. The quarantine sign had been removed and the house washed and fumigated as protection against the danger of further contagion. The saloon door was again opening and closing, and Holm began to breathe more easily again. Apparently he mourned August's departure and missed his pet more than he realized, but "we must all bend ourselves under the decrees of God," and it was, therefore, fortunate that the others were spared.

Astrid stood by the window in the living room, preoccupied, looking out on the street. It was late in the day. All afternoon she had been thinking about talking with her father, but she had not yet done so. She had made her decision. She was going away, and she knew where she would go. Two mild, intelligent eyes had greeted her in Minneapolis, and they had always looked at her so sadly when she was on her way down. She would go to those two eyes, and she would say: "I have broken with all. Now I have no one in the world to go to. Help me. Advise me." She had wanted to leave for a long time, but now, thank God, she could do it without bitterness. Even toward her father she now felt only sorrow. How wonderful it was that her old feeling of hatred was gone. Her hatred had almost bothered her the most.

The door was opened. Holm came in. Obviously, he had something on his mind. He walked back and forth a few times, then turned to Astrid: "Haven't you told Smith yet that our place is now free of infection? It seems to me—to speak candidly—strange that he hasn't come up—especially now when we have all this sorrow," he continued pathetically.

Astrid turned quietly and looked her father openly in the eyes. "Smith will never come here again," she answered slowly and emphatically.

Holm stopped still as if petrified. He grabbed the edge of the table for support. "What are you saying?" he asked huskily. "Has Smith . . ." He could say no more.

"I have concluded our relationship," she said loudly and clearly. "I have told him that I never loved him and that I would never, for all the world, be his wife."

Holm turned lemon-yellow in his face. One misfortune after the other was intruding on him. He forgot everything. He forgot that he was afraid of his daughter. He remembered only that he was a miserable, ruined man. This one certain hope had nevertheless burned for him like a star in the midst of the misery that had overwhelmed him. He did not know what he was doing. He ran up to her with raised arms as if he would strike her. Then he let them drop. "Away!" he hissed weakly. "Away!" His rage was too great for him. He could say no more.

"I shall leave," Astrid answered. She became pale. Her voice trembled. This was her father. "I'll go today, but . . ." She straightened herself proudly. "But before I go, I want to tell you the truth, father. You killed mother, and now you are furious because I won't let you kill me, too."

"What is it you are saying?" he stammered, shocked. "Did I kill your mother?"

"Yes, what else did you do?" Astrid began passionately. Her mother's suffering face stood before her as large as life. She herself had always kept silent. One day her daughter would speak for her. "Mother was like a delicate flower, father. You trampled on her with your clumsy feet until she died from it. It was grief that mother died from—grief that was never given words."

When her father did not reply but just stared at her with a blank expression of resentment and horror, she continued: "Did you never think what you could do to make her happy? What could provide nourishment for her soul? Didn't you let her hunger and thirst herself to death? You were the man in the house and she was supposed to be content because you had taken a lowly actress for a wife. After all, what more could she expect? But this you should know," she continued vehemently. "All the good that I have received in life has come through her, and all the evil life has brought me has come from you. And while I respect her memory as that of my good angel, so . . . yes, so . . ." She lowered her voice. "There are times when I have been tempted to look upon you as my evil . . ."

Holm stared at her in actual terror. Drops of sweat formed beads on his forehead.

"Everything you have done to me, father, I can forgive you, but what you have done to mother I don't think I can ever forgive you." Then she broke into tears.

"You are mistaken, Astrid," he tried to say. "Your mother has never . . ."

Astrid pulled herself together. She would not be overpowered. This one time she would speak out. "On her deathbed mother allowed me to perceive, however dimly, what she had suffered in those twenty long years of marriage, and I looked into a life so joyless, so filled with incomprehensible pain and suffering, that it was as if my own youth disappeared because of what I saw. From that time on I was no longer your daughter. I was not by nature like my mother. I was shocked while she yielded to her husband in humiliating self-denial. I was stubborn while she suffered quietly. That's why, father . . ." and she threw her head back proudly, "it won't work when you try to handle me as you did mother. I shall fight for my life, and I'm just as strong as you are. I have vacillated, but now that is past. And so I shall leave. It will be best for us two not to be together. Perhaps we can then think a little more generously of each other. But," she continued more softly, "be careful with Harald. He is the only one you have left now. He is not a bad boy. Try, for mother's sake at least, to see to it that he is not ruined."

Holm did not answer. He could not. His wife's apparition rose threateningly before him in his accusing daughter's shape. He trembled in his cowardice at this powerful accusation. He collapsed on a chair, feeling like an abandoned and unhappy old man.

Astrid looked at him with a frown. What agony to see her father sit there so lonely and unhappy and yet be unable to feel as a daughter should, unable to comfort him and help him. It was impossible for her. She could not even give him a voluntary caress if her life depended on it. But she could try to forgive him and think of him without bitterness.

She went into her room, selected a few articles of clothing, and packed them in a small valise. Then she put on her traveling clothes and took the valise in hand. In the doorway she cast a long serious look around her. Then she went from the room that had been witness to so much suffering and misery. She looked over at the bed where her little dead brother had so recently lain. "Good-bye, August," she whispered. "Now I am going out into life to be true to what I vowed when I sat by your deathbed."

Annie was in the kitchen, blowing into the stove, with a tear-stained face. Astrid took the old one in her arms and hugged her. She, who had stayed with them loyally, had loved her mother and had dedicated her last strength to her mother's children.

"Annie, now I am leaving you," Astrid whispered.

"Lord God," said the old lady, tears running down her wrinkled cheeks. "What shall I do when you leave, Miss?" She showed no surprise. Apparently she found it natural that the young lady could no longer continue there.

"You must take care of Harald. You are a better mother for him than I, and then you must also watch over father, poor thing. It isn't so easy for him either. But I can't stay here longer. I must see about amounting to something good in the world, and then you shall join me, Annie, and you shall stay with me the rest of your life."

"But where are you going, Miss? And with so few clothes?" She looked alarmed at the little valise.

"I'll be back, Annie," said Astrid calmly, "and you'll get to know how I'm getting along. But I must go in to Harald."

Harald had lain down on the bed and now slept soundly. He was not aware that his sister knelt by his bedside, kissed him on the cheek, and sobbed. Now she was leaving him. Was that right? And yet she could not do anything else. They would both be defeated if she stayed here. If she amounted to anything good, then she could probably help him later. He was still sleeping when his sister walked quietly out of the room.

"Greet Harald and say I'll return to see how he is. Tell him to be a good boy." Once more she hugged the old woman and patted her on the cheek. "Good-bye, my friend, and thank you for everything." She ran down the stairs without looking back.

Annie stood at the top of the stairs, looking down long after the slight figure had disappeared. She wiped her eyes with her apron. "Lord Jesus, for a long time this is what I thought would happen. Haven't I heard her so many nights lying there and sobbing like a child? No, no," she said, shaking her head, "that was no husband for my young Miss."

Darkness descended on the living room, and Holm was still sitting in the same chair. He heard his daughter run down the stairs, and he understood that she went in earnest. He was afraid to get up. Two pairs of eyes stared at him through the darkness. One was gentle, but it looked full of sorrow and pain. It said, "You have killed me. You never understood me. My soul longed for beauty and insight, and you . . . you thought only of yourself, letting me starve to death." The other pair was proud and bright. It said, "Now you want to kill me as you have killed mother, but look . . . it won't work. I'm no longer your daughter." And then came the worst of all: "All the evil in me I have from you. Sometimes I have believed you were my evil angel." The last was barely whispered. It was, of course, all too horrible—a daughter who could say such things to her father. But he must have become weak from the misfortunes of the past days, for he did not try to rise. He screamed: "It's a lie—all of it. It's a damned lie." And now she was gone, and August lay under the snow.

Astrid walked hurriedly up the street, never looking back. Now it was done, and she hastened forward. She knew Helene Nielsen's address. Helene had once given Astrid her calling card and asked Astrid to visit her. When she reached Nicollet Avenue, two elegantly dressed ladies came directly toward her. She knew them. It was Mrs. Rask and one of her friends. She tried to get by without them seeing her, but no such luck. The light from the brightly lit store fell right on Astrid.

"Ah, Miss Holm! How long it has been since I last saw you. It really makes me happy to see you again." They came toward her with outstretched hands and friendly smiles. "Maybe you already are Mrs. Smith? Wasn't it just now you were going to have the wedding?"

"No, Mrs. Rask, I am not Mrs. Smith, and I never will be," answered Astrid coldly.

"Why?" exclaimed Mrs. Rask thunderstruck. Her warm handshake suddenly grew limp. "I don't understand . . ."

"Mr. Smith and I have agreed that it was best for us to sever our relations." She thought she could repair a little of her injustice toward him by not telling the whole truth.

"Oh, so that's the way it is." The smile stiffened and became half-hearted, and her hand fell down weakly. Her eyes had an ice-cold look. "Come, Hanna. I'm freezing. It's really cold." Then with a proud nod of her head to Astrid and an "Adieu, Miss Holm," she and Hanna continued down the street.

"He finally came to his senses, poor fellow," Mrs. Rask said to her friend. "There must have been some truth in that bad reputation she had. There is seldom smoke without fire."

"And now she says they have agreed," said the other, laughing loudly.

"Well, yes! I heard that, too. No, it's all really too comical. As if anyone would be so stupid as to believe that! Poor child."

Astrid stood there a moment looking after them. They were the ones who had been so friendly and smiling as long as she was insincere and detestable. Now that she was trying to be genuine, the smile stiffened and the warm handshake went limp. "How much evil and ugliness there is in the world," she thought with a painful smile. She was invaded by a sense of the suffering and struggle that would befall everyone who chose to go against the stream and fight to protect her better self. The realization crept over her like an ice-cold hand and placed itself around the warm, new life that was sprouting in her with thousands of budding flowers. "Ugh," she said involuntarily. "Ugh! I won't think about it any more. It is detestable!" She walked on quickly as if to shake the ugly thought from her mind.

Helene Nielsen was in her consulting room, which also served as her living room. She had just come home from a couple of sick calls. Her practice was not large since, as a woman doctor, she was usually regarded by her countrymen as a charlatan. Her main practice was among the poor who could pay nothing.

She had just placed a little kettle of water on the coal stove when she heard light, quick steps coming up the stairs. There was a knock at the door. She went over to open it. There stood Astrid. Surprised, Helene opened the door wide. "Astrid Holm!" She saw the valise Astrid held in her hand. She looked at her large eyes that told a long history of hardship.

Astrid leaned against the door frame. "May I come in?" she half whispered.

"Come, come." Helene pulled her in and closed the door. "What is it? What happened? I can see that something has happened." She looked anxiously into Astrid's eyes.

"What has happened," Astrid answered quietly, "is that I have left everything behind me and have now come to you to ask you to help me. I have no one in the world to go to but you."

Tears welled up in Helene's eyes. "You have severed all ties?" There was deep joy in her voice. "And you come to me? Then I haven't lived in vain when the unfortunate and forlorn turn to me. This is the happiest moment of my life. It makes up for many, many disappointments. So you found the courage to break off with that man," she continued, taking Astrid's hat and coat and moving an easy chair near the stove for Astrid to sit in. "Oh, God, how happy that makes me!" She sat down beside Astrid, warming Astrid's cold hands in hers. "You have no idea how I have been drawn to you ever since the first time I saw you. Oh, how it cut my heart when I saw you being destroyed. Yes, you would have been destroyed if you hadn't broken it off. But now all will be well."

Astrid's head fell back on the chair. Her eyes were closed. After all the suffering, all those sleepless nights, all the sorrow, and all the tension—to feel a warm, soft hand take hers and see two mild eyes look lovingly and sympathetically into hers was all too wonderful, almost too much.

Helene saw how pale she was. "Now you are not to talk at all. I don't want to hear any more this evening. Just rest, and after you have had a little warm tea you may go to bed. I'm a doctor, you know," she added smilingly, "and you must obey doctor's orders."

Astrid did not answer. She just opened her eyes and looked at Helene with an expression of indescribable gratitude. Then she closed them again. Helene puttered around quietly. She forced her to drink the warm tea, led her into the little bedroom beyond the office, and helped her to bed.

Several hours later when Helene came in with the lamp to go to bed, the light fell right on Astrid's face. Helene held up the lamp and looked at her a long time. Astrid's nightgown had slid up and her strong, plump arm lay thrown over her head. Her hands were buried in her black curls. She had not put up her hair for the night, and it lay around her in a disheveled mass, forming a strange frame around the pale, young face. Her long eyelashes lay on her cheeks, giving her a child-like appearance, but her lips would sometimes twitch as if in pain. Her whole body spoke of a deathlike weariness and of her experience with pain. Helene was deeply touched. "Poor child," she whispered. "She has suffered much, but she is young and strong, and she'll recover." Astrid did not move when Helene lay down beside her.

When Astrid awoke the next morning, she was alone. At first she looked around bewildered. Then it all came back to her. Her head sank down calmly on the pillow again. Thank God! She was here! She had been rescued! She saw once more Helene's mild face and heard the deep ring in her voice when she said, "The unhappy and forlorn turn to me. This is the happiest moment in my life." At that moment she had looked into the heart of a woman so pure and noble and so dedicated to self-sacrifice that it reconciled her to all the ugliness that she had been confronted with. Now she would remember only this.

Helene opened the door. Astrid stretched out her arms to her. "Are you awake?" She closed the door after her and came over to Astrid. "How soundly you have slept." She took a chair and sat beside the bed, lovingly brushing the hair from Astrid's cheeks.

"I have slept wonderfully. Now I'm strong again, and you must let me tell you everything."

Helene nodded. She sat quietly and held Astrid's hand while Astrid, in a subdued voice, told about her agonies and about how at last in desperation she had thrown herself into the arms of the man who was supposed to have become her spouse. She told about the evening when Smith had taken her by surprise in her room and forced himself on her in a passionate embrace. She blushed to think and speak about it, but she wanted Helene to hear it all. "That was the evening of the party at Mrs. Hammer's."

"I saw you were fighting something that evening," interrupted Helene. "My heart ached because I could do nothing to help you, but I was unable to say anything."

Astrid squeezed Helene's hand and continued: "Then as Bjørnson talked about Tannhäuser, I thought I would lose my mind. I remember I bit my handkerchief into shreds in order not to cry out aloud. And that night I put an end to it." Then she told of her meeting with Bjørnson and how after talking with him she had made a decision to find a mission in life to which she could dedicate herself. She especially wanted to remove everything that stood in the way of reaching her goal. Then she went on to relate how the decision had been reinforced at her brother's deathbed.

"I had to leave home, of course. If I'd stayed there in those same sur-roundings, I would not have dared to trust myself. And I knew of no one in the world to turn to but you. Will you help me and advise me? I shall try anything you think is right. I shall help you out and do what work I am ca-pable of to begin with so that someday I can reach my goal. Will you help me?" Child-like, she looked up pleadingly at Helene, who felt her heart overflow with compassion and love for this anguished, persecuted creature who had sought refuge with her.

"Be assured I shall do all I can for you, and if I can help you reach your destination, it will be my deepest joy." She looked seriously into Astrid's eyes.

Astrid felt that she could depend on that look for life. Helene sat quietly, and Astrid lay there and looked at her. She could see that she was thinking of something.

Finally, Helene said: "At first you must remain here with me. I don't have such a large practice, but it is still large enough so that we two won't go hun-gry if we are modest. You may assist me." She motioned to Astrid, who was trying to interrupt her, not to speak. "You can keep the rooms clean, wash my medical instruments, and make breakfast and supper for us. We'll eat out together at noon. And you will accompany me on my house calls to my poor patients. The time that is left you will need to study English and read. Later maybe we can find something better for you. Are you satisfied with this suggestion?"

Astrid took Helene's hands in hers. "Thank you," she whispered. "How good you are. If only I can repay you for it some day." Her eyes sparkled as she pulled Helene down and kissed her sincerely.

Thus did these two women, who had both left their places in society, make a pact for life.

{ 20 }

O ne evening half a year later Meyer was sitting in a little back room in Lundberg's beer parlor. He had taken up one of the Swedish newspapers lying on the table and was reading in it. Suddenly he became fiery red in his face and emitted a surprised outburst. He read: "Thursday evening at eight o'clock Miss Astrid Holm will lecture on the temperance issue at Carlson's Hall, Washington Avenue."

He let the newspaper fall. Was it she? It could be no one else. He had heard that Smith had broken off the engagement and that she had run away from home and joined forces with another half-demented woman. He had occasionally met her on the street but she had always looked at him coldly as if he were a stranger. What made him most furious was that it was impossible for him to get her to notice him. There was not the least sign of recognition, so superior was her glance, with no blush showing on her cheeks. One thing was clear: he no longer existed for her. In some incredible fashion she had managed to get over it all. He still thought that he had made a deep enough impression to be remembered. But she had forgotten— even though her slap still burned his cheeks. He detested Smith almost as sincerely as he hated her because, by getting engaged to her, he had taken all the sting out of his own revenge. What an insult it had been to see her received in the very circles that gradually had rejected him.

He had gloated when he heard that the engagement was broken off. He knew those people well enough to know that she would be a victim of gossip and that her reputation would be torn apart. Therefore, it was all the more irritating to see her so unmoved and poised and without a trace of recognition whenever they met.

He sat a long time thinking and holding the newspaper in his hand. His

most unattractive and despicable traits had been brought to life by the notice. So that's the way it was. She was stronger than ever. She dared to defy
her station as a saloonkeeper's daughter to such a degree that she would
stand up publicly as a temperance speaker.

He clenched his hands on the table. The veins in his forehead were blue
and swollen, his bloated face was deep red, and his eyes were livid. He had
evidently given up his elegant appearance along with his distinguished acquaintances. His clothes were shabby, his shirt was filthy, tobacco juice had
stained the corners of his mouth, and he looked flabby. Here in the saloon,
however, he was still the superior and intelligent gentleman who stooped to
sit in such lowly and uncultured surroundings.

He was evidently pondering a plan. Suddenly he broke out in a loud
laugh. The others looked at him to see what was up.

"Yes, now it looks bad for your business, Lundberg. You might just as well
close down right away," he shouted to the proprietor, who stood behind the
bar in the saloon.

"What's going on?" grunted a deep bass voice. A tall heavyset man with
a white apron over his fat stomach lumbered across the floor and stationed
himself in the open door.

"Well, the women have begun to preach temperance here, too, and it's
bound to take effect sometime. You know these women are dangerous when
they get going. You may fill my glass, Lundberg," he continued conde-
scendingly, holding out his glass to him.

"These damned women! They are always putting their noses into everything," cursed the proprietor while he dutifully went in and filled the glass
with the foaming fluid.

"Can you guess who it is?" Meyer shouted out to him. "It's the daughter
of Holm, you know, the saloonkeeper."

Lundberg stood with his mouth wide open. "Yes, you bet I know him,
the cocky rascal. He takes on airs and thinks he's better than the rest of us
saloonkeepers. Just as if we're not all in the same business. And now his
daughter is preaching *temperance*," he continued contemptuously, spitting a
long streak of tobacco juice across the floor.

"Yes, isn't that the way of the world?" Meyer remarked casually. With a
fine nonchalance he walked into the saloon. "Her father makes his living
selling beer and whisky, and his daughter preaches temperance."

"I'll damned well teach her to preach," screamed Lundberg, pounding the bar so the glasses clattered. "Come with me to the temperance meeting, boys. When and where is it, Meyer?"

"Thursday evening at eight in Carlson's Hall," answered Meyer, smiling maliciously. He could see that his plan would succeed.

"All right, then. We'll go up there, and we'll teach her to preach temperance so she loses her appetite for it. There'll be drinks on the house afterward for all who join me! How about it, boys?"

"Yes, yes, that'll be fun," came from all corners.

"Okay, then. Be on time and bring many others with you. Tell them there will be a good time and treats."

In the commotion and turmoil that followed these words Meyer sneaked away. There were two or three other saloons he wanted to patronize this evening and bring the same welcome news.

⌁

IT HAD INDEED BEEN ASTRID WHO HAD ADVERTISED a temperance lecture. During the past seven months she had worked intensely. Helene obtained books for her from the Athenaeum where she was a member. At five every morning Astrid would get up to read in them for a few hours before breakfast.

In those morning hours there was always such a pleasant quietness around her. Every thought came back so clearly and lodged in her mind as her own possession, and it was wonderful to feel her vision expand and her mind develop from day to day. She especially liked to study history. Nothing satisfied her so much as to follow the great intellectual movements as they spread through various countries. At the same time she was horrified to read of all the cruelty and terrible suffering that narrow-minded fanaticism and brutality and ignorance had brought to humanity. But there was also progress, and each generation was coming a little closer to the truth than the one before. Should one generation go under because of their sins and the sins of their parents, then some new movement would crest, full of spirit and life, to bring about suffering humanity's deliverance. Astrid enthusiastically followed the lives of great men and women who had been the means of improving the world.

Thus it was that the person of Jesus of Nazareth in all his human grandeur and beauty came to symbolize the new life for humanity, and his story filled her with intense enthusiasm. Never before had she been able to grasp his significance. He had always been so distant, so far removed. He was said to be God, and yet he was a human. She had previously paid no attention to him. But now in reading history independently she came to look at him as a human being, a persecuted and mocked human being, who dared to speak the truth and confront the powerful and mighty. With his fearless championship of truth and his love for the depressed and despised he regenerated the world and gave it a mission so large that even the best men and women were still stumbling over it. Yes, she loved him and fervently prayed to the spirit that is in all things for a tiny drop of his pure enthusiasm and for the courage to speak the truth. More and more frequently the idea came to her that she should become a minister like the one Bjørnson had spoken of. She would be a minister who took as her mission the defense of the oppressed and who taught her fellow beings that the main purpose in life was a noble life. But could she speak so others would be moved? Was her own enthusiasm pure enough and strong enough for her to influence others? Would those who heard her grow in their desire to live higher and nobler lives?

These were the questions that always faced her. And if she became quite certain of her mission, how would she ever be able to reach that goal? She talked with Helene about it—just as she talked about everything with her. Helene said she should just wait and keep on working as she was now doing. Once she became sure of herself a way would be opened up.

In the afternoons Astrid generally accompanied Helene on her house calls, and she often came into the most wretched part of Minneapolis, where squalor and humiliation were at home. She was deeply moved when she saw how often drunkenness was to blame for this misery. When they looked into a situation more closely, they often discovered that drunkenness lay at the bottom of the family's difficulty. To her it was dreadful to see how this vice was so ingrained in the Norwegian character. When she realized that her father was prospering on this misery and how she herself, even if against her will, had lived on it for a long time, then she felt the need to atone for her sin by helping the poor and forsaken wives and mothers, even though her own sin could never be fully expiated. She became convinced that she should speak publicly for temperance. There would be no break with her plan to enter the ministry. In fact, this might help her to reach it more easily. If she could bring about some actual blessing for someone by doing it, then she would not desire anything higher. From the moment she made her decision she used all the time she could spare to familiarize herself with the topic. And now she had announced her first lecture.

⁓

THURSDAY EVENING HAD ARRIVED. THE LARGE HALL was filled, and people came unusually early. Anyone who had looked closely at the audience would have found it strange that so many coarse and inflamed faces were there. It was, after all, an audience that had gathered to listen to a lecture on temperance. An occasional vulgar exclamation could be heard. Something explosive was in the air. Unrest filled the room.

In the first row nearest the stage sat Meyer, leaning back arrogantly, his arms crossed, looking with an indescribably ironic smile up at the podium, which was still empty. He could just sit quietly and enjoy his triumph. The others would handle the affair. Behind him sat Lundberg, gasping and panting, in a black overcoat with a sky-blue tie wrapped around his thick bull neck. His bloated face was copper red in anticipation of the moment he would give the sign.

A little before eight Astrid and Helene entered from a side door and sat down on two chairs on the platform. Astrid wore a plain black wool dress with a plain white collar. She was pale and serious. She became still more pale as she sat there looking out over the crowd. She glanced anxiously at Helene, who understood her and quietly squeezed her hand. At eight o'clock Helene stood up, took Astrid by the hand, led her to the podium, and introduced her to the public with a few words.

Astrid wanted to begin, but it was as if the power of speech had deserted her. This audience reminded her of one of the most terrible evenings in her life, the theater performance at Turner Hall. There were the same crude faces—indeed, worse—and here they were sitting and looking at her with malicious pleasure. She looked at the first row and saw Meyer, who was gloating as he sat staring at her. This time she was taken by surprise, and he had the delight of seeing her waver and involuntarily grab the lectern. A suspicion of a plot against her went through her, and the same fear that she had experienced that evening at Turner Hall returned to her. She could have screamed and run away. With a strong determination of will she pulled herself together, took a glass of water from the lectern, and drank. Her hands shook, but otherwise she looked quite calm. She straightened her back and looked proudly out over the audience. But when she opened her mouth to speak, Lundberg stood up. He spit across the floor and loudly cleared his throat. Astrid looked over at him. Then he said with a defiant face: "We Scandinavians have come here to say that we don't want this American practice of letting women preach forced on us. They can mind their own business, and we'll take care of ours."

Astrid glared at him. "Those who don't want to listen to me are free to leave," she said in a high voice. "I have rented this hall for this evening, so I think we'll turn to the topic we are gathered to talk about."

Lundberg sat down astonished. "These damned women," he mumbled, scratching himself behind his ears.

For a moment all became quite still, and Astrid began to speak. Fear had given her courage, and she forgot everything except that she was speaking for a cause that she loved. She impressed them with her calm, erect bearing. A power emanated from her that subdued the rowdy temperaments. Meyer began to fear that his plan would fail. Astrid had talked for a while, and the hall was quiet.

Then Meyer turned around and looked at Lundberg with a sneering smile. Lundberg saw it, and he broke out in a fury with a "Hey, there, boys!" and raised his whistle to his lips. With that the spell was broken. A hissing sound interrupted Astrid—first one, then one more. Soon it came from all sides accompanied by clapping of hands and tramping of feet. It was impossible for Astrid to get a word out. She stood quite still, waiting for it to end. Finally, the noise stopped. Astrid began where she left off as though nothing had happened. But as soon as she had spoken a few words, the same spectacle began. She stopped again, looking out at them calmly. Only the nervous contraction of her eyebrows and the quivering of her nostrils showed that she was angry. Meyer sat enjoying her predicament. He recognized these signals from a previous time, but now the situation was changed. When the noise finally subsided and Astrid began again, a loud voice was heard from far back in the hall: "You had better preach to your father first. Her father is a saloonkeeper," he yelled to the audience.

Astrid became chalk white. There it was. She thought she had freed herself from her past, but no—her past was the first thing to be thrown in her face whenever she wanted to try to do something. Nothing would ever be successful for her. Her past would always drag her down in the depths again. She looked around, confused.

Among the clapping and whistles in the hall could be heard voices that shouted: "Down with her! Away with the saloonkeeper's wench!" Some tried to hush those voices, but the noise was so tremendous that they were lost in the loud din. A Norwegian policeman walked up to Astrid.

"It's best you leave, Miss. They won't stop. It's no use trying to talk sense to them. They're mad."

"Are you a policeman and yet you cannot assure my right to speak in a hall I have rented?" Astrid asked with trembling lips.

The police officer shrugged his shoulders. He had too many friends in the audience to want to use force on them. "The awkward thing, you see, Miss, is that they have been told that your own father runs a saloon. It is better you quit preaching temperance as long as he is in business," he answered.

"Come, Astrid," said Helene behind her. "Come now. It's of no use." She pulled Astrid down from the rostrum, led her quietly into a side room, and locked the door after them. The crowd's noisy confusion, shouts of bravo, and clapping could be heard. Astrid looked helplessly at Helene.

"Come, come," continued Helene. "Let's just get home as quickly as possible." She led her quietly down the back steps and they were already down the street when the crowd came staggering noisily down the steps.

Astrid did not say one word all the way home. She just squeezed Helene's arm firmly, and Helene felt her shaking. Finally, they were home. Helene breathed easier now that she had got her there. Astrid sank into the armchair, and Helene sat beside her, taking Astrid's head and laying it on her breast and tenderly stroking her hair without saying a word.

"Oh, no, it's no use for me," Astrid burst out in desperation. "I may just as well give everything up. The curse follows me."

"You don't mean what you're saying, Astrid. You know just as well as I do that you cannot and must not give up."

"Oh, yes, I know that, of course, but tell me what I should do. Wherever I turn, my past follows me, and that's the way it'll always be no matter what I attempt to do," she spoke bitterly, her voice still shaking with fear.

"I know, and here it will always be in your way," Helene answered calmly. "That's why I've been thinking that you should get away from here, Astrid."

Astrid raised her head suddenly and looked Helene in the eyes. "Oh, God, Helene, don't you think I have thought the same thing? But how? How? Can you tell me that?"

"Yes, I have a plan."

Astrid stared at her.

"I have often thought about it, but first I wanted you to have full confidence in yourself. This evening I think we both will agree that you are committed to going ahead and that you won't stop before you have reached your goal."

Astrid nodded.

Helene continued. "Actually, I'm happy about this evening since it forces us to make a decision. Tomorrow you and I will drive over to St. Paul to speak with the Reverend William Gannett, the Unitarian minister there. I know him, and I am certain that when I explain your position to him, he will be interested in helping you. I'll ask him to write to the president of the Unitarian university in Meadville, Pennsylvania, to see if he can find a scholarship for you at the school. Perhaps by working on the side at his house you can pay for your board and room. During the long summer vacations you may be able to earn enough to clothe yourself, and if that's not enough, then you know that I will help you as long as I have something. I'll get your travel money together myself. I have some savings, and I know of several who will give us a helping hand if I ask them. What do you think of that?"

Astrid had placed her elbows on the arms of her chair. She stared intently in Helene's face. Tears glittered in her eyes. "Tell me, Helene," she finally said gently, "what would I have done in this world without you?" She kissed Helene's hand, the hand that lived only to serve and help others.

The next day they went to St. Paul where they found the Reverend Gannett at home. He was a man with a pleasant face and two dark eyes. Most noticeable about him was his smile. It was melancholy, yet so mild and warm that it moved anyone who saw it. Helene told him as much of Astrid's history as she thought necessary to bring him to an understanding of her character and her needs and to see how necessary it was for her to go away.

He cast a critical glance at Astrid. "I don't doubt that I will be successful in getting Mr. Livermore interested in your case," he said in a friendly voice.

"We don't have such an abundance of young enthusiastic and dynamic people that we can afford to let any go to waste." Again he smiled in the way that struck Astrid as so remarkable. How many endured agonies and battles of his soul it told of! But it also indicated an achieved peace and an infinite love for all human beings.

"How the matter may best be arranged, I'll leave up to him," he continued. "I know he'll find a solution when he hears how the matter stands. I shall write to him today. Next month the new school term begins, and it would be best if you could be there at the beginning. Is it possible for you to travel so soon if, as I take for granted, I get a favorable response from Mr. Livermore?"

Astrid looked inquiringly at Helene.

"Naturally," she answered quickly and decisively.

How happy Astrid was when they went back home. At last she was beginning to catch sight of land. She saw her future life following cleared paths where her thirst for clarity and enlightenment would be satisfied and guided by a goal that was great enough to take her through all difficulties. How she would work! With joy she felt her vibrant blood and her overflowing youth stream through her veins.

In the evening she stood in the middle of the bedroom floor. She had just taken off her dress when she happened to look at her arms. She saw that they were white and beautiful. A recollection came to her. She lifted up one arm and fondled it. How healthy and strong it was. She stroked it up and down several times before turning to Helene. "Oh, Helene, am I not fortunate? My body belongs to me, and no one else has a right to it. Just think! I am saved," she added slowly, kneeling down and laying her head in Helene's lap.

{ 21 }

Almost six years had gone by. Helene sat by the window in her room, holding a letter in her hand. Joy was written on the stern features of her face. She read:

"Who else should I turn to this evening, Helene? You embraced me at the moment of my deepest despair. You gave me shelter under the wide wings of your love. Ever since, you have been mother, sister, friend to me. This is my last evening here. Tomorrow I will venture out into the world to see what I can accomplish. I find it strange to leave this place, for so much love has been shown me here that it really has become my home. I have spent the most wonderful hours of my life in this little room.

"Outside my open window the huge maple gently waves farewell greetings to me with its green crown. The smell of spring emanates from the light-green virgin leaves glowing in the light of the sinking sun. Can you imagine anything more sacred than a spring evening when nature, rejoicing all day long in the resurrection of new life, puts itself to rest? Every leaf, every blade of grass, every flower, every bird—exhausted by joy—bows its tired head and falls asleep under the canopy of heaven, absorbing the refreshing dew sent it in the mild summer night, pregnant with fragrance. All nature knows that a new day awaits it in the morning—a new day to rejoice and be happy!

"How I love spring! I think I shall never be too old to be intoxicated by it. One morning a few days ago I was awakened at four o'clock by the songs of birds in my maple tree. It was still half dark, that marvelous festive time of morning when nature lies expectant. The birds trill their songs of love. The blades of grass perk up, drops of dew still glimmering on them. All await the arrival of the Prince—the Bearer of Light, the Messenger of God.

"I could not lie in bed. I, too, had to get up to receive Him. When I came outside, everything around me was enveloped in a fragrant white bridal veil. During the night the cherry trees and wild flowers had blossomed as if by the touch of a magic wand. And then came that first golden band over the top of the forest, breaking up the dark silence with its flaming brilliance. Birds flew out of the woods with a jubilant warble. Frogs and grasshoppers and thousands of unfamiliar voices sang in praise of the sun. Soon everything around me was bathed in the morning sun. The forest of white blossoms trembled in the golden beams. Dewdrops glittered like diamonds. What a fairyland splendor! I can well understand the old heathen worship of the sun as God! I know that my whole being bowed in inexpressible joyful adoration.

"But now you are laughing at me. How like Astrid this is, you are thinking. On my last evening here I ought to gather my thoughts and look back over these years to see, as far as this is possible, what I may expect in the future. You are, you know, my spiritual confessor. And here I am singing a hymn to spring! That wasn't exactly my intention. But now I shall begin, calmly and in orderly fashion.

"Tomorrow I shall leave this place. What, then, have I achieved in all these years? This evening I feel like a child who has climbed a high mountain. She has always imagined that once she reached the top, could she only get there, yes, then she could look out over the whole wide world and all its glory. But now that she is there she can still see only a tiny little piece of it. She is not disappointed, however. The air is so easy to breathe. The flowers have stronger colors and richer fragrances. The heavens are bluer. Everything below her lies as if enshrined in the peace and quiet of a Sunday afternoon. Above her she can see mountain after mountain in the distance. She still has the notion that could she only get up there, she would see more. I am like that child. I do not see as far as I have dreamed. So much still lies veiled in uncertainty and mystery. Yet I have come a little farther on my way. I breathe purer air, have higher goals and greater visions. And I know that no happiness on earth is equal to that which comes from finding a mission that can fill me completely—one to which I can dedicate my life with undivided attention.

"Tomorrow I shall leave this place to begin my mission. These years have sped by like a wonderful dream. They have healed my wounds and removed the bitterness from my heart and replaced it with the value and the joy of work. This has become the fundamental harmony of my soul. Sitting here in my little room, working on some problem or other, I have felt my own being grow and expand as I sought to solve it. Then I have often, with rapture, felt life pulsing in my veins. This was what my soul coveted. This was happiness!

"Listen, now, Helene. I want you to know what at times has been the secret dread of my soul. Not that my work was too demanding. I loved it too much for that. Anyway, I believe that the task you love with all your strength you will, to some extent, be successful at. Rather, what I feared was that I was too free, too daring in my thoughts to give something positive to those who need me—something for them to live and die by. You see, I cannot give them a God who is exactly this or that, formed according to our human concepts. Then He would drown in my own doubt. No, God must always be infinitely larger than my own ideas of him. In our highest moments we may only see Him as a faint idea and glimpse, perhaps, only the hem of His garment, as I did that spring morning when I bent my knees on seeing so beautiful a revelation of nature. Whenever I have feared that this was my weakness, that I might stumble on this stone, then the person who came to help me in the most miserable hours of my life has helped me again. For in these lines by Bjørnstjerne Bjørnson I have found my creed:

> That You are, I am aware,
> For I know You are there
> As the voice crying out in my soul—it is You!
> Seeking justice and light,
> Seeking all that is right
> In the new life we find—it is You, it is You!
> Every law that we see
> Or glimpse vaguely to be—
> Even all that we never perceive—it is You!
> And my life is inured,
> Free from troubles assured,
> And I cry out in joy: it is You! it is You!

With that creed I leave this place tomorrow in confidence.

"The first winter I was here I heard a lecture on these words of Jesus: 'And as ye would that men should do to you, do ye also to them likewise.' The speaker did not wonder that people had forgotten this golden rule because, after all, the church, which ought to hold this saying out to the world as the first and highest commandment of Christianity, as the guiding ideal principle, had itself forgotten it. Instead, it had taken as its first commandment: 'Believe as I do, or you will be condemned.' And if anyone now comes to acclaim these words of Jesus as the first Christian commandment, he said, then all will cast stones at her and say: 'She doesn't preach Christianity. She preaches ethics.' And yet it is the very words of Jesus that this person proclaims. From the time I heard that lecture I knew the way I wanted to go. I wanted to preach this commandment and the other commandments of Jesus in his Sermon on the Mount. If only those who hear me will set these as the goals of their lives, then I will ask for nothing more. If I am accused of preaching ethics instead of Christianity, then Jesus did not proclaim Christianity either. And I feel confident when I preach in his spirit. This, then, is the program I have now set up for myself.

"Where shall I go? First to Chicago. Beyond that I am not sure, but most likely I will go west and take over an American congregation. It is possible that someday I may be able to have a mixed Norwegian and American congregation—once our fellow countrymen finally reach the stage where they can accept a woman preaching to them.

"You will come to me, won't you, when I have my own home, and then we shall work together, each in her own calling. And you will bring faithful old Annie with you. You must be more lonely where you are now than ever before. You gave yourself for me, the despised outcast.

"And I hope I will be able to do something for Harald. When I get settled, I will demand that my father sends him to me. I think he will do that gladly because he now has other responsibilities placed on him. To think of my father this evening is the only thing that is difficult for me. Yet even in that I am happy because all the hate and bitterness that arose in me whenever I thought of him before are gone. Now I feel only sorrow. His new wife tyrannizes him. I think he now looks at mother through different eyes. Yes, my mother! Tonight I feel as if she is close to me. Now she will be happy about her daughter.

"Many disappointments, many hardships, can and will confront me, but never any that I will lose heart over. I have known despair. It was dreadful.

God help everyone who experiences that same emptiness of soul. May they be saved, as I was, by the caress of a lovely woman's hands and by sharp, brilliant eyes that told me that it is better to die than to surrender your human dignity. If only I can now do the same thing for women who forget themselves and their challenge to be human!

"It is growing dark here where I sit and write. Outside, the stars are beginning to sparkle, one by one. All is so quiet—so quiet. It is also quiet in my soul. I am filled only with gratitude and happiness this last evening here. I take only cheerful, loving thoughts with me from this home."

∼

THERE WAS A CELEBRATION IN UNITY CHURCH on the north side of Chicago. The large church was splendidly lit up and decorated. The platform where the lectern stood was adorned with beautiful flowers—white lilies and red and yellow roses flaming against the dark green background of tropical plants. Every seat was occupied. A Norwegian woman was being ordained as a minister that evening. The simple ceremony was just concluded, and Astrid welcomed into the church. The mighty organ burst out in that marvelous song of praise, "Nearer My God to Thee, Nearer to Thee," and the entire congregation stood and sang. There was a powerful jubilation in the song.

Astrid went over to the lectern. She had become as if taller and stronger during these years. Physical and spiritual courage were hers, and one could see that she went to her task with all her soul. Those large, gray-blue eyes looked about seriously. A shudder went through her when she remembered the audience she once had in front of her when she had tried to speak. How frightening it was! And now? Now she saw before her a sea of friendly faces, tear-filled eyes, as all welcomed her and waited, quietly and expectantly, to hear what she had to say. Two tears ran slowly down her cheeks and smeared the manuscript in front of her. She had as her text: "Blessed are they which do hunger and thirst after righteousness: for they shall be filled." She had herself hungered and thirsted almost to death, but now she was filled. She raised her head and looked out over the congregation. She felt that her words had power. She was at home here. She had not mistaken her call.

She had reached her destination.

{ }

Notes

Page 4 *The Feast at Solhoug Gildet på Solhaug,* one of Henrik Ibsen's early plays (1855–56). The mention of the play and its main character, Dame Margit, is the first suggestion of one of the central themes in the novel.

Page 5 **Kristiania** The capital of Norway, renamed Oslo in 1925. Up to 1877, the year when internal evidence suggests that Astrid and her father went to Bergen, it had been spelled "Christiania." At that time most roads were very primitive. Their route would have been through the Valdres valley, over the mountain pass of Fillefjell, down the narrow valley of Lærdal to the Sognefjord, and by steamboat to Balestrand further west, on the north side of the fjord. From Balestrand the steamboat would go out the fjord and then south to Bergen. There were no roads from the Sognefjord to Bergen at that time.

Page 6 **Svartediket** A dammed-up lake (the name means "black tarn"), now within the city limits, cradled between steep mountainsides. It is one of the city's sources of water.

Page 7 **the theater** The visit to the theater and Astrid's strong reaction may have been suggested by a scene in Bjørnstjerne Bjørnson's novel *Fiskerjenten* (1868, translated as *The Fisher Maiden* [1869]), where the first theater experience of Petra, the naive young protagonist, has a powerful influence on her. Petra has just come to Bergen from extreme poverty in a coastal village. She is at first very bewildered, but when others explain the concept of theater to her and "she finally fully comprehended what a drama was, and what great actors could do, she said, as she drew herself up, 'This is the grandest calling upon earth! It shall be mine!'" (112–113). It may be that one reason why Drude Janson did not have Astrid pursue a theater career was that this would have led to criticism for plagiarism.

The play seen by Astrid and her father, *Hærmændene paa Helgeland* (The Vikings at Helgeland) is an early play by Henrik Ibsen (1858). The slight differences between Swedish and Norwegian would not have caused difficulties for the audience.

Page 8 *Olaf Kyrre* Named for a king who reigned from 1066 to 1093, the *Olaf Kyrre* was one of several steamships in regular traffic between Kristiania and Bergen.

Page 10 **Mrs. Hvasser** Elise (Ebba Charlotta Elisa) Hvasser (1831–1894), one of the great Swedish actresses, is particularly remembered for her interpretations of Ibsen.

Page 14 **Charles XV** From 1814 to 1905 Sweden and Norway were joined in a union with a common king, foreign policy, and defense but with separate political institutions. Charles XV ("Karl" in Scandinavian languages) was king of Norway and Sweden from 1859 to 1879. The king's main residence was in Stockholm, but there was also a royal palace in Kristiania; it was there, no doubt, where August Holm waltzed with Queen Louise.

Page 21 **Kristiansand** A coastal city in southern Norway. The common route for immigrants in the 1860s and 1870s was by steamer from a Norwegian port to Hull and from there by rail to Liverpool, where they would board a passenger steamer bound for New York, usually with a stopover at Queenstown, now Cobh, to take on Irish immigrants. Early steamers would also be fitted with sails.

Page 25 **Moody's and Sankey's hymns** Dwight Lyman Moody (1837–1899) became a full-time evangelist in 1860, touring both the United States and Britain with great success. He met Ira David Sankey (1840–1908) at a YMCA convention in Indianapolis in 1870 and became so impressed by Sankey's voice that he persuaded him to join his evangelizing campaign. They attracted large audiences here and abroad, in particular in the British Isles. The popular hymns from their meetings were collected in many volumes.

Wennerberg Gunnar Wennerberg (1817–1910), Swedish poet, composer, scholar, and politician, primarily remembered for his *Gluntarne* (1848–51), a collection of duets for male voices, narrating and celebrating student life at Upsala University. A statue of Wennerberg was erected in Minnehaha Park, Minneapolis, in 1915.

that eternal crochet work Drude Janson had a strong dislike of needlework. "Such work always taxed Drude's patience; her niece, Dina Kolderup, has said that Drude thought embroidering such folderol and a waste of time" (Nina Draxten, *Kristofer Janson in America* [Boston, 1976], 118).

Page 27 **Such was Astrid's entrance to the New World.** At this time immigrants entered the United States through Castle Garden in the southern end of Manhattan. Ellis Island was opened in January 1892.

Page 28 **strange painted wooden figures** The so-called wooden Indians, used to advertise tobacco stores.

a strange, unpleasant odor The author reacted strongly to the smell of saloons. In her autobiographical novel, *Mira* (Copenhagen, 1897), she writes of the "evil-smelling saloon" (25).

Page 42 **a law office** A common path to the bar examination was still a kind of on-the-job training that was open to gifted and ambitious young men without a formal education. A good friend of the Jansons, Andreas Ueland, came to Minnesota from Norway in 1871 with only elementary education and no knowledge of English. In his memoirs he writes: "I shall not recount the struggles [of] the following five years with hard work summers and some schooling winters until I got a chance to study law in a law office, and then the struggle with law books and poverty." He was admitted to the bar in 1877. (*Recollections of an Immigrant* [New York, 1929], 35).

Page 46 **the familiar pronoun** In Norwegian, as in many other languages (e.g., French and German), the first person singular pronoun (*du,* thou) was used only for relatives and intimate friends. Others were addressed, more respectfully, with the pronoun in the first person plural (*De,* you). This usage is now in the process of changing.

Page 46 **Peter and Inger** *Petter og Inger,* a popular play or vaudeville frequently performed by Scandinavian theater groups in Minneapolis. See Carl G. O. Hansen, *My Minneapolis* (Minneapolis, 1956), 52, 82.

Bjørnson Bjørnstjerne Bjørnson (1832–1910) was a towering public figure in the second half of the nineteenth century in Norway. He wrote in all literary genres and was an important spokesman for liberal causes on the European as well as the national scene. He enjoyed international fame, and on his visit to the United States in 1880–81 he spent the first three and a half months in Cambridge, where he was welcomed by the intellectual and social elite, before he went on a lecture tour among the Norwegian Americans in the Midwest (see Eva Haugen and Einar Haugen, eds., *Land of the Free: Bjørnstjerne Bjørnson's America Letters, 1880–1881* [Northfield, Minn., 1978], 27–137). His political views and religious beliefs became increasingly liberal throughout his life. In 1903 he was awarded the Nobel Prize for Literature. In spite of his contemporary standing, his reputation can no longer be compared to that of his contemporary Henrik Ibsen.

The Newlyweds Bjørnson's play *De nygifte* was published in 1865. There are several translations, with varying titles. The character Laura is a young, immature woman, married to Axel two days before the opening of the play, who comes to a rather sudden awareness of the meaning of love and marriage at the very end of the play after reading a novel that turns out to have been authored by her friend and companion, Mathilde. There is very little action; what plot there is seems implausible and far from the experience of the audience in Turner Hall. Laura's doting and ineffectual, wealthy and conservative parents, Mr. and Mrs. Lee, are caricatures of types with whom Astrid's immigrant audience were hardly acquainted. The unrest in the audience is understandable; the choice of play less so. *De nygifte* was performed by a Norwegian-American company in Scandia Hall, Chicago, in 1891 (*Budstikken,* October 21) and 1926 (Orm Øverland, *The Western Home: A Literary History of Norwegian America* [Northfield, Minn., 1996], 95).

Page 47 **Turner Hall** The "turn" or gymnastics movement originated in Germany. Among German Americans the *Turnverein* (gymnastics associations) became an important network of social and cultural associations in the United States. The Minneapolis Turner Hall was frequently used by Norwegian-American dramatic societies (Hansen, *My Minneapolis,* 83). Drude Janson had personal experience from setting up a theatrical there. In *Budstikken,* April 21, 1885, there is an advertisement for a dramatic performance for "the benefit of the Scandinavian-Unitarian Church in Turner Hall." The play was by Kristofer Janson, and the production was favorably reviewed May 12.

Refreshments during the performance and the following ball were common practice. In his memoirs, Kristofer Janson tells of an experience during his first American lecture tour in Wisconsin that may be echoed in Drude's account of Astrid Holm's dramatic experience. He had come to lecture, he writes, someplace in Wisconsin. "The older settlers came to listen, but the young people remained outside having fun. They couldn't be bothered with listening to some nonsense from the old worthless country. But no sooner had I completed my lecture than they came rushing in, opened the windows, threw the benches out through them, and shouted: 'Now we shall have a *meeting.*' They organized a dance" (*Hvad jeg har oplevet: Livserindringer* [Kristiania, Norway, 1913], 179–180).

Page 48 **Maecenas** Gaius Maecenas (70–8 B.C.), a wealthy Roman, was a patron of the arts, supporting poets such as Virgil and Horace. His name has entered many languages meaning "a patron of the arts."

Page 56 **sharing his bed** Sleeping more than one in a bed was quite common. Drude Janson's friend Andreas Ueland writes of sharing a bed with two others in a 10 x 12 room, where they also did their cooking, during his early years in Minneapolis (*Recollections of an Immigrant,* 33).

Page 59 **Blackstone** Sir William Blackstone (1723–1780) was the author of *Commentaries on the Laws of England,* 4 vols. (1765–69), a work that became the basis for legal education in both Britain and the United States.

Page 62 **streetcar** The streetcars of Minneapolis were at this time drawn by mules or horses. The first electric line was opened in 1889.

Page 64 **Robert Ingersoll** Ingersoll (1833–1899) was primarily known for his popular public lectures and books criticizing orthodox readings of the Bible and propagating a rationalistic view of life.

"Yes, there's no doubt about it." The phrase in the original, "det skal være ganske vist," echoes a Hans Christian Andersen story about scandal mongering, "Det er ganske vist," translated as "There Is No Doubt about It." The story is an animal fable set in a chicken coop and concludes with the words "one little feather may easily grow into five hens." Drude Janson surely expected most readers to make the appropriate connection.

Page 69 **"Why a young girl more than a young man, Madame?"** The conversation here touches upon the controversial theme of Bjørnson's play *En handske* (A gauntlet) (1883), the double standard in sexual ethics for men and women. Bjørnson had sent his new play to the Jansons. Kristofer wrote to him that he was going to "read it for a small group he and Drude were entertaining in a few days" (Draxten, *Kristofer Janson in America,* 102). This was an important issue for both Jansons, and Kristofer contributed to the debate in Europe with an article, "Sædelighedsspørgsmaalet" (The sexual morality question), in the Copenhagen journal *Kvinden og Samfunnet.*

Page 84 **Keene** (The original has "Keen.") Thomas Wallace Keene (1840–1898) became a professional actor in his teens and toured the United States and England. In the early 1880s he began a long series of annual tours with a repertory that included such Shakespearean characters as Richard III, Hamlet, Othello, and Romeo. As the years went on, he became less popular and played in small towns rather than major cities. "For modern plays, as for the modern method of acting them, he had little sympathy" (*Dictionary of American Biography* 10:284–285). Mr. Smith's enthusiasm for Keene may suggest his lack of true appreciation of the contemporary theater.

Page 87 **Lake Minnetonka** A twelve-mile-long lake and park area in the western part of Hennepin County. Hansen describes the lake in *My Minneapolis:* "Minnetonka with its shoreline of a hundred miles beneath wooded hillsides and its numerous bays, inlets, points and islands, early in the history of the region attracted tourists from all parts of the country. In the eighties and nineties four large hotels at the lake had full house during the summer. They were Lake Park on Gideon Bay, Excelsior in the village by that name, St. Louis at Deephaven, and Lafayette on Minnetonka Beach. Large excursion steamers were plying the lake all summer" (152). In the spring of 1884, when the Swedish singer Christina Nilsson visited Minneapolis, the all-Scandinavian entertainment included a tour to Minnetonka and a lunch at the Lake Park Hotel (114). The Jansons would have been present, and the visit may have suggested the use of this setting for Drude's novel.

Page 87 **Gone, however, were the white tents** Such sentimentalizing of the passing of the Native American is representative of nineteenth-century American poetry and fiction. Here these are the contemplations of Astrid.

Page 99 **Red-gold ring** This is said by the young character Margit quite early in Ibsen's play *The Feast at Solhoug,* after she has sung a song in traditional folk ballad style about the "Mountain King" with the intention, as she says, to "lighten care." She is in despair because of an unhappy marriage, and in the translation by William Archer and Mary Morrison (*The Works of Henrik Ibsen* [New York, 1911], 218), she sings:

> *He is my husband! I am his wife!*
> *How long, how long lasts a woman's life?*
> *Sixty years, mayhap—God pity me*
> *Who am not yet full twenty-three.*

After singing, however, she suddenly realizes that the sad story of the ballad applies to her own situation. After the two lines remembered by Astrid, Margit says, "Woe! Woe! I myself am the Hill-King's wife! / And there cometh none to free me from the prison of my life."

This ballad, which echoes in Astrid's mind through much of the novel, is related to a tradition in Norwegian folklore of supernatural beings who live underground, in hills and mountains, and who enchant young people, in particular young women, to enter their underground domain. They are then lost to the human world. With brave assistance, such spells could be broken.

Page 101 **Bjørnstjerne Bjørnson is coming to town** Bjørnson came to Minneapolis in January 1881 and gave his first public lecture in the Pence Opera House on January 11, "to a crowd of nearly nine hundred. It was said to have been the largest Scandinavian audience so far in the history of the city." He lived in the home of Dr. Karl Bendeke. Bendeke was a close friend of the Jansons, as were the members of the Minneapolis organizing committee for Bjørnson's visit, Luth Jæger, editor of the newspaper *Budstikken,* and Andreas Ueland (Haugen and Haugen, *Land of the Free,* 159–160). He gave three lectures in Minneapolis, the first on politics and the second on "the prophets." The third, on Grundtvig, was given February 10, in Association Hall.

Page 103 **Market Hall** On the corner of Hennepin Avenue and First Street North. Although the author is mistaken in having Bjørnson give his first lecture here (see the previous note), she would have attended another major event in Market Hall before she began work on her first novel: a celebration of the famed Swedish soprano Christina Nilsson on March 14, 1884 (Hansen, *My Minneapolis*, 113).

Page 104 **Grundtvig** The Danish Lutheran theologian, bishop, and poet N. F. S. Grundtvig (1783–1872) was the founder of the folk high school (*folkehøyskole*) movement and the main inspiration behind the school that Kristofer Janson taught at in Norway. Bjørnson had identified himself with a Grundtvigian theology and church tradition before he developed the more rationalistic faith he had by the time of his American tour.

Page 109 *skald* An Old Norse word for poet.

Page 110 **the Ninth of June resolution** In the 1870s there was a growing political conflict between the Norwegian parliament (the Storting) and King Oscar and the cabinet (then answerable to the monarch, not to the Storting). One of the contested issues involved the royal veto. According to the 1814 Norwegian constitution, the king had a limited power to veto an act of the Storting: after being passed a third time, it would become law even without the king's signature. The conservative interpretation, the position of King Oscar and his cabinet, was that since the constitution did not speak of a limited veto for amendments to the constitution, the king had an absolute veto. The liberal interpretation, the position of the majority of the Storting, was that since the constitution made no exception for constitutional amendments, the king had a limited veto also in such cases. In March of 1880 the Storting for the third time passed a constitutional amendment that would allow members of the cabinet to take part in the debates of the Storting. When the king vetoed the amendment, insisting on his absolute veto, the Storting passed a resolution on June 9 declaring that the amendment was now part of the constitution without the king's signature. This was the first step toward an impeachment of cabinet members in 1884, a parliamentary system of government, and the eventual dissolution of the union with Sweden in 1905.

Page 119 **Stuart Mill** John Stuart Mill (1806–1873) was a British philosopher and economist, among whose many important works are *Principles of Political Economy* (1848) and *On Liberty* (1859). Both Bjørnson and Drude Janson would have found him particularly attractive for his strong interest in the liberation of women. Mill was one of the founders of the first British women's suffrage society in 1867 and the author of a key text in nineteenth-century feminism, *On the Subjection of Women*, published in 1869 and translated into Danish by Georg Brandes, a friend of both Bjørnson and Drude Janson, that same year.

Herbert Spencer A British philosopher and sociologist (1820–1903) and proponent of the theory of evolution. Spencer coined the phrase "survival of the fittest" (*Principles of Biology*, 1864) and was very influential in American political and economic thought in the late nineteenth century for his use of Darwinian concepts for an understanding of society (*The Man versus the State*, 1884). Spencer had been important for the development of Bjørnson's views, and Bjørnson was actually reading him in Minneapolis (Haugen and Haugen, *Land of the Free*, 165).

Page 120 "**How blessed is the little flock**" "Hvor salig er den lille flokk" is the first line and the title of a Norwegian hymn by Nils Johannes Holm, the minister of a pietist congregation in Kristiania. He died in 1845. The hymn may be found in *Landstad salmebok* (Oslo, 1926) or *Salmebog for lutherske kristne i Amerika* (Minneapolis, 1895). In prose translation, the first four lines are

> *How blessed is the little flock*
> *that is acknowledged by Jesus!*
> *In him, their Savior, they have all they need*
> *Now and in eternity.*

> *(Hvor salig er den lille flokk*
> *Som Jesus kjennes ved!*
> *I ham, sin Frelser, har den nok*
> *Nu og i evighet.)*

Pontoppidan The Danish-Norwegian theologian and bishop Erik Pontoppidan published his explanation of Martin Luther's *Small Catechism, Truth Unto Godliness*, in 1737. "Virtually a national reader for many generations, especially in Norway, this 'layman's dogmatics' combined Law and Gospel, orthodoxy and Pietism, in such a manner that its power persisted into 20th-century American Lutheranism" ("Pontoppidan, Erik," Britannica Online, <http://www.eb.com:180/cgi-bin/g?DocF=index/po/nto/5.html>).

When Bjørnson says, "All they care about is to have people with their last breath to swear upon Pontoppidan," he is criticizing both the practice of so-called deathbed conversions and a stifling dogmatism.

a minister like those found here in America In one of Bjørnson's letters from Cambridge, dated November 30, 1880, and printed in the Kristiania newspaper *Dagbladet*, January 22, 1881, he wrote about American clergy: "I have met a great many ministers here; it is no problem, because they have heard that I am interested in religion. They have a characteristic in common that is different from that of European ministers: they are men who have *chosen* their life work and who themselves have been *chosen;* they are strong, free men with great talent and tremendous zeal. I can most closely compare them to the best folk high-school teachers at home, and their task is also just that of folk high-school teachers; they want to bring sound human enlightenment, and they want to inculcate a love of mankind and a sense of duty" (Haugen and Haugen, *Land of the Free*, 119).

Page 121 **I met so many noble women** In 1885 Drude Janson attended the convention of the Women's Suffrage Association in Minneapolis (see Introduction). Here she has Bjørnson express her own high opinion of American feminists.

Page 139 **the person of Jesus of Nazareth** Drude Janson had arrived at a view of Jesus as a great human being before her husband embraced a Unitarian faith. Kristofer Janson remained engrossed by the greatness of Jesus and wrote many poems on him, some of which are collected in his book *Jesus-sangene* (1893).

Page 141 **her first lecture** Prohibition was becoming an important political issue in the 1880s. In the 1889 election in North Dakota, for instance, it was the single most important issue, and the majority voted for prohibition. The temperance movement was well organized among the Norwegian immigrants, and a strictly realistic approach to fiction would have given Astrid the support of a strong organization. Other considerations were obviously more important for the author. The cause of temperance interested both Kristofer and Drude Janson. Kristofer wrote an article, "Om Temperancesagen og Temperancebevægelsen i Amerika" (On the issue of temperance and the temperance movement in America), for *Budstikken,* October 13 and 20, 1885.

Page 144 **Gannett** William Channing Gannett, a prominent Unitarian clergyman, minister of the Unity Church in St. Paul, was very supportive of Kristofer Janson when the latter began his Unitarian ministry among Norwegian immigrants in Minneapolis in November 1881.

Meadville Several of the Norwegian immigrants that Kristofer Janson recruited for the Unitarian ministry went to the Unitarian seminary in Meadville, Pennsylvania, now the Meadville/Lombard Theological School in Chicago.

Mr. Livermore Abiel Abbot Livermore (1811–1892) began to serve in a Congregational church after graduating from Harvard University and then, in 1836, from Cambridge Divinity School. From 1850 he was a Unitarian minister and in 1863 became president of the Meadville Theological School. He published profusely, with books on theology as well as on social and political issues, for instance *The War with Mexico Reviewed* (1850), for which he was awarded a prize by the American Peace Society. The year after he became president, the school in Meadville began to accept women students. Among his other innovations were a course in comparative religion and the introduction of courses in the social sciences.

Page 148 **That You are** This is the first "solo" section of the third of three "Psalms," first included in the second edition of Bjørnson's *Digte og sange* (Copenhagen, 1880; translated by Arthur H. Palmer as *Poems and Songs* [New York, 1915]). The three "Psalms" express Bjørnson's faith after he ceased to believe in the Christian God and are addressed to a divine principle rather than to an anthropomorphic god. The most often anthologized one, the second, is in praise of a Darwinian life principle.

"And as ye would that men" Luke 6:31.

Page 150 **"Blessed are they"** Matthew 5:6.